Martin

THE COLOURED CHAMELEON

First published in the UK in paperback by Delizioso Publishing 2020

Copyright © 2012 - 2020 Martin Sanderson

Martin Sanderson has asserted his right under the Copyright, Designs and Patents Act 1988 to be identified as the author of this work.

ISBN 978-1-8381088-0-9

Printed and bound in the UK by Mixam UK Ltd.

CHAPTER 1

Michelle's engagement to Grant was no more than a month old, and the inevitable meeting with his parents was mere minutes away. Grant was driving the car, its headlights illuminating the hedges bordering the narrow road. Streetlights were long gone as they travelled deeper into the Surrey countryside. She noticed that Grant was unusually tense and they had progressed for some miles without exchanging a word. Reflected light from overhead tree canopies occasionally flashed on the skin of her hands, displaying evidence of her African origins. They turned off the road onto a gravel driveway which led to a grand freestanding house. The lights were on in the lower level, but the floor above was in darkness. He parked the car, and they walked together to the front door where he rang the bell.

'Grant, darling,' Gloria Fortescue greeted her son with a kiss on each cheek, as they came through the door, 'I've been looking forward to this for so long.'

'This is Michelle Simpson,' Grant said, moving to one side.

Grant's mother hesitated a moment looking at Michelle.

'Do come in,' she said rather formally contrasting with the warm welcome she gave her son.

Passing through the hallway into the living room, Michelle noticed the antique furnishings and stylish décor. Tastefully selected it gave an impression of British upper-middle-class status A promise of tradition and wealth. Visible were some oil paintings depicting ancestors of military and aristocratic bearing, seen posing with the males standing and the women seated in elegant dresses. Grant's father, Bernard dressed in tweed, more like a country gentleman than a business executive, with a cut-glass tumbler of whisky in his hand greeted her with a warm smile and handshake. When asked what she would drink, Michelle chose a Sherry an evening ritual introduced to her by her father.

'Now come and sit down and tell me about yourself,' Gloria Fortescue said.

Michelle hesitated just long enough to allow Grant's parents to sit in their usual chairs before choosing an easy-chair for herself next to Grant's father but facing Gloria Fortescue.

'Tell me, Michelle. What do you do for a living?' she asked.

'I'm a medical researcher.'

'From your accent, I can tell that you're not from England.'

'No, I'm from Northern Rhodesia originally from the mining town of Ndola.'

'So, you're a native African,' Gloria commented, raising her eyebrows.

'Well my father is European from here in England, but my mother, who passed away five years ago was an African.'

'Is your father in the colonial service,' she asked, 'my brother is in the Colonial Service in Kenya and played a major role in the defeat of the Mau Mau uprising.'

'No, he's a geologist now retired to our home in Sumbu, on the southern shore of Lake Tanganyika.'

'Did he have his own business?'

'No, he worked for a mining company,' Michelle replied, beginning to resent the woman's attitude, 'My brother has a fishing business in Sumbu.' Michelle added, feeling as if she was under interrogation.

'That's interesting,' Bernard Fortescue commented, 'what kind of fish do you have in the lake?'

While she described the fishing activities around the lake, Gloria glared at her husband, got up and left the room with Grant following close behind, perhaps as the result of a signal. She heard their muffled voices coming from the hallway.

'You're not seriously going to marry this girl?' Gloria Fortescue growled at her son.

'Well she's quite a wonderful girl, and…'

'That's beside the point. You know that she's coloured?'

'Of course, what does that matter?'

'Don't be an idiot you're the eldest son in the family. Do you really want to introduce someone like this into the Fortescue family? We might end up with a black grandchild.' Her voice was becoming shrill with anger.

'But she's so beautiful …'

'I don't care if she's a Nubian Princess. It's out of the question. If you do this, don't expect to come back here. I'll have your position in the business reviewed. I'll make sure of that.'

Michelle saw Bernard Fortescue's head droop as his wife's voice carried through to the living room, embarrassing him and humiliating Michelle.

'I'm sorry about that,' he said ruefully.

'So am I,' Michelle replied, 'I'm leaving now and don't worry, I won't be back.'

She picked up her handbag, walked through into the hall, straight past Gloria Fortescue and her son, and out the front door without uttering a word. By the time she had walked down the driveway and out onto the road, she heard the car engine start, followed by the crunching of the tyres on the gravel driveway as Grant set out to follow her.

She was so angry, at first she refused to get into the car but relented, not knowing exactly where she was, realising it might be a long walk to the nearest station.

'Sorry about that,' Grant muttered once she was seated. Michelle took off the ring and dropped it into the car ashtray. 'Please, Michelle, don't be so hasty. We can work this out.'

'Don't think for a moment that I intend to spend the rest of my life being humiliated by your family. No Grant, it's over. Just take me to the nearest station and drop off my suitcase at the office on Monday morning. And another thing, if I were a Nubian Princess, I certainly wouldn't marry into your family.'

That's how it ended, the ring consigned to the ashtray, with Grant protesting, appealing, almost begging her to reconsider. It wasn't his fault she knew that, but even if he loved her as he claimed, and she had her doubts about that, eventually his loyalty to his family would prevail, and that would leave her out in the cold.

Emotionally it hurt her, but she was not surprised. Over time she had better prepared herself for this kind of reaction to her racial origins. Something she was always expecting, or if not, was able to counter with silent contempt. Not to say it didn't make her angry, it did. It made her cynical but protected her from severe humiliation. But what about Grant? Looking back, she now realised that all this hidden self-consciousness about her colour prevented her from falling in love with him. A built-in defence mechanism that she hid behind her acknowledged beauty. She had never slept with Grant. Did that mean she was destined never to marry? Did her emotional self-protection mask prevent her from engaging in a truly intimate relationship?

Before Grant, she had not had a man in her life if she disregarded her relationship with Alex James, her Rastafarian friend from Jamaica. They met at an Anti-Apartheid Rally she attended at the urgings of some of her students at the University. Tall with long dreadlocks it was difficult not to notice him at the side of the road as they marched in Trafalgar Square. He joined the marchers working his way towards her as they marched, causing a few people to stumble and mutter. At her side, his friendly extroverted personality radiated a broad smile as he regarded her with darting dark eyes.

'What's apartheid?' he asked as they marched.

'If you don't know, why are you marching?' she laughed.

'Oh man, because you are.'

That summed him up. Apolitical and unemployed, his life was one long happy party, reggae music, cannabis, and Bob Marley. His way of life contradicted everything she stood for, work ethic, commitment, responsibility, service, and striving for success. He and his lifestyle became an escape, a happy way to relax and forget for a short while the demanding research problems that dominated her thoughts. Cannabis helped her to float away on a feather of pleasure, enveloping her in a bubble of illusion. But she was not prepared to continue inhaling smoke into her lungs to achieve that state, so she soon abandoned it. Alex was enough of an intoxication to sustain her enjoyment. Jokes, light-hearted banter, smiles, laughter, music, and love. They made love in that carefree uncommitted way with no expectation of it leading anywhere. She knew that this hedonistic lifestyle could not last and that he was not a potential long-term partner, but for the moment, it suited her. When he visited her, she never allowed him to stay over-night. What he did during the day while she was at work, she never discovered, but he always seemed to have enough money to survive. Eventually, it ended when he announced that he had run out of money and was returning to Jamaica. Two days later, he was gone.

The morning after the Fortescue incident, she arrived at the office in Dorking deliberately erasing all thoughts of Grant from her mind. On her desk, the headlines on the front page of the newspaper screamed 'United Nations Secretary-General, Dag Hammarskjold dies in air crash near Ndola.' She wondered what the Secretary-General was doing there and resolved to read the report a little later when she had time. It was some time since she was there in Northern Rhodesia following her arrival in England to study medicine at the University in London. When she graduated, she joined the Dorking Pharmaceutical Company as a junior researcher. As the only woman in the team, she found it difficult in the beginning. The others didn't take her seriously. In time, without the distraction of a man in her life, she learned that she could more than hold her own. Working in the lab after hours and often over the weekends, she produced results that were at the forefront of their research efforts. Not everybody appreciated her success, and a number of the men ostracised her. She experienced the meaning of professional jealousy accompanied by the suspicion that her race also played a role. In the end, her boss Clive Francis appointed her team leader, a position she worked hard to retain.

'Michelle, your in vitro results on project "Heartburn" are very encouraging,' Clive Francis said entering her office.

Michelle looked up from where she was transcribing the results of her latest tests into a report. She marvelled at the industrial espionage inspired names management dreamed up for their projects.

'Yes, but these I'm working on now are conclusive.'

'Excellent, when can you let me have them?'

'I'll bring them up tomorrow morning for your assistant to type.'

'What about the compounds the other members of the team have been working on?'

'I've been checking the test results, but there is nothing to compare with what we have here. I'd like you to check theirs out as well. It's up to you to decide between the candidate compounds.'

'I've already examined them, and there's no doubt. You've identified the one we need.'

Michelle knew that his enthusiasm would aggravate her tenuous relationship with some of the other researchers.

Especially Graham Samuels who produced some fine work but seemed to continuously fall short.

'I think you should compare what I've done with Graham's work.'

'Let's get him to bring his latest result through right now.'

'Please be diplomatic,' Michelle pleaded.

'I'll be truthful, that's all I can promise.' He picked up the phone, dialled his assistant's extension number, and when she replied asked her to get Graham Samuels to come through to Michelle's office. 'Ask him to bring through his latest research results,' he added.

They sat around Michelle's desk with Clive Francis studying Samuels' research file, making comments in the margins of the pages as he went along. After an initial curt greeting, Samuels ignored Michelle, looking intently at Clive Francis.

'There's some good work here, Graham. These results are reasonable, but we need to decide between yours and Michelle's.' He handed Michelle's file to Samuels and his to Michelle allowing each to study the other's latest results. When he could see that each had finished perusing the other's report, he asked Michelle to comment.

'I agree, Graham has done some good work here, and I think you should decide which of the two we should adopt,' she suggested, although she was confident hers were superior.

'What do you think, Graham?' Clive Francis asked.

'I think my results are as good if not better than hers.'

'Can you explain how you arrive at that conclusion?'

'Can't you see it for yourself?' Samuels complained.

Michelle could see that Samuels's evasiveness irritated Clive Francis.

'Alright, I'm not going to sit here and explain to you why the compound Michelle has developed is producing safer results than yours. You have seen the results, and they are self-evident.'

'If you give me a bit more time I'm sure I can improve it,' Samuels said, almost pleading.

'No, all work on your compound is suspended. We need to start a new project. I'm satisfied with the efficacy of Michelle's tests, so I'm promoting project "Heartburn" to a phase one trial using some healthy volunteers. We'll also start the patent application process.'

Later in the afternoon when everyone in research had left having no reason to stay late to work on project 'Heartburn', Samuels returned to the office carrying a camera slung over his shoulder concealed under his jacket, ostensibly to protect it from the rain outside. It was dark, and all the lights were still on. The cleaning staff would switch them off when they had finished their work.

He signed in at security in the lobby and passed through with the camera undetected. The spare films were in his pockets. He needed to find Janice, who he knew had a crush on him to get the key to Michelle's office. No one was surprised that he was there; people frequently worked late. Wandering through the ground floor, he found the young blonde-haired girl busy cleaning the passage outside one of the offices.

'Janice, be a sweetheart, give me a kiss,' he teased her.

'Not here we'll be seen. I'll lose my job,' she giggled.

He drew her into the open office she was about to clean and kissed her while she was still holding the broom.

'I need the keys to the offices.'

'Why? Do you want to lock us in?'

'Not tonight some other time, I need to get my pen from Michelle Simpson's office,' he lied feeling in her overall pocket.

'Stop it,' she laughed, pulling his hand away but reaching in for the keys herself.

'Show me which one it is.'

Leaving Janice to her cleaning, he made his way to Michelle's office, unlocked the door, and when he was in locked it again from the inside. It only took him a few minutes to locate Michelle's research file, which he recognised from that morning's meeting. Her neat writing was on one side of each page, which made his task more straightforward. He managed to lay out ten pages side by side across the desk, took off his jacket to free the thirty-five-millimetre camera, set the aperture and shutter speed using the light-meter, focused the lens, and commenced photographing the pages from left to right. He continued photographing them laying down sets of ten pages at a time until he had photographed the complete document. By the time he had finished, he had filled three films. He carefully replaced the pages in the file and returned it to the filing cabinet. With the camera back hidden under his jacket and the films in his pocket, he relocked the door as he left the room, and went off again in search of Janice.

'You're a real honey,' he said, giving her another kiss and returning the keys to her pocket with a little squeeze to her thigh. 'You won't tell anyone I was here, will you?'

'Of course not, as long as we can meet like this again when nobody's around,' she said conspiratorially. With that reassurance, Samuels left her and passed out through security into the night air his heart thumping with an adrenaline rush.

During the following week, Michelle received numerous phone calls from Grant until she refused to take any calls at all. On two occasions, he was waiting outside the front office for her to leave in the evening. She chose instead to depart by the back exit to the car park and have one of her co-workers take her by car to the station.

Eventually, Grant's attempts to phone or meet her stopped, but then the letters started to arrive. Michelle immediately passed the letters through the shredder, ignoring the compulsion to read them. He even knocked on the door of her flat in Earls Court, but she recognised him through the peephole and silently refused to open it. His persistence was flattering in a way, but she was sure he did not love her. His relentless pursuit was more likely the result of dented pride.

His pursuit of Michelle finally stopped by which time she was fully engrossed in the challenges presented by project 'Wounded Knee.' The letter from her brother when it came was to redirect her attention.

Dear Michelle,

It grieves me to have to write you this letter, but I know that father doesn't want to concern you. He has been unwell for a few months now and I finally insisted and took him to the hospital in Ndola for tests. We were there for a week, the results came back positive, and the prognosis is not good. He has advanced pancreatic cancer and the doctors say that they are not able to treat it at this late stage. He remains mobile at present and the painkillers keep him comfortable, but I do not know how long he has, and the doctors said it could be weeks or months.
I cannot imagine what life here will be like without him, but I'll just have to manage and try to keep going as usual. It would be unfair to ask you to come back permanently but if you can come for a short while for a visit, it would be a great help. I'm not sure I can look after him by myself as I'm out with the boat almost every day.
Sorry to bring you such sad news.

Your loving brother,
Jeffery

Although it was right in the middle of their new research project Michelle didn't hesitate. Clive Francis was quite understanding and agreed that she take leave for an extended period. He couldn't ask her how long she'd be away, so he left it open with a guarantee that she would still have a job when she returned. Her experience and knowledge of their developments were too valuable to risk losing. She could soon obtain employment with a competitor, and he had no desire to consider the complications of their confidentiality and restraint agreements. Once she had used up her leave, he agreed to keep up the rental payments on her flat as a retainer.

Three days later, she was on a plane headed for Lusaka in Northern Rhodesia. One person who was pleased to see her go was Graham Samuels who had plans of his own.

CHAPTER 2

In a military operation with the Katanga Mercenary Commandos, Dominic Harrison had driven north from Elizabethville some two hundred and eighty miles to the town of Pweto and continued north to engage what they thought was a UN supported military unit. He was driving the command vehicle with the major in the other seat conducting the operation, issuing commands on the radio. The major was acting as a forward scout keeping his men a long way back making sure where the enemy was, intending to direct his force in an out-flanking manoeuvre. He believed the opposing unit would expect them to come straight along the road. Usually, Major van der Walt would send forward one or two of their regular scout vehicles to reconnoitre the forward positions. But he was a professional South African soldier who regretted that he had never experienced combat during his career and was determined to remedy that before he became too old. There was much speculation about whether he resigned to join the Mercenary Commandos or was on a sabbatical. On that day he had decided to lead from the front to make sure that if there were a contact, he would be in the thick of it. They had stopped again as they did every two hundred yards or so to survey the terrain up ahead through binoculars.

'Up ahead in the trees on the left,' Dominic pointed.

'I see them,' the major replied then picking up the radio handpiece he shouted, 'Delta, we have visual here on the left of the road, join us immediately.'

While looking through the binoculars, Dominic noticed that the uniform the enemy unit was wearing was not representative of the UN nor the Congolese forces the UN was supporting.

So anxious to experience an engagement and before Dominic could say a word, the major stood and fired his FN rifle in the direction of the opposing soldiers. Immediately, a hail of bullets raised dust in front of them some thudding into the Jeep.

'Turn around let's get out of here,' the major ordered.

Suddenly the radio crackled to life with a report coming through from the main force to the rear.

'Major, we have a problem back here. UN forces have surrounded us. Must we fight our way through to join you?'

'Negative, do not engage the UN. I repeat, do not engage,' the major shouted over the radio.

'Roger.'

As Dominic was turning the Jeep, the major picked up his FN automatic, stood up and fired again in the direction of the partly hidden unit. The return fire was even fiercer than the first. Bullets were hissing past all around them, and Dominic heard the thuds and clinks as they hit the Jeep. The radiator went in a hiss of steam, and the steering went heavy as the tires deflated and it stalled and wouldn't restart. Before Dominic could take any further action, the major slumped down against the door and slid partway into the foot-well. A bullet had caught him just above the right eye, leaving brain matter with his beret on the back of his seat. Opening the door, he grabbed the backpack, the map and his FN automatic and ran with his head down. To avoid being hit, he ran, keeping the vehicle between himself and the line of fire. At first, he had thought the blood on his side was from the dead major, but as he ran the pain in his side intensified and blood seeped through the material of his tunic. A moment of guilt gripped him as he fled; should he stand and fight. But the opposing force so outnumbered him that the outcome was predictable, death or capture, and he was not ready for either.

He continued running away from the road into the trees in a south-easterly direction. After about fifteen minutes, he sat down, breathing heavily with his back resting against a tree. Making sure there were no pursuers he unfolded the map, spread it out over his lap and tried to estimate his position to decide what he should do. The enemy unit in the north, and the UN around Pweto in the south, cut him off in both directions. Capture by the UN in the south was preferable to capture by the force they had just fired on who might merely execute him. Even the UN option, although not life-threatening, had unknown consequences. He decided to escape somehow. Escape over the border out of the Congo.

Studying the map, he saw that Northern Rhodesia and Lake Tanganyika were to the east, the closest border from where he was. His first task was to get as far away from Pweto as quickly as he could in that direction. On the map, there was a road shown travelling parallel to the Northern Rhodesia border for about 50 miles to a village called Kimpalapala. If he left the road somewhere between Kikalengu and Kimpalapala and walked in a south-easterly direction, he should be able to get to Sumbu. It was the nearest small town on the southern shore of Lake Tanganyika, a distance of about seventy miles. The walk would be challenging, but he had covered distances like this in his military training. The first step was to cut across country to intersect with the road and then try to board a bus to get as quickly as possible away from Pweto. He removed the small compass from a side pocket of the backpack and then rotated the map to align it to magnetic north. Placing the compass on what he estimated to be his position, he read off the bearing of the route he wanted to take to the road. He folded up the map and stored it in the backpack.

He was ready to cast aside the burden of the FN automatic, somewhere where he could recover it if that became necessary.

Using the compass to maintain his direction as he walked, he finally reached the road after about two hours. Looking left and right along the road, all he could see were trees on either side. He needed to turn left to walk along the road in the correct direction, but not in full view in case a UN contingent came along especially as he was dressed in combat fatigues and carrying an FN rifle.

Moving back into the trees, he resumed walking, but this time parallel to the road sufficiently hidden from any passing traffic. From time to time, when a car or lorry approached, he lay down in the grass and waited for it to pass. On one occasion a rider on a bicycle who came along quietly surprised him, passing by before he could go to ground. There was no sign the cyclist saw him. After a while, he stumbled on a dry stream that entered a culvert passing under the road. He walked towards its entrance along the stream, removed the magazine from the FN automatic, crawled in and left the weapon in the middle.

Continuing his walk, he shed bullets periodically in the bush as he went along. Eventually, he threw the empty magazine into a thicket. Freed of these burdens his pace quickened.

Around midday, he reached a small village. Along the edge of the road were a few small stalls selling fruit, vegetables, warm soft drinks, and cigarettes. Mainly to passing travellers he suspected.

'Does the bus stop here, going to Kikalengu?' he asked one of the stall owners. He received a reply in French that left him none the wiser. A few people joined in, all chatting away in French. Someone pointed excitedly at his clothes. He remembered that the blood was seeping through the right side of his tunic. It was getting a bit out of hand until a young man appeared, as if from nowhere, and said,

'I am speaking a little English, please speak slowly.'

'*Merci*, does the bus stop here going to Kikalengu?' Dominic asked, pointing in that direction.

'Yes, stops, goes that way.'

'When does it come?'

'Maybe at two o'clock.'

Dominic thanked him, took a few Belgian Francs from his pocket and gave it to him. The crowd dispersed seemingly quite pleased with the outcome. A warm soft drink tasted terrible but helped quench his thirst. Surprisingly the bus arrived on time, and once the waiting passengers loaded additional luggage, to join the assortment of suitcases, blanket wrapped bundles, bicycles and chickens on the roof, they set off down the road churning up a cloud of dust behind them.

They stopped at Kikalengu where passengers left and joined the bus. About twenty minutes after they left Kikalengu right in the middle of nowhere, Dominic asked the driver to stop and drop him off. When the bus halted, the passengers' voices increased in volume at this strange turn of events. A bus did not just stop here. Why would anybody want to get off? There was nothing for miles. As the bus drew away, he saw the astonished faces looking back at him from the windows of the bus. Setting the compass to the required bearing, he walked into the trees. That night he slept amongst the trees using the backpack as a pillow feeling hungry but more worrying he had run out of water.

When he resumed his walk in the morning before sunrise, his foremost thought was to find water. He tried to dig in the sandy bottoms of the streams he crossed, but they were all dry, or if there was water, it was deeper than he could dig by hand.

Smoke filtering through the trees was the first indication that he was not alone in this part of the forest. It hung almost motionless in the upper leaves. The smell of cooking confirmed that it had human origins. It crossed his mind that it might be wiser to bypass what he assumed would be a camp of some sort.

There were no trees cleared in the vicinity, so it was unlikely to be a small village. He could not find any reason why there would be anyone here, but the water bottle was empty, and he had found nowhere during his journey that morning to re-fill it. A matter of concern to him was that his appearance and dress might alarm whoever it was in the camp. Being white and with limited French, he would be identified as one of Moise Chombe's mercenaries the moment he spoke. He was concerned he might be in trouble having only a Walther P38 in his belt, if whoever was there were armed. The last thing he needed was to provoke a firefight. Perhaps he would regret abandoning his automatic the previous day.

He approached the camp in a stooped position until he was about fifty yards away and crawled forward on his stomach until he was at the edge of a small clearing in the trees. Peering through the grass, he could see a few makeshift shelters made out of branches. Two young women were busy around a fire one stirring the contents of a pot whilst the other wielded a small axe splitting away kindling from a sizeable dry log. The carcass of a small antelope hung in the shade from the branch of a nearby tree. Strips of meat were hanging out to dry between two trees. Against one of the shelters, some canvas water bags were hanging, and he could tell from the dark stain on each that they were full of drinking water. The slow evaporation at the surface of the canvas would keep the water inside pleasantly cool even in the midday heat. It seemed a perfect scene of domestic peace out in the forest, but men's clothing on a washing line was a warning that trouble might not be far away.

He lay there waiting until two men appeared from the far end of the camp. They were dressed only in shorts and shoes, their torsos muscularly well defined, lumbering wearily towards the shelters sweat glistening on their black skin. They needed to be fit and robust because each carried a large elephant tusk on one shoulder and a hunting rifle over the other. The two women stood up in greeting, laughed and clapped their hands, while the men returned their welcome in a local dialect that Dominic could not understand. They lowered the tusks to the ground, rested the hunting rifles against one of the shelters, and joined the young women at the fire sitting on two wooden stools fashioned from a log.

One of the women poured what he took to be tea into two mugs adding generous spoons of sugar, handing the first to the taller of the two men who had a stubbly beard. For a while, the two men sat in silence, sipping their tea, and he could see that they were physically tired. Watching them drinking reminded him of his own thirst. He needed to refill his water bottle. Now that he had seen the tusks and knew they were poachers, he was a danger to them. To enter the camp in these circumstances would put him at risk.

The women ladled food onto two metal plates, and the men ate in silence with the two women sitting a short distance away in the shade outside the nearest shelter. The tall, older of the two men, the one with the stubbly beard, when halfway through his meal barked an instruction at the two women. They rose, walked to the tusks and one at a time carried them into the shelter. It took the two of them to lift and carry each tusk straining under the load. When they had deposited the tusks in the shelter, they pulled a branch across the entrance hiding the evidence. Dominic wondered how many more tusks were in the shelter and how they got them from here to the next link down the chain. Right now, somewhere quite far from here, the vultures were feeding.

There was a chance that he might be shot entering the camp were the tusks not hidden in the shelter. If he did not take on water here, he would never make it to the border. The more difficult decision concerned the pistol. Should he enter the camp armed or not? If not, he would be unable to defend himself against the two men. With the pistol, his chances were not too good against two men each with a hunting rifle. He decided to go in without the pistol but needed to hide it somewhere outside the camp to retrieve if he was fortunate enough to leave alive. It would be sensible to hide the pistol and backpack, on the side of the camp where he would depart in the direction of the border. If he left from the direction from where he had come, the two men would be fearful that he was making his way back towards the authorities.

Overall it took him half an hour to make his way around the camp, hide the pistol and backpack next to a small rocky outcrop, and back to a position where he could enter the camp. He brought with him a packet of Camel cigarettes he found in a side pocket of the backpack and the military issue metal water bottle. He did not smoke. During his escape from the firefight, he must have grabbed the Major's backpack mistaking it for his own.

Approaching the camp from the West and a fair distance off, he made as much noise as possible hoping this would give the impression that he was not around to witness what they hid in the shelter.

'Bonjour monsieur,' he shouted, as loudly and as amiably as he could walking cautiously into the camp. The two women immediately fled into the nearest shelter, whilst stubble beard leapt to his feet, shouting something in French that Dominic could not understand. The second man's move towards the rifles surely meant it was a command. Before he reached the rifles, Dominic continued, his voice rasping from his dry throat.

'Please, do you have water?' he rasped.

The second man had reached and raised one of the rifles, but stubble beard restrained him with a backward motion of his palm. For a moment they stood facing each other hesitantly, with the taller man eyeing Dominic rapidly and in detail.

'Do you speak English?' Dominic asked, moving cautiously forward.

'What are you doing here?' Stubble beard responded as an affirmative.

His English was fluent without a Congolese French accent.

'I'm trying to get to the border to enter Northern Rhodesia.'

'That's a long way from here, where have you come from?'

'Just west of here north of Pweto.' Dominic knew that it was obvious what he had been doing there, so he continued, 'I was with the Katanga Mercenary Commandos working for Tshombe. We were involved in a heavy firefight. Most of our group were captured by United Nations forces, but I managed to get away.'

It was a risk saying this without knowing where Stubble-beard's allegiances lay. But he reasoned that this man's English was too good to be a Congolese. Stubble-beard smiled, a bright white smile, then he visibly relaxed and said,

'Ah, Tshombe is a good leader trying to prevent the Government in Kinshasa from grabbing his mines.'

'Yes, you're right, that's the reason for the fighting.'

'You need water and a meal if you are going to make it to the border, come and sit down.' He called out in the vernacular, and the two women reappeared from the shelter glancing curiously at the dirty and dishevelled white man before handing Dominic one of the water bags from its hanging place in a tree.

The meal consisted of thick cassava dumplings with venison and gravy which Dominic chewed on whilst Stubble-beard lit up one of the Camel cigarettes, lighting it by igniting a twig in the fire. The venison was fresh but jaw straining having had no time to hang and become tender.

'My name is Dominic Harrison.'

'Daniel Ngosa, hunter,' Stubble-beard offered which surprised Dominic. There was good reason for him to remain anonymous. 'There's blood on your shirt,' he continued, 'is the wound serious?'

Dominic lifted his shirt and examined his throbbing right side just below the ribs. Being preoccupied with his escape, it was the first opportunity he'd had to investigate the wound closely. It looked a mess but appeared to be a flesh wound.

'It doesn't look too bad, but it could become infected then it will be a problem,' Daniel suggested scratching his beard. Looking back at the younger of the two women, he waved his hand in the direction of one of the shelters and gave an instruction. She went into the shelter for a while and returned with a cloth, a bottle, and a small metal bowl. At the fire, she poured some hot water from the kettle into the bowl and added a small amount of the liquid from the bottle. When Dominic had finished eating, she came and kneeled next to him with the bowl.

'What is it? Dominic asked.

'Dettol, it will hopefully clean and disinfect the wound, but I'm sure it will hurt a bit', he grinned, 'it's all we bring with us to treat any wounds we receive ourselves.' The woman looked at Dominic for a sign, so he nodded. After about five minutes she was finished, took away the bowl and rejoined the other young woman.

'That looks better,' Daniel said, 'sorry we have no bandages, but hopefully that will help.'

'It's better than I could have expected out here in the bush,' Dominic noted, standing up from where he had been sitting. 'I'm thankful but have no way of rewarding you or returning your kindness.'

'No need. Take this water bag, and here is some dried meat. A bit salty, so be careful not to get too thirsty.'

They shook hands, and Daniel patted his upper arm as the two men's eyes met in an unexpected bond of friendship.

'Good luck,' he shouted as Dominic departed the camp at the east side of the clearing.

The feeling of fraternity remained with him long after he had picked up the backpack and pistol and was forcing his way through the forest towards the border. He'd probably never see the man again.

After two days walking through the forest and on the third day as darkness approached, he heard rustling in the undergrowth but could not discern what animal it might be. By now, he had finished the last of the water, and he was having moments of dizziness. His body ached, his legs felt weak, his lips were chapped, and the heat was sapping his energy. Having not eaten since leaving Daniel's camp, the salted meat proving too salty and difficult to swallow, he knew he needed food but felt no hunger. The terrain had been rising for the past few hours slowing his progress as he laboured uphill gaining altitude. Exhaustion and an overwhelming need to sleep were overtaking him, and he started looking for a place to rest for the night, or at least a part of the night until the moon was up and he could walk further in the slightly cooler moonlight that filtered through the canopy of the forest.

He finally found a small clearing that he chose as a resting place where he could perhaps get some sleep to temporarily relieve him from the burning thirst that raged in his mouth and throat making it almost impossible to swallow. Removing the backpack, he set it down as a pillow on which to rest his head, first removing the battery torch from a side pocket. Having used it sparingly there remained sufficient power in the batteries to cast a beam up to about twenty yards. Gazing upward from where he lay, he could just make out the position of the full moon above the canopy.

In his dream, strange sounds yelped from a dark well from which he was trying to draw water and the faces of demons reflected off the water at the bottom. A foul smell rose upward, so he moved back from the opening. Something brushed against his leg, waking him with a start. It was breathing close to where he lay. He could smell its breath. Without moving, he switched on the torch his eyes dazzled for just a second before focusing on a fully grown hyena. It leapt back startled by the light but only a few paces from his feet before moving speculatively towards him.

Although he was now fully awake, reaching for and unclipping the pistol, it felt like the actions were taking place in treacle, his movements seemed that slow. A race to beat the hyena as it closed in on his feet. It would tear flesh from his leg with its powerful jaws and retreat, leaving him immobile and vulnerable to the next assault that would come from the rest of the pack. They would undoubtedly be there now emboldened by their leader. The pistol let out a loud crack as he discharged it, followed by the scurrying sound of the pack of hyenas as they fled. But they would be back having smelled his blood. As was their nature they would now pursue him relentlessly, timidly harassing him until one of them got in a bite. Once immobile, that would be the end.

Traversing the edges of the clearing with the torch, pairs of red eyes reflected back from where the hyenas had retreated into the trees. Here they felt safe for the moment but would gradually recover enough courage to advance again towards their prey. From where he was, as long as the torch had power, traversing a circle with it would expose the advancing hyenas. But he knew the torch would not last until daylight if he used it continuously. He lifted the backpack and slipped into its harness. Holding the torch in one hand and the pistol in the other, he made his way to the edge of the clearing. There he sought and found a tree he could climb, all the while scanning to-and-fro with the torch.

Scaling the tree when he found it was a huge effort and he eventually had to leave the backpack at its base, hoping the hyenas would not carry it away. Once in the tree, he found a suitable but hardly comfortable branch on which he could stretch out with his back to the trunk. Fearing he might fall asleep or pass out and fall to the ground before sunrise he lengthened his belt and passed it under the branch and secured it around his waist. The hyenas gradually assembled themselves beneath the tree in the belief that he would eventually come down.

During the night he passed in and out of sleep or unconsciousness, and the demons returned in hideous forms, climbing the tree and terrorizing him by slowly consuming his flesh. The piranhas arrived and darted in and out of the wound in his side, spewing blood in all directions. Pain racked his body, and he writhed restlessly on a bed of broken glass which lacerated his back. There was a buzzing in his ears, and he awoke with flies circling his head with others crawling over his side where the blood seeped slowly from the wound. His body was so stiff it took him a few minutes to revive the circulation in his legs and loosen the muscles in his back. Looking down, he saw that the hyenas were still there lying around at the bottom of the tree as was the backpack where he had left it. The sun was rising although he could not see it from within the forest. Soft light was filtering through the leaves, the air absolutely still. Again, he unclipped the pistol and aimed it down at the hyena, but not at any particular animal. There seemed little sense in wounding one as it would make no difference, the pack would pursue him anyway. They scattered in all directions as the pistol discharged, but this time he could see where each one was located. Reaching the bottom of the tree, he harnessed the backpack and set off again in an easterly direction orienting himself using the hand compass, which pointed towards the source of the sun streaming into the forest. Looking back, he saw the hyenas following a short way behind him.

Plodding eastward through the forest he felt the gradient of the terrain increasing until he found himself climbing a consistently steep slope. His breathing became more laboured, and his progress slowed. If his memory served him correctly one of the maps that he'd left behind in the Jeep showed an escarpment on the western shore of Lake Tanganyika. If he could reach the top, it would be downhill all the way to the lake and the water that was his only chance of survival. Since he left Daniel's camp there had been no sign of any human presence, no cultivated or fallow fields, no footpaths, not even abandoned huts, so it seemed unlikely that anyone had ever lived in the area where he was walking. Passing through the few clearings he came across, the only life he found, were a few antelope who took flight, fearful of his presence but also of the hyenas shadowing him as he came. On several occasions, their leader had trotted towards him speculatively, but Dominic aimed a shot in his direction, causing a retreat to an ever-closer following point.

They were becoming bolder and more confident as time passed. Could they sense that he was reaching the end of his endurance? A condition being tested against the military training he had endured as a non-regular conscript in Rhodesia before he joined the mercenaries. He wondered where the hyenas found water here in the forest, likewise the antelope that occasionally appeared. If he could follow the antelope until evening, they would lead him to water, but he knew this would be impossible. They moved too quickly, merging with and disappearing into the undergrowth, aided by their natural camouflage.

Now the terrain was becoming rockier, and the trees were thinning presenting an exhausting obstacle course, causing him to scramble over the boulders on all fours.

A few times, he fell and lacerated his hands in his effort to remain upright. His feet and calves were cramping, and his tongue was so dry it clung to the inside of his mouth. Ignoring the pain, he forced himself onward until he slipped descending from a small rocky ridge, falling heavily at the bottom. Winded and dazed, his eyes closed, and he felt remarkably relaxed as his body surrendered to the comfort of approaching sleep. It was a satisfying feeling, but one of the demons returned, and he recovered with a start, just as the lead hyena came running towards him. It was so close when he discharged the pistol that the bullet caught it in the middle of the chest. There was a yelp, and the hyena ran a short way away and collapsed to the ground and lay motionless. Dominic rose and turned through three hundred and sixty degrees to see where the rest of the animals were, to find them running directly towards him, jumping over the rocks as they came. They were coming from all directions, so he had no chance of stopping them all, but could only wait until the next one reached him and try to deal with them one by one. But there were so many he had no chance.

Two of the animals ran right past him, followed by a third as they headed for their fallen leader. The whole pack descended on the prostrate hyena milling around him, raising dust that obscured their intentions. Strange sounds emerged from the melee, and soon he could hear the crunching of bones as the hyenas cannibalized one of their brothers. 'I hope that the bullet was fatal.' Dominic thought as he watched the horrifying scene from a short way off. He realized that he should make as much progress away from this disgusting sight whilst the hyenas were distracted. Perhaps he could eventually lose them.

After about half an hour, the terrain levelled out, and he had left the rocks behind for it became grassy and more even underfoot. A short while later he caught the first view of the lake between the lower trunks of the trees. And soon after that, the terrain fell away, sloping steeply down towards the lake. It spread out below a vast body of water shimmering blue into the distant horizon. Excitement increased his heart rate as he realized he might yet survive this journey of escape he'd embarked on, without any idea of just how arduous and life-threatening it would be.

Making his way down to the lake, he soon discovered how difficult and physically demanding this was to be. His legs were under continuous strain to prevent him from running downhill out of control. Now and again he lost his footing, slipping on the grass and falling backwards onto the backpack, causing him to use his hands to prevent himself from sliding forward uncontrollably.

When he reached the bottom, he collapsed and crawled the last few yards to the edge of the lake where the waves lapped gently on the shore. The dizziness returned, and the world revolved, causing him to wretch, convulsing his body as he reached out, immersing his fingers in the water. Cupping his hand, he brought a small amount of water to his mouth. Sucking it in, he could hardly swallow the dryness was so intense, and he knew that he had reached a dangerous level of dehydration and would need to take only a little water at a time or his stomach would cramp. Even though the African sun had set behind him, the temperature remained high, and the humidity was almost suffocating.

He looked north and south along the shore but saw no signs of human life, only clumps of rocks at the foot of the hills where they met the water. Straight across the lake in the far distance, hazy hills rose at the horizon. Looking north, he could see the water stretched as far as he could see. For a moment, he became concerned that there might be crocodiles lurking just below the surface where he was lying. He reasoned that there was no evidence that animals came here to drink, so he was probably safe from that threat. Other than the lapping of the small waves on the shore, it was silent. There was not even the sound of the birds. Something he occasionally heard, as he laboured through the forest and down the escarpment to the lake.

Now, his legs were cramping badly, and he rolled up the legs of his military fatigues and attempted to massage the blood down from the top of his thighs. His hands had become too weak to be effective. Having stopped walking and climbing his body was beginning to cool, and his legs felt like huge weights hanging from his body down to his burning feet. Sitting up, he managed to separate himself from the backpack, falling back with his head resting on it. This effort was enough to remind him of the wound in his side, which throbbed incessantly.

He started to wonder how he would find someone, anyone to help him from here. Perhaps if he walked south along the shore, he would eventually reach a village, but he could go no further now as nightfall approached with the sun setting in the west and the shadows lengthening out into the lake. He needed to sleep, and perhaps in the morning if he awoke with enough energy, he could attempt it. As he contemplated this course of action, a movement above him on the slope caught his eye. The pack of hyenas was back and approaching rapidly down the escarpment. He unclipped the pistol once again and prepared the battery torch, but he knew he would not have the energy to climb another tree.

The pack surrounded and hemmed him in against the water of the lake. A few of them drinking thirstily on either side. Two of the large males advanced determinedly, directly towards where he lay. He aimed the pistol at the larger one determined to kill it as a distraction to the others. Perhaps if he could kill them one-by-one, they would become sated with their own family's blood. As he pressed the trigger of the pistol, all that he heard was a sharp click. The magazine was empty, and he had neither more bullets nor another magazine.

CHAPTER 3

The next morning Jeffery Simpson prepared his breakfast cracking two eggs into the pan on the gas stove and adding bacon and tomato. Two slices of bread smeared with butter and a generous layer of marmalade completed his preparation. An aluminium coffee percolator bubbled and hissed on the hot plate, and a mug with two spoons-full of condensed milk waited on the table. He prepared some sandwiches using cheese he took from the paraffin-powered fridge, adding slices of tomato from some left to ripen on the windowsill. These he slipped into a brown paper bag. From the kitchen window, he looked out north over Cameron Bay where the water had a grey tone reflecting the semi-darkness of the sky just before dawn. His father and sister were still asleep although he knew that his sister often lay awake with her eyes closed, waiting for him to leave before arising herself. Already dressed in denim jeans, a white T-shirt and a pair of tennis shoes without socks, he was ready for work.

Flames from the stove provided just enough soft light to illuminate the kitchen. Later in the evening, one of them would start the diesel generator to provide electric power. Originally, they had needed this for not only the electric lights but also to power the valve-driven wireless which they had recently replaced with a transistor one that ran off batteries. For now, he chose to sit at the kitchen table to eat his breakfast, rather than use the more formal dining room. His father still insisted they sit down there to dinner in the evening at the large mahogany table with is pierced back chairs. During the day while Jeffery was away, he would spend his time sitting on the veranda that looked out over the bay reading, listening to the radio and dozing. The family's boat, moored at the jetty, was a short distance to the west in the small town of Sumbu.

As he ate, he wondered what it was that Omar wanted to discuss. He had phoned in the morning two days before planning to drive the truck from Ndola to Sumbu. They arranged to meet at the jetty this morning. Omar had begun to explain over the phone, but the line was poor, and Jeffery could not hear clearly. Their longstanding agreement was proving beneficial to them both and Omar drove to Sumbu every two weeks to buy the fish that Jeffery had accumulated during the intervening fortnight. The last time he came up was only a week ago so there would not be enough fish to make a full load although some of the supplies that Jeffery needed for resale would be on board with a batch of hessian bags to store the dried fish.

He finished his breakfast, drained the last of the coffee in the mug, washed it with the plate, knife and fork, then poured the hot water remaining in the kettle into the frying pan, and left it to soak. Stuffing his wallet into the pocket of his jeans, he walked out onto the veranda. As the sun was rising, he took a deep breath, and descended the steps into the warmth of a cloudless sky.

When he arrived at the jetty, he found Omar seated on a barrel close to the moored boat smoking a cigarette.

'Greetings,' Omar said with a smile emerging from his thick grizzled beard, 'it's sooner than I thought we would meet again.'

'Welcome. How was the drive up?' Jeffery asked, shaking his hand.

'Oh, you know, as usual, the truck-stop food was terrible and the prostitutes ugly,' he chuckled.

'In that case, you had better join us for dinner this evening. I am sure we can rustle up something better than a truck stop.'

'Thank you for your kind offer, but I need to get back with whatever fish you have for me as soon as I can. There is an increasing demand, and the wholesale distributor is threatening to place his orders with someone else unless I can increase the volume. That's why I've come up a week earlier than usual.'

'Then you will understand that I've only got half a load for you,' Jeffery warned with concern.

'Yes, I knew that would be the case, and even though half a load increases the cost per bag and I can't sell them for more, I want to give you a chance to see if you can increase the volume.'

'That's generous. I'll see what I can do to increase it to a truckload a week. For the moment I'll reduce my selling price to compensate you for carrying half a load,' Jeffery offered, his smile displaying white teeth shining in contrast against his black skin.

'Allah be praised, that will not be necessary for this trip, let's load up the sacks and conclude our business. You have to catch more fish, and I have to get back to Ndola.'

The two men walked back along the jetty chatting amiably as they went until they reached a small warehouse near its entrance. Constructed of corrugated iron, it was one of a number in a row, each more like a large shed than a warehouse. Some had their doors open, while others remained locked. A small group of men lounged about in the vicinity hoping to pick up some work, mainly loading and unloading of cargo from the small boats arriving and departing from the jetty.

Jeffery unlocked the doors of the warehouse with a key that he extracted from his wallet. A strong smell of fish greeted them as he swung the doors open. It contained hessian sacks packed with the salted and sun-dried kapenta, the fresh-water sardines that populate Lake Tanganyika in large shoals. These filled about an eighth of the space in the warehouse. Down the right-side Jeffery had built some shelves extending up to the roof. A wooden stepladder leaning unsecured against the shelves about halfway down provided access to items placed near the top. Paraffin, in five-gallon-cans, was stored on the shelves below. Above were bottles of cooking oil; packets of salt; tins of Bisto; cigarettes and matches; blankets; net twine; adzes; axes and hoes; a selection of knives and scissors; a selection of electric batteries; paraffin lamps; soap; toothpaste; razor blades and shaving cream; aspirin; mosquito nets; and non-prescription medications; most items the villages along the shore of the lake might require.

Omar backed the lorry close to the entrance to the warehouse, alighted from the cab and hinged down the sides of the vehicle to make it easier to load. Two of the casual workers came over to help, and Jeffery nodded to them and pointed at the bags in the warehouse. From previous experience, they needed no instructions knowing what was required. They carried and loaded the sacks, packing them carefully on the flat exposed floor of the lorry while Omar counted them. When they were all loaded Jeffery removed his wallet and paid them while Omar raised and secured the sides and pulled a green coloured tarpaulin over the cargo as protection from the dust that would rise and settle on the lorry as he drove back to Ndola. Jeffery fetched a notebook from the warehouse, and he and Omar confirmed the number of sacks loaded, and reconciled what they owed each other. Omar paid him in cash which Jeffery inserted into his wallet, thanking him with a smile.

'I'll be back for more the same time next week', Omar promised, offering his hand.

They shook hands and Jeffery wished him a safe journey, reminding him to bring his order of supplies at the same time. As the lorry passed out of sight down the road, he wondered how he might increase the number of sacks of kapenta. Before he closed and locked the warehouse he called over one of the casual labourers, he knew him only as Jimmy and had him remove from the shelves a collection of supplies. Then together they made a few trips between the warehouse and the boat to load it.

The boat was wooden, sixteen feet long, and uncovered except for a small storage space in the bow. There was a single outboard motor at the stern. On such a large lake it would have been preferable to have twin motors in case one failed, but cost prohibited this precaution. Instead, onboard was a pair of paddles for use in an emergency to get to shore. What he would do in this event if he reached shore and there was no one there was something he preferred not to contemplate as he had no flares or other means of communication. In the storage area in the bow, he kept some tools, a small anchor and chain, bailing tins, tarpaulin, hull planks and a tin of tar in case he needed to make emergency repairs. It tended to leak but not sufficiently to harm the cargo.

Jimmy stood by to unhitch the mooring rope whilst Jeffery pulled on the starter cord of the outboard motor until it spluttered, expelled blue smoke, and gradually gained motor speed. Once Jimmy was onboard, he released the clutch churning up water at the stern as he steered the boat away from the jetty towards the open bay. As they came into the open water, the boat pounded on the small waves until Jeffery throttled back to a steady cruise speed. Jimmy made himself comfortable lying back amongst the cargo.

If he navigated in a north-westerly direction across the lake, Jeffery would reach the western shore, where the first of the villages were located. Once there he would make his way up the coast stopping at each settlement to collect the sacks of salted kapenta, inspecting the contents, weighing each bag, and making payment in cash. With the payments made and the bags loaded onto the boat, he would open shop selling the supplies that he had brought with him. Much of the cash returned to his wallet. When he first visited the villages, they only caught enough fish for their own needs, and he promoted the idea that they might earn money by collecting a surplus of their fish for sale. The villagers accepted his concept with enthusiasm, but once they had the cash in hand, there was nowhere nearby where they could spend it. Jeffery realised that he could provide them with supplies when collecting the fish, thereby improving his small enterprise.

Cruising on his usual course, he noticed a huge forest fire that was raging up the escarpment to the west. Dark smoke billowed high in the sky. The fire had already passed over the top on its way to who knew where. It left a black scar on the face of the mountains. He had travelled past that area in search of villages when he first set out on his venture and knew that the steep slope of the escarpment fell directly into the lake leaving only a narrow rocky shoreline with no potential for establishing a village. He was aware that lightning started forest fires, but there had been no such storm the previous night. The only other cause in this part of the world was human negligence or burning of previously cultivated areas to clear them of old dried crops and their accompanying pests. He should investigate, but he needed to collect more fish, and he might need to increase the number of trips he made up the coast to two per day if he could persuade the villagers to catch more. This would mean travelling in the dark either there or on the way back depending on how he could arrange it. Without a reliable employee to make one of the trips on his behalf, he would not be able to sustain such long working hours. He held his course and advanced the throttle to increase his speed. This would shorten the travel time, but he had no idea of the effect this would have on the motor.

He continued on his course for another fifteen minutes, but the fire worried him. By now, most people in Sumbu would be aware of the enormous fire and plume of smoke over the mountains, and in no time, the news would reach the District Commissioner. Knowing that Jeffery travelled almost daily up the lake, he would seek him out later in the afternoon and ask if he knew what was going on. To admit that he was out on the lake but did not take the time to investigate was going to be hard to explain. The DC expected his community to act as his eyes and ears in matters such as this. He turned the boat and headed west towards the source of the fire.

Jeffery reached the southernmost point where the fire had blackened the face of the foothills. The wind was blowing gently from a northerly direction so he figured that if he started from the south and worked north, he would pass the point where the fire started. Jimmy stood up in the bow, scanning the shoreline, not knowing quite what Jeffery expected him to find.

'We might find a boat moored here somewhere,' Jeffery called to him from the tiller, 'it might be concealed in some way.'

He manoeuvred the boat as close to the shore as he dared, looking ahead to avoid any rocks protruding out into the water. The water was so clear that looking directly down, the bottom and the shadow of the boat was clearly visible. It was easy to judge the clearance from the keel. Progress was slow as he could not risk striking a rock at speed. Thick grey and black ash lay in layers up the slope of the foothills, and there was a strong smell of burned grass. Above, high in the sky, the smoke rose above them, now thinning to a light-yellow colour. There was bound to be a spectacular sunset that evening as the smoke dispersed over a wider area.

Half an hour passed and then an hour. It was hotter as the sun rose higher in the clear blue sky. Travelling so slowly the air did not pass quickly enough over the boat to have a cooling effect, and the land radiated heat back in their faces. Jeffery took a sandwich from the brown paper bag and beckoned Jimmy to fetch it from him in the stern. No sooner had Jimmy reached him than he noticed something on the shore ahead, pointing to direct Jimmy's attention.

'Something there, Boss,' Jimmy yelled, 'looks like someone sleeping.'

'Unhitch the anchor and get ready to wade ashore and secure it in the rocks,' Jeffery said. He turned the boat away from the shore and turned back around, aiming the bow at the point where the body lay. He throttled right back, coming in as slowly as he could. Jimmy jumped into the water when it was waist high and waded in and secured the anchor in the rocks.

'How does he look?' Jeffery asked.

'Not good, maybe dead.'

Jeffery cut the motor, slipped into the water and waded ashore to see for himself.

The man lay on his back, his head turned to one side, resting on the rocks. His body and clothes were covered in ash, and his exposed flesh stained grey. A brown stain showed through on his right side. Next to him was a backpack, a pistol and a Zippo cigarette lighter.

'A white man,' Jimmy exclaimed.

'Yes, a soldier, but you can hardly tell he's such a mess.'

'How did he get here?' Jimmy asked.

'No idea, perhaps somebody dropped him off. But why here.'

Jeffery knelt and took the man's wrist feeling for a pulse. He had seen his mother do it often. Make sure you do not feel your own pulse; she would caution him when he tried. After a while, he felt a weak pulse, but if the man was breathing, it was so shallow that his chest did not appear to move. He shook him gently and asked, 'Can you hear me? If you can, move your fingers,' but there was no response. His body was limp but warm.

'He's alive but in bad shape,' Jeffery announced, 'we need to get him back to Sumbu as soon as possible. You take his feet, and I'll take him under the shoulders. Be careful, it's very uneven over the rocks, and we don't want to drop him into the water.'

They carried the man into the water, Jeffery wading backwards as carefully as he could. The tennis shoes helped to protect his feet, but he could see that Jimmy was grimacing as his bare feet pinched between the rocks as they went. When they reached the boat, it moved away from them as they tried to lift the man in.

'We need to turn the boat so that the side is against the rocks on the shore,' Jeffery instructed. They manoeuvred the boat around carrying the man with them until it presented a firm side over which they could lower his body. Once he was in the boat Jeffery went back to collect the backpack. He slipped the Zippo into his pocket, the pistol into the backpack and returned with it to the boat storing it in the bow.

Meanwhile, Jimmy made the man as secure and comfortable as he could, on the bottom of the boat, using some blankets from their cargo. Although he doubted the man would feel anything, he didn't need to be injured any further by the speed induced pounding of the waves on the hull as they travelled

Once they had him safely in the boat, Jimmy waded back to release the anchor and turned the boat, so that it's stern faced outward away from the shore. By now, Jeffery had the motor running, and when Jimmy took up his position again in the bow, he reversed the boat out and turned in the direction of Sumbu. There was no compass in the boat, but Jeffery knew every distant feature to aid his navigation with corrections as smaller, more precise landmarks appeared. He set the throttle to full speed, and they skimmed over the small waves the bow lifting and falling rhythmically.

It took them just under an hour to reach the Jetty at Sumbu. After they had moored the boat, Jeffery left Jimmy to watch over the unconscious man and ran to the house.

'What's the hurry?' Michelle asked as he ran up the steps to the veranda.

'We need an ambulance from the hospital to take care of a man we have in the boat.'

'Who's hurt?'

'Don't know. We found him on the shore below the escarpment where the fire started.'

He ran inside to the phone, lifted it, and waited for the operator. It rang for some time until eventually, she answered.

'Put me through to the hospital,' he demanded.

She complied, and he waited again this time for an answer from the clinic. When he got a reply, he explained, and they said they would get an ambulance there immediately; it would take about fifteen minutes.

'I'm going back to the boat to meet them,' Jeffery said to Michelle, 'I'll be back as soon as we've returned our cargo to the warehouse. We didn't make it to the villages this morning, and it's too late to go now.'

CHAPTER 4

In Sumbu, Michelle Simpson listened to her brother Jeffery that morning as he prepared breakfast and readied himself for the day. She thought he had made an enormous effort these past few years to make a success of his fishing business. She felt proud of him because while she was studying at university in London, she had no idea of quite what he was doing. Her father's letters recorded that Jeff was doing fine without providing any details. In retrospect, she should have taken more interest and prompted her father to tell her more about his activities. But her studies distracted her. She was determined to do well, and Jeffery faded into the background. Of the two of them, she had been the more academically inclined, and her father decided that she should further her education at university at a time when females usually became housewives to support their husbands.

Her father, Harold Simpson, was a geologist who came to Northern Rhodesia from England before the Second World War catching a boat from Southampton bound for Cape Town, travelling by rail and road from there to the Copper Belt. An international mining company recruited him to conduct exploration in areas away from the Copperbelt where they expected there might be gold and other minerals. He married a nurse he met whilst in hospital in Fort Rosebery while recovering from a bout of malaria. Michelle was born before the war. Before she went to school, wherever the company decided to conduct exploration, they camped out in the bush. Her mother, a Bemba woman, was educated at a mission school and then at a nurse's training college but did not work during these exploration trips. At the outbreak of hostilities her father volunteered and joined up with Rhodesian and South African forces fighting in the Northern Desert. While he was away, the children started primary school, and her mother resumed work, scanning miners to detect evidence of tuberculosis. When he returned to his wife and family after the war, Michelle had just started high school, and Jeffery was still at primary school.

Michelle loved to camp with her father during school holidays, following him through the bush taking rock samples that he studied and analysed when they got back each evening. Her mother and Jeffery stayed in Ndola so that her mother could continue working. When it came to what she might study at university, encouraged by her mother, she chose medicine. Entitled to a British passport through her father, she chose a university in England. Eventually, the University accepted her application to study there, and she said a sad farewell to her parents and brother but left excited about the future.

In her second year at university, she received a telegram from her father telling her that her mother was seriously ill, and she should expect the worst. In tears, she composed a reply stating that she would leave London immediately and return home. Eventually, her father arranged a phone call and persuaded her that her mother was insistent that she should stay in London and finish her studies. He read out the message her mother had given him to read:

'Your father and I have worked all these years to ensure you received the best education we can afford. If you return, it will be difficult for us to finance your return journey to London. Just remember me as I was and make the best of your life. I love you as always.'

Michelle sobbed and put down the phone. She just could not carry on talking to her father. Three days later, she received a telegram that her mother had died from pneumonia.

She stayed and continued with her studies. She had intended to return home as soon as she graduated, but she received a job offer with a reputable pharmaceutical company in Dorking, Surrey, as a junior researcher. They also agreed to pay her to continue postgraduate studies at the university on a part-time basis. If she returned to Sumbu, she would have to work as a general practitioner in a Government hospital whereas she had excelled in research. Her main field of study was the development of new drugs. Later, pop culture with its bold fashion and beat music emerged; she found the thought of leaving the excitement of living in London difficult to contemplate. Africa seemed so primitive and far away, although she missed the warm weather and glorious African sunsets.

Now back home with her father and brother, she felt a relief and a sense of purpose that transcended her life in London. This morning after Jeffery left to go down to the boat, she got out of bed and had a cold shower. They still used a wood burning boiler attached to the house as the generator did not produce enough power to heat an electric geyser. Later in the afternoon when he started work their manservant George, would clean out the brick grate, load in more wood, and light the fire assisted by some methylated spirits. After about half an hour, the water would be close to boiling and hot enough for the family's bathing and other needs in the late afternoon and evening. There was enough dry wood in the forests not too far away, mainly from trees pushed over by elephants. Every two weeks or so, Jeffery would take some of the casual labourers and drive them in his four-wheel-drive Land Rover along the main road in a southerly direction until he found a favourable spot to collect firewood. The wood tended to be hard, so using hand axes took some time to cut the fallen trees into small enough pieces to fit onto the truck. The hardwood burned slowly and produced considerable heat. Once George finished firing the boiler he would don his cook's white uniform and headgear, tidy the kitchen of anything leftover from the morning or lunch, re-stoke the stove, and prepare the evening meal laying the table in between. George trained as an assistant to the chef at the District Commissioner's official residence. His wife Elizabeth, not her real name but chosen as an alias to her tribal name, which was difficult for Europeans to pronounce, acted as a housekeeper.

She came to the house each morning, worked until lunchtime, and then walked back to the village where she and George lived.

When she finished her shower, Michelle dressed and went to her father's bedroom, knocked, and asked if he was ready for breakfast. She found him already dressed sitting on the bed gazing out of the window, a far-away look in his eyes.

'Good morning father, where would you like your breakfast?' She asked. It would be one of three places, depending on how he felt that morning, either the dining room, bedroom, or on the veranda.

'Michelle, thank you, on the veranda this morning I think.'

'Have you taken your pills?' she asked, and he nodded.

When Michelle left to make breakfast, Harold Simpson picked up the transistor radio on the small table next to his bed and made his way out onto the veranda. Chairs lined the veranda facing out onto the bay. He sat down next to one of the tables and looked out across the water. The sun was up, and the lake sparkled in the early morning light.

Busy in the kitchen Michelle heard music coming from the veranda; Brenda Lee was singing, "I'm Sorry". It was a mournful song, which made her feel sad. She had left it on that station the previous evening before she returned the radio to her father's bedroom. It would not stay on that station for long she knew that, and sure enough, a political discussion soon came on from the BBC General Overseas Service. The news would follow on the hour. He would listen all day, and she was happy that it distracted him from his illness. In the evening, he would relate to her and discuss the latest news and the economic and political issues occupying minds worldwide.

A cease-fire agreed following a week of heavy fighting in Katanga meant it was now quiet in Elizabethville. The OAS blew up a TV station in Algiers the capital of the French colony of Algeria moments before President Charles de Gaulle was due to deliver a message. Efforts to contain the tensions between the West and Russia continued in the United Nations.

As they sat on the veranda later that afternoon after Jeffery had met the ambulance and ensured it safely removed the injured man, Michelle asked him what had happened.

'If he is a soldier, as you say, how did he get there? Was there any sign of fighting in the vicinity?' she asked.

'No, it's so remote there it seems unlikely that there would be any reason for a military engagement. He must have walked there from somewhere, what other explanation can there be. Why would anybody take him by boat and drop him there?'

'We only have police here, so it's not one of ours,' her father added.

'I'll visit the hospital each day to see how he is progressing. He is missing from somewhere so I'll see if I can help,' Jeffery said.

CHAPTER 5

Voices mumbled just within earshot, forming a background to the playful chatter of birds. Somewhere children were laughing. The sound of plates and cutlery rattled into his consciousness. Something was flickering through his eyelids like the frames of a moving film projector. He opened his eyes to see a fan rotating above his head, contrasted against a white ceiling. A slight breeze brushed over his face, and the curtain at the window to his left moved slightly back and forth. There was a strong smell of disinfectant. He felt no pain, but his body ached, and his eyesight was not completely clear, forcing him to blink frequently. His mouth was dry, and he felt incredibly tired and weak. To his left and above him, hanging from a stand, was a bottle of liquid with a tube running down to where a rolled-up pyjama sleeve exposed his left arm. The sheet and blanket on the bed covered him up to the middle of his chest, and his first reaction was to try to loosen them to relieve the heat that enveloped his body. Tucked in tight, they acted as a restraint, so he desisted and examined the room in more detail, but there was not much to see. Next to the bed on his right was a small cupboard. On it was a bottle of water and a glass. He was very thirsty, so he reached out for the glass with his right hand, but his fingers fumbled uncontrollably, and the glass fell from his grasp onto the linoleum floor with a low ringing sound without breaking. An African nurse in a neat and clean white uniform appeared at his side as if from nowhere.

'You're awake,' she said, taking a clean glass and filling it with water from the bottle. 'Here, take just a few sips,' she continued holding the glass to his lips. He managed to lift his head just enough to bring his lips to the glass.

'Where am I?' he asked.

'In a clinic,' she replied with surprise.

'Yes, I figured that out, but where am I, in which place?'

'Sorry, I thought you knew. You're in Sumbu on Lake Tanganyika.'

'Northern Rhodesia?'

'Yes.'

Dominic fell back on the pillow without answering and closed his eyes. He was alive. Before he could ask how he came to be there and for how long, he felt himself drifting away until his whole body was completely relaxed and he fell asleep. The nurse took his pulse, temperature, and blood pressure and noted them on the chart. Satisfied, she left the room.

Someone was gently shaking his shoulder, and a voice urged, 'Come on, you have to wake up.' He opened his eyes, and standing there was a man in a white coat with a stethoscope around his neck. His blue eyes examined Dominic critically through a pair of wire-rimmed spectacles.

'I'm Doctor van Rensburg,' he said, 'you need to wake up now and have something to eat.' Dominic tried to raise himself on his elbows, but it was too much of an effort. The Doctor and nurse positioned themselves on either side of him and lifted him forward, placing two more pillows behind his back. For a moment, he felt dizzy, but it soon cleared, and he found he could move his arms although the drip slightly restricted the movement of his left one. The doctor reached inside his pyjama jacket and raised the dog tags from where they lay on his chest and lifted them by the chain over his head.

'Dominic Harrison,' he read aloud from the dog tag in the palm of his hand.

'That's right,' Dominic confirmed as the doctor checked against the name recorded on the chart.

'We found no other identification in your clothes, no papers, just the British Pounds and Belgian Francs in your pocket. Your money is in the draw there.'

Dominic remembered setting fire to the grass with the Zippo he found in the backpack; how the hyenas hesitated as the small flames spread towards them crackling and growing in height. There was little wind coming off the lake, but convection drew air into the flames, increasing the intensity of the fire. The hyenas loped away slowly at first, but as the fire spread up the face of the escarpment, they scrambled more urgently to escape until he saw them above the flames climbing upward. Had there been a strong wind blowing off the lake, they would not have been so lucky. The fire hissed and crackled as it progressed away from him and the lake. It was the last thing he remembered. What had happened to the backpack?

'How did I get here?' he asked the doctor.

'You're an extraordinarily lucky man. A local fisherman Jeffery Simpson found you on a remote part of the shore. He went to investigate the source of the fire.'

'Well, I need to thank him then.'

'I'm sure he'll come by. He has every day since you've been here.'

'How long is that?' Dominic asked.

'This is the third day,' the doctor replied, 'but no more discussion, we need to look at that wound and apply a new dressing.'

When the nurse removed the old one, Dominic glanced down at the wound. It was clean with a slightly inflamed swelling around the groove the bullet had carved out of his flesh.

'Surprisingly there was little infection, but we have been giving you penicillin injections just as a precaution,' the doctor said.

Whilst the nurse was busy, he listened intently, at different points over Dominic's chest. When he had finished with that, he lifted the covers to expose his feet.

'You've lost a couple of toenails,' he said, 'we've treated them as best we can, but they'll be sore for a while.'

He picked up the chart and studied the graphs the nurse had recorded. While he was busy, another woman entered the room with a tray which she placed on the top of the small cabinet on his right.

'When he has eaten, make sure he gets up and help him walk around the room,' he instructed the nurse. Addressing Dominic, he said, 'I have to let the police know that you are now awake so you can expect a visit from them sometime soon. I'm required to report any suspected assault casualties, and a bullet wound falls into that category. If I feel you're strong enough to walk out of here by yourself tomorrow, we'll discharge you. I'll come by and check in the morning. One other thing, no travelling for at least a week and come by here each day for the nurse to change the dressing.'

After the doctor left, the nurse placed the tray on his lap and asked how he preferred his tea which she promised would follow once he had eaten his meal.

Now, the sight and smell of the food, while it was quite simple, made him feel desperately hungry. On the plate, there was a liberal helping of what the nurse called *ubwali*. Dominic knew it by its Rhodesian Shona name as *sadza*, a maize meal preparation that was similar to what the Americans called grits. Completing the meal was some grated cabbage and pieces of fried chicken covered in dark gravy. He ate it all.

Later in the day, a messenger of the court, an African police sergeant, arrived at his bedside carrying a notebook. He was a tall, wiry man with a shaven head and a thin moustache.

'Mr. Harrison?' he enquired.

'Yes,' Dominic answered from where he sat in a dressing gown on the edge of the bed. At which point, the Sergeant drew up a chair and sat down.

'Sir, I'm required to ask you a few questions.' It sounded like a phrase he had rehearsed and used many times. He opened the notebook, retrieved a Biro pen from the top pocket of his tunic and wrote carefully at the top of the page.

'Do you have any means of identification?' he asked.

'Only those dog tags on the cupboard next to the bed.' The sergeant picked them up and copied the contents onto the page.

'What Nationality?'

'British,' Dominic replied.

'Where are you normally a resident?'

'Salisbury, Rhodesia.'

'What is your address?'

'I don't have one,' Dominic offered.

'No fixed abode,' the sergeant said as he wrote it down.

'What is your occupation?'

'Accountant,' Dominic replied. The sergeant hesitated. It seemed most unlikely. He waited for an explanation which was not forthcoming.

'Sorry, Sir, but the hospital tells me that you arrived here in a military uniform,' the sergeant prompted.

'Quite right, I was in temporary employment, but that's over, so I'm unemployed.'

'I understand a fisherman found you on the shore of the lake. How did you get there?'

'I travelled here from Salisbury via the Congo,' Dominic explained evasively, not wishing to provide too much detail.

'But you have a bullet wound, where did that happen and in what circumstances?'

Dominic thought carefully about this question.

'There's nothing to worry about. It happened outside your jurisdiction, there was no crime committed, and if I wished to lay a charge in connection with my injury, I would not be able to here in Northern Rhodesia.' The sergeant nodded realising that this could well be a correct legal interpretation of the situation. He wrote the answer in his notebook, but he was not so sure that the District Commissioner would be happy with this when he read the report.

'Did you start the fire on the western shore of the lake on Wednesday? You know it's an offence?'

'I had good reason,' Dominic replied, describing the danger from the hyenas. The sergeant wrote slowly and carefully in his notebook for a while.

'I have one last question,' he said, 'Do you have a passport in your possession?'

'I had one, but I believe I've lost it,' Dominic answered, by now it could be anywhere in the backpack in the Congo.

'Sorry, Sir, but I need to take your dog-tags with me. You may collect them in due course.' He picked them up from the top of the small cupboard as he left.

The nurse returned later to remove the drip from his arm and for the remainder of the afternoon, Dominic sat or sometimes lay on the bed, walking around the room at regular intervals. His strength was returning rapidly, and he was becoming bored. Eventually, he made his way out into the passage to find a book to read.

At the rear of the clinic, he found a nurses' recreation room with tables and chairs. There was evidence that the nurses used it as a canteen at mealtimes or more likely times when they could fit in a meal between their duties. Some women's magazines were stacked neatly on a table against one wall and a bookcase against another. The books were of a reasonably recent publication, and after browsing through them, he selected James A. Michener's "Hawaii." Returning to the ward, he sat in the chair and started to read becoming engrossed in Michener's description of the volcanic birth of islands in the Pacific. After a while, his grip on the book relaxed, and it slipped into his lap as he fell asleep.

'Mister Harrison, you have a visitor,' the nurse's voice announced as Dominic stirred from his sleep. Standing there was an African man in denim jeans, a white T-shirt and a broad smile on his face. Possibly in his late twenties, he was in great physical shape.

'I'm Jeffery Simpson,' he said, offering his hand. Dominic took the firm grip and said, 'I believe I owe you a debt of gratitude. You saved my life.'

'You had me worried out there for a while. I was beginning to think you wouldn't make it. How are you feeling?'

'I'm feeling much better. I'm hoping the doctor will let me come out to-morrow.'

'That's good news. But tell me, what happened out there with the fire.'

Dominic told him how he had walked out of the Congo across the border and down to the lake. Described how the hyenas had encircled him on the shore and having run out of bullets how he had set fire to the grass with a cigarette lighter and then passed out.

'Well, not only did the fire save you from the hyenas, but without it nobody would have come to investigate and you would most likely have died right there,' Jeffery remarked.

'You're probably right,' Dominic acknowledged.

'Look, it's none of my business, but what are your plans when you get out of the hospital. Where do you usually live? How will you get home?'

'Well, I'm from Salisbury, but the doctor has advised me not to travel for at least a week, and I need to come back each day for a new dressing. So, I need to stay for a while.'

'There are a few guesthouses around, but they are usually full at this time of the year. You are welcome to stay with us until you're fit to travel.'

'I don't want to impose on you any further. You've already saved my life.'

'Really, it's no problem. It would be nice for us to have a guest.'

Dominic turned this suggestion over in his mind. It would give him a few days to decide what he wanted to do and how he might travel back to Salisbury. When he got back there, it would not be easy to find a job. An incident from before he had joined the mercenaries would weigh against him. His parents had a farm in the Banket area, and his sister and her husband assisted them in running it. He had declined the opportunity to take over the farm in the future. So, his sister went on to study at the Agricultural College. He had no desire to end up on the farm.

'Alright thanks, it will give me a few days to plan my return to Salisbury.'

'That's decided then. I've brought your combat clothes back. They've been washed, but perhaps you would prefer some civilian attire otherwise you'll make the locals nervous,' he said with a chuckle. 'I'm a little smaller than you, but some of my father's clothes should fit until you can get some of your own.'

'I'd also prefer that. I'm not exactly anxious to draw attention to myself.'

'Good, I'll come by in the morning and pick you up.'

The official residence of the District Commissioner lay at the boundary of the *boma,* that collection of district administration buildings which included the police headquarters, prison and the court. A gravel road network ran through the *boma* area between and leading to the fronts of the buildings. Football-sized white painted stones placed every few yards marked the edges of the roads and parking places. Indigenous trees provided shade in the open areas whilst neatly trimmed lawn carpeted the sunny parts.

After lunch, with his wife, DC Arthur Cameron walked the short distance from the residence to his office in the court building. Tall, and with a military bearing, he looked impressive and immediately identifiable by his all-white tunic, brass buttons and white pith helmet. His face was clean-shaven other than the neatly trimmed moustache. He had served in Burma during the war rising to the rank of major. After the war, he joined the Colonial Office, studied law, and accepted a position as an assistant district officer in Northern Rhodesia. Technically in the legal services. Assigned to a remote rural area, he soon discovered that his duties were to cover all branches of administration. This was much to his liking, and he immersed himself in whatever challenges arose. His superiors noticed this enthusiasm and he rose quickly through the ranks to his present position.

Now his primary responsibility was to act as magistrate hearing both civil and criminal cases with those of a more severe nature referred to the high court. Recently though, he had also become involved in security and intelligence activities, brought on by the potential for unrest threatened by the emerging African political movements based in Lusaka. The secession and declaration of independence of Katanga from the rest of the Congo just across the border came after the Congo gained independence from Belgium. Fighting on the other side of the border had the potential to spill armaments, refugees and combatants into Northern Rhodesia. He was expecting to find a report on his desk of just such an incident.

When he arrived at his office, he ran through the roster of cases due to be heard that Friday. There were three cases of assault, two of theft and one of fraud. Prosecutor Mills would present evidence and call witnesses for the state while the accused tended to conduct their own defence. For some time he had neglected to read through the Government Gazettes which kept him up to date on new and amended legislation. Perusing the Gazettes, there was only one amendment that attracted his attention, and that was a change to legislation, which outlawed racial discrimination in all public eating establishments and movie theatres. He considered this for a moment and wondered how long it would take before an African brought a case of discrimination before the court. Perhaps it depended on how active the African Political Movements were in the district because the average person would have no awareness of the change and anyway there were so few restaurants, other than local taverns which were African, and no cinemas. His habit of imagining scenarios used to anticipate what might confront him in court led him to consider an African complaining that the local country club denied him access. There the members were exclusively European. Although he would be sympathetic to such a complaint, the club was within its legal rights since by law it was not considered a public place. At the next country club committee meeting, he resolved to raise the matter. Why should they not consider some suitable African's membership application? The club's constitution did not explicitly exclude anyone, but there was an unwritten rule that excluded any non-European. Smiling to himself, he made a note in his diary. This was just the beginning of the 'Winds of Change' forewarning issued by British Prime Minister Harold Macmillan as a prelude to the dissolution of the Colonial Empire.

Later in the day, the court sergeant delivered to the DC's desk the report he'd compiled regarding the suspected mercenary who appeared to have crossed into Northern Rhodesia from the Congo without completing immigration formalities and was now in the clinic in Sumbu. It also suggested that he face a charge of arson. Delivered with the report were the dog tags belonging to the suspected mercenary. 'I need to hear what this fellow has to say for himself,' the DC thought. He turned to the next item that required his attention, a letter from the Colonial Office, which he opened and read.

This is to advise you that an aerial photography reconnaissance mission has been carried out covering the Northern Rhodesia Congo border area. This will lead to the production of a new more up-to-date series of maps to aid in the administration of the Northern Province of Northern Rhodesia. To this end, we are sending two surveyors who will be working in your district to undertake the ground survey work needed to produce the mapping. They are instructed to contact you when they arrive to present their credentials.
Any assistance you can render to assist them in their duties would be very much appreciated.

DC Cameron screwed up the envelope, threw it into the waste-paper basket, walked across his office, unlocked his confidential cupboard and filed the letter.

Then he picked up the dog tag examining it more closely. Impressed into the metal was the inscription: Dominic Harrison – Commando Unit – 4631960. He took out a pre-printed form from his desk and composed a message on it. As the destination, he wrote the address of police headquarters in Salisbury and their telex number. He pressed a button on a small board on his desk which activated a barely audible buzzer in the main office. A few moments later, the same sergeant arrived at the DC's desk and gave a smart salute.

'Have the operator send this telex message to Salisbury Police Headquarters. Let's find out if your suspect has a criminal record.'

It was late afternoon when Jeffery arrived back at the house. He parked the Land Rover and joined his father and sister where they were sitting on the veranda. For a change as a compromise between his father and sister, Michelle had tuned the radio to Voice of America and the Dave Brubeck Quartet was playing 'Take Five'.

'Come and sit down with us,' his father said.

'Can I pour you a drink?' his sister added. He declined the offer, and she left to pour their father another whisky. 'He shouldn't be drinking on top of the painkillers,' she thought, 'but what difference would it make.'

'What have you been up to?' Michelle asked her brother.

'I went to the clinic to see how that guy is getting on. He's conscious at last.'

'That's good,' she responded.

'Yes, his name is Dominic. He's coming out tomorrow and has to stay in town for a week until he's well enough to travel. I told him he could stay with us for a few days.'

'Why did you do that? He's a mercenary, a Rhodesian, he's a racist,' Michelle blurted angrily, 'I met up with some of them in London.'

'But he's been fighting with Tshombe's men in the Congo, they're all black.'

'That doesn't mean a thing. He's killing people for money.'

'Other soldiers, yes, it's a war.'

'And no poor civilians get killed. You believe that?' She snapped angrily.

Jeffery remained silent, looking out over the lake. Even although the fire was now a few days ago, the sunset was a beautiful deep red. The icy silence continued for a few minutes, the tension rising.

'Well, I respect your feelings, Michelle,' her father said, 'but Jeffery has already offered our hospitality, I don't see how he can now refuse him.'

'I'll just stay out of the way,' she muttered unhappily.

Jeffery left them both on the veranda and went to his bedroom that doubled as an office. He did some bookkeeping to bring the business records up to date. The ringing of a hand-held brass bell announced that George was ready to serve the evening meal. There was not too much talk at the table that evening, perhaps he should have checked with Michelle before inviting Dominic to stay, but he normally decided these things himself as she was usually not there.

After dinner, Michelle and her father returned to the veranda to have coffee. It was a beautiful evening, and the moon remained hidden somewhere below the horizon whilst the Milky Way glittered like an infinite number of diamonds spread across a black satin sky. Michelle had forgotten how brilliant the stars were out here in the African bush. In London, even at night when the sky was cloudless, the lights of the city washed them away.

Harold Simpson took two tablets and washed them down with a sip of coffee to subdue the fierce pain that was eating into his body.

'Michelle, I loved your mother very much, but sometimes I wonder if it was not a bit selfish to subject my children to the results of a mixed marriage. Being occasionally confronted by bigotry and racism must be hard.'

'It just makes me so angry. What makes those people think they are so superior?'

'Well, you've lived in London a cosmopolitan city with many different races and nationalities living there together, but there are prejudices based on culture, religion, language and in your case, even gender. Look at the class system in England where history has institutionalised privilege and perceived superiority. Yet, even so, there is less racialism there than there is here. Social upward mobility is most clearly defined by education. And yes, I admit that you are disadvantaged by your gender and your race, but times are changing. During your lifetime, things will change for the better. In the end, if you have an advantage, it's your education.'

'I have you and mother to thank for that,' she conceded, 'but what about Jeffery?'

'It's interesting. Unlike you, Jeffery looks like and is a true African. He has little social contact with Europeans, so he experiences no racism here in Sumbu being remote from the cities. He is mighty confident and comfortable with himself in this environment, has a successful business and no ambitions to be anywhere else. Excuse the pun, but he would be like a fish out of water in London,' he smiled.

'Are you suggesting that I have an advantage because I'm lighter-skinned? Aren't you being racist?' Michelle muttered.

'No, but I recognise that racism exists in many different degrees and preferences. Some white men find black women attractive like me, but not all white men feel that way. Likewise, some white women find black men attractive. They have a reputation for being sexually desirable and well endowed.'

Michelle did not respond.

It was peaceful sitting there on the veranda in the warm evening air. The only sounds were the chirping of the cicadas and the dull hum of the diesel generator. Far in the distance, without the moon and just visible, the shore of the lake was defined by the lights carried by the kapenta fishing dugouts operating a few hundred yards out from the villages. But large sections of the shore were invisible because the mountains rose straight out of the water, leaving the shore unpopulated. Michelle turned on the radio and tuned in to a shortwave music station. The Shirelles were singing 'Will you love me tomorrow?' which made her feel lonely even though she was with the family she loved so much. London was far away, so she had none of her closest friends to share her deeper emotions. Tears welled up in her eyes, and there was a thickness in her throat. She should have been crying for her father, but he seemed so much in control of himself, she cried for herself.

'I'm going to bed,' her father said, 'ask Jeffery to turn off the generator when you're ready to go in.'

CHAPTER 6

Dominic and Jeffery arrived at the house in the Land Rover a little after ten in the morning, later than Jeffery had hoped. The doctor had been attending an emergency, delaying a final examination and the authorisation of Dominic's discharge. Entering the house up the veranda steps, Dominic met an elderly emaciated looking white man introduced to him as Jeffery's father. He expected him to be an African. They shook hands and Dominic thanked him for lending him some clothes, but the old man shook his head and said that Dominic should keep them, as well as whatever clothing there was in the wardrobe in the spare room.

'He's not got long to live,' Jeffery whispered to Dominic as they entered the kitchen.

'I'm sorry,' replied Dominic.

'I'm not much help to him as I'm out on the lake most days. My sister has come out from London to help.' Jeffery said, noting that she had made herself absent following up on her promise.

'I look forward to meeting her. I've never been to London,' Dominic remarked.

'Me neither. If you need to make tea or coffee or to make a sandwich, you'll find what you need here. The fridge is working so if you're looking for butter or cheese and the like, it's in there.'

They went down a passage to a spare room, and Jeffery said, 'I hope this is alright as a bedroom.'

'Thanks, it's just fine,' Dominic replied.

'Look I'll leave you here to settle in, but when you're ready if you feel up to it come down to the jetty and I'll show you around. I also have your backpack stored in the boat. I'll be down there most of the day, so you could bring it back here and unpack. If you walk back along the road, just take a right at the fork.'

'Sounds a good idea, I'll be along later then.'

When Jeffery had left, he examined the room. There was not much to look at, a single bed with a side table and an electric lamp. A small desk, one of those you find in schools where the seat is attached, and the desktop hinges up to expose space for storing the student's books and writing materials. At the right on the back edge were two cylindrical holes that had formerly contained inkwells and grooves along its length to hold pens and pencils. A towel lay neatly folded on the desk. The wardrobe had double doors with full-length mirrors and appeared to be made of oak, probably imported from Europe at some time in the past. An imitation woven Persian rug covered about half of the cement plastered floor area. The window looked out into the back garden of the house where there were some pawpaw and mango trees. Grass grew in between them long enough to reach up to his knees. Looking at himself in the mirror, he was shocked at his appearance. Unshaven, lips split, bloodshot eyes and greasy, short, dark hair.

Looking in the wardrobe, he found no dressing gown, so he undressed and wrapped the towel around himself from the chest down to the middle of his thighs. Padding with bare feet through the house in search of the shower he hoped he would not bump into Jeffery's sister. What was her name? Jeffery didn't say. The shower was in the bathroom, so he locked the door and turned on the water. It was unheated but warm enough that within a minute, his body felt comfortable the same temperature as the water. Lathered with soap he allowed the shower to cascade over him for quite a long time, standing there naked with his eyes closed until there could be no doubt all the soap washed away. After he had dried himself, he padded his way back to his room and dressed again, pulling on his combat boots.

He needed to find a store where he could buy a razor, blades, toothbrush and toothpaste for a start. Some tennis shoes like those that Jeffery wore would be preferable to the combat boots. He stuffed his money into his pocket and made his way through the house and out onto the veranda. There, a political discussion was in progress on the radio.

'Meet my daughter Michelle,' the old man said, waving his hand in her direction.

Dominic stood there quite astonished as he gazed at this beautiful girl, in her mid-twenties he estimated, with flawless skin, no makeup, and long black hair tied back in a ponytail. She wore shorts and a white T-shirt and sandals.

'Dominic,' he said, extending his hand as he approached her.

'Hi, I must be on my way,' she said dismissively, turning away before he could reach her, leaving him standing with his hand extended. Embarrassed, he looked towards the old man, but he just shrugged. Dominic's immediate reaction was a desire to get away from the house as fast as he could, but he thought better of it and decided to spend some time with the old man before he went off to meet Jeffery.

'Sir, I'm going to make myself some coffee. Would you like a cup?'

'Yes, that's a splendid idea, black with one teaspoon of sugar will be fine,' he said, shifting painfully in his chair to see Dominic more easily. The young man went away, and for a while, the old man could hear him busy in the kitchen. A heated debate was in progress on the radio regarding the pros-and-cons of Britain joining the European Community with the protagonists talking over each other. Dominic returned with the two cups of coffee, setting one down on the table next to the old man who was quietly gazing out over the lake.

'What do you think about the future of the British colonies?' the old man asked, turning down the volume on the radio.

'I must confess I've not given it much thought, Sir,' Dominic replied, sipping his coffee. He was surprised at the question because he was expecting the old man to ask him who he was and how he came to be there. Perhaps he already knew.

'There are going to be changes. Independence is coming, and there is no knowing whether that change will be peaceful or not. A country seeking independence will hold elections. But based on what type of constitution? Will we have a democracy? Or will the situation descend into a war between different tribes? Northern Rhodesia has mineral wealth, and the mines on the Copper Belt generate most of the revenues for the country, but the mines are in the hands of private enterprise. The Russians are funding some of the African National Liberation movements which may encourage them to introduce a communist political system and nationalise the mines. Britain and the West may resist if this is without compensation. A war directly or by proxy could result; much like what is happening in the Congo. For us, the cold war could turn into a hot war. You have some experience with this?'

'A little, Sir,' Dominic replied without elaborating, waiting for a more probing question, but it did not come. Instead, the old man turned up the radio again as if to indicate that their short conversation was at an end and sat with his eyes closed listening intently.

Dominic got up, picked up the cups from the table, took them through to the kitchen, washed and dried them and stored them away in the kitchen cupboard. When he came out again onto the veranda, the old man was as he had left him, lost in his thoughts with the radio droning next to him, oblivious of Dominic's presence.

When he reached the fork in the road that Jeffery had mentioned, instead of taking the right branch that led down to the Jetty, he carried on straight towards the centre of the small town. His legs were sore and stiff, but his feet hurt most, so he progressed relatively slowly. It wasn't too difficult to find a General Dealer's Store in the main street. There was a choice of three. The one he entered was typical of most stores one could find in small African towns. An aroma of spices greeted him as he passed through the door into a cool and subduedly lit interior. One could not easily describe the choice of goods that were for sale. It was more a case of you name it we have it, and if not, we can get it for you. Vegetables, fruit, meat and other fresh products brought in from the countryside, were not available. One could buy these at the open market, but there were bins containing sugar, maize meal and wheat flour which could be scooped out into brown paper bags, weighed and sold by the pound.

As might be expected, the shopkeeper was Asian most likely of Indian origin a testimony to their impressive history and success as traders. He greeted Dominic with the typical friendliness characteristic of his profession. His wife, identifiable by the red spot on her forehead dressed in a simple sari hovered behind him ready to offer any assistance that might be required. It turned out that Mr Patel was also a moneychanger. 'No problem,' he said when Dominic asked if he would accept Belgian Francs. Half an hour later, Dominic left the store with a paper carrier bag containing his personal supplies plus some fresh bread, coffee and a variety of canned foods for the house. A small contribution, but it was the least he could do.

When he arrived at the Jetty, he could not see Jeffery anywhere. In the parking area a few trucks stood next to a concrete loading ramp taking on cargo, mostly hessian sacks of dried fish. The drivers, predominantly Indians, had assembled on one side relaxing and talking. The Jetty was a wooden structure extending some two hundred yards out into the water. Old motor tyres secured along the sides of the jetty protected the boats as they rose and fell on the swell. Walking along the Jetty past the moored boats he thought he might find Jeffery on one of them. Labourers were busy offloading a variety of goods, carrying them to the warehouses or trucks.

'Do you know which boat belongs to Jeffery Simpson?' he asked a group of men working nearby. One of them pointed up the Jetty.

'That one with the blue on the bow,' he replied.

Dominic walked along the Jetty until he reached it and clambered aboard.

It was well worn, and there was a little water swirling around in the bottom, evidence of small leaks. Otherwise, it looked sound. There was an outboard motor attached to the stern with two red fuel tanks situated under the operator's seat. He moved forward to the storage compartment in the bow, opened the door, and removed the backpack. It confirmed he was on the right boat.

'Someone told me there was a trespasser on my boat,' Jeffery jested with a smile.

'Yes, I was looking for you but not sure where you were, looks like everything's safe here with so many eyes watching out,' Dominic remarked.

'You're quite right there.'

'Quite busy here, where do these boats come from?'

'They bring cargo through from Mpulungu. It's about fifty miles to the east by boat from here, the biggest town on our part of the lake. There's a commercial fishing operation there. It's on the main road route down to Lusaka in the south, so they transport most of their fish that way. But some of it they bring by boat to here and road transport it down to the copper-belt. It's a shorter road route.'

'You mean they take the pontoon ferry across the Luapula River at Chembe, drive through the Congo pedicle strip and come out at Mufulira on the copper-belt?' Dominic asked.

'Yes, it's a much shorter drive.'

'What about your operation?'

'Well, I don't do any fishing. I take my boat up along the western shore where the villagers catch kapenta from dugout canoes. They salt the fish and lay them out to sun dry on reed mats along the beach, then collect and store them in hessian bags. I buy the fish, bring the bags back here and store them in my warehouse waiting for Omar to come through from Ndola.'

'Who's Omar?'

'Omar drives up from Ndola to buy the fish from me, and I buy supplies from him to sell to the villagers.'

'Sounds like a reasonable business,' Dominic observed.

'It is, but Omar needs larger quantities; otherwise, I could lose out to other suppliers. I'm trying to make more trips which is demanding and I have to encourage the villagers to catch more.'

'Aren't there more villages along the coast?'

'No, I'm collecting from all the villages for twenty-five miles as far as the border.'

'What about further north beyond the border into the Congo.'

'The escarpment is so steep for two hundred miles up to Moba Port that there are no villages of any importance.'

'What about the eastern shore?'

'It's the main transport route up to Kigoma about three hundred miles north. Cargo and passenger ferries are operating all the way. From there, there is a rail link through to the Indian Ocean port of Dar es Salaam. It's too far for me to operate in such a small boat.'

Dominic thought this over for a while. It certainly seemed that Jeffery had a problem.

'Is there anything I can help you with?' Dominic asked.

'No, thanks, it's too late to go out now. Anyway, you need to get better. You're still not looking that great. Perhaps you should get back to the house and rest. I'll be up later to take you back to the clinic to have that dressing changed.'

Dominic shouldered the backpack, picked up his brown paper packet of shopping, said he'd see Jeffery later and left for the house.

Back there Dominic found that the old man and Michelle were not on the veranda. The old man was probably sleeping, and he didn't know what Michelle did during the day, so she could be anywhere. He put the backpack on his bed and took the groceries through to the kitchen after removing his personal items. Once he had made a cup of coffee, he went back to his room, sat in the chair and reviewed his day. Meeting Michelle that morning had been a bit of a disappointment, not that he had reason to have any expectations. But her behaviour had been, well, not exactly hostile but not friendly either. Such a beautiful girl was bound to have suitors wherever she went.

There were no rings on her fingers, but that didn't mean she was not attached or engaged. Perhaps right now, she was visiting one of her male friends. The thought disturbed him, which was quite absurd. He didn't even know her, so why did it concern him. But the thought persisted until he had to acknowledge that he had an overwhelming desire to get know her better, at least to talk to her. Perhaps the opportunity would arise in the next few days before he moved on, but what if she had gone away for a week or two. He would leave without ever having even spoken to a girl who for some reason he could not explain, captivated him. It was something he had never experienced before. He would just have to wait and see.

Then there was Jeffery whose entrepreneurial spirit he was beginning to appreciate and respect. The same spirit had led him across the lake to save Dominic's life. He felt he owed Jeffery but was it even possible to repay him.

Finally, the old man, whose insight and wisdom had impressed him, sitting there on the veranda that morning. A man who was anticipating a future that he was not destined to experience.

Dominic went through to the bathroom with his towel and newly purchased toiletries, shaved, brushed his teeth and took a shower, trying not to wet the dressing.

Back in his room, he applied some of the ointment he received from the clinic to his inflamed and blackened toes. Once he had dressed, he sat back in the chair and continued reading Hawaii.

Half an hour later, Jeffery arrived back, and they set off for the clinic in his Land Rover. It was the long-wheelbase version which meant there was a fair amount of space at the rear for carrying goods or whatever. The gearbox made it an ideal vehicle for travelling over open terrain away from the roads, with a yellow lever to engage low range, and a red one to engage four-wheel-drive.

'I'll take you each day,' Jeffery said, 'but from tomorrow it will have to be much later. I'm going to be making more trips from now on to try to increase the amount of fish I'm bringing in.'

'That makes for a long day I can walk there it's not that far,' Dominic replied, thinking that it was nothing compared to how far he had walked to get to Sumbu.

'I'm sure you're strong enough, but it's your feet you need to look after. If you walk too much, you'll only make them worse and delay your recovery.'

'Alright, perhaps you're right,' Dominic conceded. He wondered why Michelle couldn't help. Was she away, if not, was it really that much trouble? Perhaps he would find out in due course.

Changing the dressing took no more than ten minutes after a wait of fifteen minutes for the nurse to arrive from her ward duties. They soon returned to the house where Jeffery reminded him to listen for the bell and join them for dinner.

Back in his room, Dominic turned to the backpack and started to unpack it. Inside he found the maps on top of which was the pistol. Jeffery must have picked it up on the shore and placed it there. Underneath that were the major's spare clothes, a blanket, first aid kit, a bag of toiletries, a metal mug and plate, and some utensils. At the very bottom, there was a large wallet and a notebook held together by two broad elastic bands.

Slipping off the elastic bands, he separated the notebook from the wallet, unfastening the clip and folding back the flap. Inside he found a wad of pound notes in denominations ranging from ten shillings to ten pounds but mostly ten-pound notes.

For a moment, he could not quite appreciate what he was seeing. It was more money in cash than he had ever seen other than with the tellers at a bank. Opening the notebook, he browsed through the pages that turned out to be a cashbook that recorded the receipts and payments made in respect of the Katanga Mercenary Commandos. Turning to the last entries made in the book, he read off the last recorded balance. The date was the day before the incident in which the major died. The figure was two thousand three hundred and forty-four pounds, ten shillings. He knew from the meticulously kept entries that there was no need to count the notes. There were no coins, with all transactions recorded in multiples of ten shillings. He was now holding a considerable fortune in his hands. What should he do with the money? First of all, having captured a unit of the mercenary group, the UN would press forward to try to rescue the major and his driver. They would find the Jeep with the body of the major and the driver missing. By then the rebels would have pillaged the Jeep taking the major's FN rifle, the radio and Dominic's backpack. Whoever investigated the incident would be recording the Major as killed in action and the driver as missing, not immediately presumed dead, but perhaps captured. For all anyone knew the rebels had taken the major's backpack. As far as the police in Sumbu were concerned, he had arrived at the hospital without any possessions other than what he was wearing. A watch, a wallet containing money in his pocket and the dog tags around his neck. It presented opportunities, but on the other hand, keeping the money would be dishonest.

The bell rang for dinner. He placed the pistol in the drawer next to his bed, the rest he returned to the backpack. For a few minutes, he delayed leaving, not wanting to be the first to arrive. When he did get there, he found the old man waiting patiently at the head of the table with a portly black man dressed all in white standing to one side whom he introduced as George, the cook.

'Can I offer you a sherry?' the old man asked when Dominic sat down.

'Yes Sir, that would be nice.'

The old man motioned to George who came forward and poured the sherry into a small cut glass goblet. Dominic waited not wanting to take a sip until the old man did in case there was some family ritual attached to it. Perhaps his children needed to be present for an evening toast. Would Michelle appear? There was an almost Victorian formality about the whole scene in the dining room right down to the dresser with family silver on display. There was a silver candelabra in the centre of the table and place settings made up with silver cutlery and starched serviettes flanked by glasses.

'Ring the bell again, George,' the old man prompted, looking impatiently at his watch. He took a sip of his sherry, so Dominic followed suit.

Jeffery and Michelle came in with an apology each, said their good-evenings and took their seats. Dominic's heartbeat quickened slightly at the sight of this beautiful girl seated diagonally opposite him at the table. George served two more glasses of sherry and went out of the room and returned carrying four plates held deftly in his hands, setting them down at each place. He followed this with three bowls of vegetables brought through on a tray with a gravy boat. Dominic wondered how George managed to do the cooking, keep the food warm in the kitchen, and serve as well. Jeffery engaged his father in a lively conversation as the meal progressed with Dominic listening and stealing an occasional glance at Michelle. She sat there, silently engrossed in her meal without once looking in his direction. Had she looked his way, he would have opened a conversation. Was it shyness? But he knew that was a futile hope. For some reason, she did not wish to have anything to do with him.

CHAPTER 7

As the days passed, Dominic rapidly regained his mobility. His legs were back to their former strength, and the wound in his side had healed enough for him to apply new dressings himself. Only his feet were still a bit tender. Two visits Michelle had from a senior game ranger who arrived to pick her up in his Land Rover dispelled any thoughts he might have about her being shy. The old man introduced him as Misheck Ozumba. They left together laughing and talking happily, Michelle touching him occasionally on his forearm. He couldn't understand what they were discussing because they were speaking in the vernacular. It was now time Dominic realised to travel back to Salisbury. These days Jeffery was getting up well before dawn, so Dominic joined him in the kitchen, and they had breakfast together before he was due to make his way down to the boat.

'Jeffery, I have much to thank you for, but I cannot impose myself on your hospitality any longer. I need to get back to Salisbury.'

'I understand. You must have someone to get back to.'

'No, actually I don't, but when I get there, I'll look around for a job.'

Jeffery thought for a moment and then said, 'You know I can't keep up the pace I'm working at now to bring in more fish. If you don't have a job to go back to, why not stay on here and work with me? We can certainly make enough money for both of us.'

'Are you serious?' Dominic asked.

'Look, you can't get out of here so easily. You've lost your passport so you can't go back through the pedicle strip,' he warned with a devious smile.

'But I can't continue staying at the house. I sense that Michelle is seriously uncomfortable about that.'

'Yes, she's difficult but listen, I have to accept that my father has not got long. Once he's gone, there's nothing to keep Michelle here. She will go back to London, and I will be all alone here in the house. So, you see I have an ulterior motive for asking you to stay.'

'What about Misheck, they seem noticeably close?'

'With Michelle, it's difficult to know. All I know is that he's just taking her on day trips into the Game Park.'

'And you, do you have a woman to join you here? I don't want to be in the way.'

'There's no shortage of girls around here, but to find a suitable intelligent one out here is difficult. They're all in the cities. If I lived in Lusaka, it would be a different matter. Let's cross that bridge if and when I find someone.'

'But I have no idea what you do out there,' Dominic said cautiously.

'Tell you what, I have to make several trips today, come with me on my final trip, and I'll show you the ropes. I'll also introduce you to the headman at the largest village, and we'll stay there overnight so you can experience artisanal fishing and their way of life. Is that a deal?'

'A deal,' Dominic said with conviction grasping his extended hand.

'Right, I'm off now. Meet me at the Jetty at four this afternoon.'

When Jeffery had gone, he finished his breakfast and cleaned up the kitchen. It was still early, so Michelle and her father had not yet made an appearance. He made a cup of coffee, took it out onto the veranda and sat there relaxing, waiting for the sun to rise. Birds were beginning to chatter in the half-darkness. It was with a new sense of purpose that he greeted the day. Half an hour later still well before sunrise, Misheck arrived in his Land Rover, turned it around to face the way out, and then hooted briefly to announce his arrival. When he noticed Dominic sitting on the veranda, he gave a wave but remained sitting waiting in the vehicle.

Early morning game drive Dominic thought, an excellent time to see the animals. About five minutes later, Michelle appeared dressed as usual, but this time she had on a wide-brimmed straw hat and was carrying a wicker basket with the contents covered by a cloth. She briefly glanced his way but did not offer a greeting and by now, Dominic had decided that it would be better if he didn't either. She got into the vehicle placing the basket at her feet, closed the door, and they drove away. Now that he had the agreement with Jeffery, he felt better able to deal with her disapproval. She would not yet be aware of the events that morning but was sure that Jeffery would explain when he had the opportunity. As for Michelle, they would have a silent agreement between them to make their lives as comfortable as possible in the circumstances.

There was now the question of what to do about the money hidden in the backpack in his room. It was just too much money to keep in the house. He went back to his room to read the book until the agency of the National Bank opened, which he imagined would be at nine.

The entrance to the bank led into a small hall with four desks along the wall on which were a collection of pre-printed forms. Two men and a woman formed a queue at the teller's window which had an ornately carved mahogany frame with brass bars separating the public from the teller. A second window in an almost identical style, marked Enquiries, was located to one side. A heavy door near the entrance identified the manager's office. Dominic asked at enquiries if he could see the manager explaining that he wanted to make a substantial deposit. After the clerk had spoken to the manager, she asked him to wait on a chair located outside his office door. Five minutes later, the manager came out and shaking Dominic's hand introduced himself as Michael Nicholls. He was in appearance just what Dominic had expected except for the polka-dot bow tie. Probably in his early forties, a little over-weight, perfectly groomed and dressed in a pinstriped suit. His skin was that of a man who spent little time outside in the sun, unblemished but slightly pink perhaps a result of lunchtime gin-and-tonics at the club.

'Mister Harrison, what can I do for you?' he asked spreading his hands out in front of him on the desk, peering at Dominic over narrow reading glasses that he had mounted on his nose as Dominic sat down.

'I need to open two bank accounts, one a savings-account the other a cheque account,' Dominic explained placing the large wallet on the desk.

'Have you just moved here? I've not seen you before.'

'Yes, you can say that. I'm entering the fishing business,' Dominic said.

'Well first I need you to fill in this form giving your details, you know, name and address, phone number and so forth, one for each account.' Dominic took the pen he offered and filled in the forms. When he'd finished, he handed them to Michael Nicholls who read them without comment.

'Tell me what amount you want to deposit in the interest-bearing account and I'll give you a better rate than you can get at the post office. Our rates range from one-and-a-half per cent to three per cent depending on the fixed period.'

'It's more than two thousand pounds,' Dominic told him.

'That's a fair amount,' the bank manager acknowledged raising his eyebrows and looking at Dominic more closely. It wasn't often he had a young man coming in to deposit that sort of amount, especially in this remote place, but if he was going into the fishing business, who knows.

'I can offer you a twelve-month deposit savings account at three per cent,' he said.

'As long as the interest is compounded in the same account,' Dominic replied.

'Yes, it's monthly, and we will post you a statement at the end of each month,' the bank manager assured him, 'should I open the accounts?'

'If you can do that right away, I'll make the deposit.'

'That's fine, I'll do that while you wait, but just be aware that I can't issue you with a cheque book right away. I have to order it from head-office. Check with me again in two weeks. If you need to withdraw some cash from the cheque account in the meantime, don't go to the teller come directly back to me, and I'll help you.'

Michael Nicholls fetched two ledgers from his cabinet and consulting the forms that Dominic had filled in, made the required entries. Dominic handed him the money from the large wallet as the deposit. The bank manager counted the notes neatly paper clipping them into wads of one-hundred-pounds. After recounting the wads and loose notes, he announced that the amount was two thousand three hundred and forty-four pounds ten shillings, precisely the amount recorded in the notebook.

'You agree?' he asked.

'Yes,' Dominic replied.

He repeated the process for the amount that Dominic gave him for the cheque account and made the opening entries in the ledgers. Having opened the accounts, he gathered up the cash, went to a large heavy four-legged safe, rotated the combination dial according to the code sequence, swung open the door and deposited the money. Five minutes later, Dominic left the bank with two signed and stamped deposit slips. He then walked back along the road until he found a store. After about twenty minutes, he came out of the store with a couple of pairs of jeans, some shirts and a pair of tennis shoes. If he needed something more substantial for his feet, he could revert to his combat boots. He returned to the house to continue reading his book waiting for the time in the afternoon when he had agreed to meet Jeffery.

As they drove out of Sumbu, the headlights illuminated the way up from the lake. Michelle glanced at Misheck, waiting for some comment about where they were going. He was concentrating on negotiating several curves appearing in the lights of the vehicle as they progressed. It was better not to distract him until the road straightened. Eventually, in the pre-sunrise light, they were passing through successive grassy *dambos* making up a dry wetland.

'Come on, Misheck, tell me where we are going.'

'To Kaputa, it's on the north-western shore of Lake Mweru Wantipa,' he replied.

'What's there?' she asked.

'Well, it's a small town, but it's more a case of what we see on the way. We needn't go the whole way. I have to make sure the game guards make regular patrols of the northern shore of the lake. There is a large elephant population spread over that area. I thought you might want to see the elephants.'

'That's fantastic, how long will it take?' she asked excitedly.

'About half an hour to reach the lake, more a huge swamp actually,' he replied, 'so we'll make it at sunrise and drive along the north shore until we find a herd.'

Michelle sat back in the Land Rover taking in the African bush, which she had learned to appreciate during travels with her father when she was a young girl. But they had never visited anywhere as exciting as it was here. No wonder he had chosen to retire nearby at the lake. He had introduced her to Misheck having asked if he would mind showing her around. As they drove, they passed through areas of savannah woodland and out again into the *dambos*. Some cattle egrets strode along in the grass at the side of the road as they passed by.

Michelle had become fond of Misheck and felt safe in his presence. Not only with her physical safety, but they had a cultural affinity. She understood the social customs that regulated his behaviour and even felt more comfortable than the predominantly European culture she experienced in London. Nevertheless, London had the advantage of being a cosmopolitan city where she fitted comfortably into the background with only occasional racial discrimination. She found herself caught in a social no-mans-land between the two cultures, the magnificent splendour of Africa and the centuries of evolved science and democratic politics of London. She did not accept but was more used to the racial discrimination here in colonial Africa than in London. When she experienced it in London, she felt outraged because it violated her democratic rights. Usually, these insults came from Europe's colonial settlers visiting the city. Here in Northern Rhodesia, the government was denying the majority of the population their democratic rights. Like a chameleon, she changed herself to blend into either her African or European skin depending on where she was. Sometimes her confusion about her identity reminded her of the tale they would relate as children. If you put a chameleon on a checkerboard, it will explode. Now in her African skin, she gravitated towards Misheck as a potential partner, but was she in love with him? Her feelings for him grew as their time together became more frequent. But she was not sure.

As they progressed along the road, originally constructed as a series of straight sections with the occasional curve, they had to deviate around trees that elephants had pushed over. Passing around one of these chicanes, she could see how the weeds had grown in the inaccessible surface of the road that lay beneath the tree.

'A few more minutes and we'll leave the road and drive down towards the marsh,' Misheck said, interrupting her thoughts. When he stopped on the road, he pulled the red lever and engaged the four-wheel-drive. He turned off the road and headed towards a clump of trees. As he drove, passing through some long grass, he shifted forward in his seat, raising his head close to the roof, the steering wheel almost on his chest.

'I have to look out for tree-stumps in the long grass,' he explained, peering downward as they went. The vehicle rocked to-and-fro as they passed over some uneven ground. They passed through the clump of trees, and when they emerged on the other side, the swamp spread out beyond and slightly below them. And there in front of them no more than two hundred yards away was a herd of elephant. Some of them were in the swamp wading and feeding, the water up to the middle of their bodies. Nearer, they were on land just short of the papyrus reeds that marked the edge of the swamp. Misheck edged the Land Rover slowly towards them and those on land moved slowly into the water excepting one that stood its ground, shaking its head as if in refusal.

'Look, she has a baby and can't go into the water, he's too small,' Misheck said to Michelle.

'Oh, that's beautiful,' she replied in excitement, 'can we go a little closer.'

'Let's try.'

As he edged slowly further forward, Michelle could see that the elephant cow was becoming increasingly agitated, swaying with huge ears flapping. Then she charged towards them in a cloud of dust. Michelle felt her feet hard on the floor as she instinctively pressed herself back into the seat.

'It's alright,' Misheck reassured her, 'it's a mock charge to warn us not to come too close. She won't leave her baby.'

Just as he suggested, she stopped well short of them and turned back to her baby.

'Wow, you're right, I thought she would keep coming,' Michelle replied.

'I know them intimately, they're part of my life, like children.'

They sat watching the elephants for some time as the sun broke through the horizon painting the whole scene a pale pink. Some white pelicans perched on the top of a nearby tree bathed in the early morning light,.

'Shall we have breakfast?' Michelle asked.

'Great idea. I'll just reverse back into the trees so our elephant mother can relax.'

With the vehicle parked half in and half out of the trees, they could still see up-and-down the edge of the swamp. Michelle opened the basket and poured them each a cup of hot tea from the thermos flask. She handed him a bacon sandwich and took one for herself.

With the windows of the Land Rover slid open she could hear some masked weavers coming to life nearby. It was so peaceful she felt unusually relaxed. After a while, Misheck leaned over and kissed her on the cheek.

'Are you enjoying it?' he asked.

'It's wonderful,' she replied, holding him and kissing him on the lips, but immediately taking the empty mug and returning it to the basket as a signal that the intimacy should end right there. He sat back with a happy smile admiring her unselfconsciously. She squeezed his arm affectionately, finished repacking the basket and watched the elephants in the swamp.

'There's something over there just beyond those trees,' she said, pointing, 'it's white. What is it?'

'Come with me. I'll show you,' he replied.

They got out of the vehicle and Misheck unclipped the three-seven-five magnum rifle from behind the seats and hooked it over his shoulder.

As they walked along the edge of the trees, the elephants took no notice. The cow and calf had moved away from them a little further along the shore. As they approached the white object,

Michelle realised that she was looking at a large elephant skull bleached white by the sun. When she stood next to it, it reached up to her hip.

'My God,' she exclaimed, 'what happened here?'

'Poachers, but some time ago,' Misheck observed. 'Look here. You can still see where the bullet entered its head. And here you can see where they forcibly removed the tusks.'

'Does this happen often?'

'All the time, we're only about ten miles from the Congo border, so they come over here, and in no time they're back over the border with the ivory. We're fighting a losing battle, but we did catch a couple of them the other day.'

'What happens to them?'

'Well, we hold a hearing here at the district court to make sure there is sufficient evidence to refer it to the High court in Ndola or Fort Rosebury. They get up to two years in prison if found guilty.'

'Is there nothing more anyone can do to prevent it?' Michelle askcd.

'The game department is just too small to cope and even if we doubled our staff here, it would still be difficult to contain.'

As they walked back to the Land Rover, she could not imagine how Misheck carried on knowing that irrespective of his dedication, the outcome seemed inevitable. When they got back to the vehicle, Misheck stopped and pointed to the sky in the west, 'You see those vultures circling, you know what that means.'

'Another dead elephant?' she asked.

'Not necessarily, there are lions in this area, let's take a look.'

Misheck drove carefully through the trees and over open grassland back to the road, disengaged the four-wheel drive and headed towards Kaputa. On the way, she saw some antelope in the trees but did not ask what they were. She could see that Misheck was preoccupied, driving much faster than they had any time that morning. He was clenching his jaw and she could see the tension in his face. They left the road where the vultures were overhead and drove towards some trees where they could now see them balancing precariously on the top branches, their wings half spread, to maintain balance. She could smell death before they arrived at the carcase. A pack of hyenas were tearing at the flesh of the dead elephant, breaking away periodically to chase away the vultures, as if there was not enough meat for them all. A few jackals circled at a safe distance from the hyenas waiting for the opportunity to dart in and grab a piece of meat.

'Not a pretty sight, you can see that the tusks are gone,' Misheck muttered.

'Let's get out of here,' Michelle breathed softly.

Back at the road, Misheck stopped the Land Rover, got out and walked, first in one direction and then the other. When he came back, he said, 'I found their tracks in the grass leading in the direction of the border. By now they're safely on the other side.'

They drove back to Sumbu in a sombre mood.

At four o'clock, dressed in his new jeans, T-shirt and tennis shoes conforming to Jeffery's choice of attire, Dominic walked down to the jetty. There he found Jeffery and Jimmy unloading sacks of kapenta from the boat. He helped carry the bags to the warehouse where Jeffery supervised the storage arrangements. When they finished, he paid Jimmy for his day's effort telling him that he only needed to come later in the morning the next day.

'You and I will load the boat out there at the village tomorrow morning,' he said to Dominic. He locked the warehouse and he and Dominic went back down to the jetty and boarded the boat. Without a load of supplies, Jeffery having delivered them earlier in the day, the boat sat higher than usual in the water and they skimmed over the small waves out into Cameron Bay. The lake was shimmering in the afternoon sun and Dominic settled himself comfortably just short of the bow feeling relaxed. It was wonderful out here on the lake compared to his experience on the escarpment, now visibly rising out of the lake to the east. In the stern at the tiller, Jeffery leaned back smiling to himself, for whatever reason.

'It'll take about forty minutes,' Jeffery shouted over the loud hum of the engine. 'You need to come back here and take over so you can get a feel for the boat. Also, you need to take note of the direction we're going. See those two hills there in the distance on top of the mountains that look like the two humps on a camel's back,' he said pointing northeast, 'keep the boat aligned in that direction, and when we get closer, I'll give you another feature that will lead us to the village.'

Dominic went back and exchanged positions with Jeffery.

'Hold the throttle in that position for economical speed,' Jeffery said.

As they travelled further out into the lake, the waves became a little larger, causing some spray to reach Dominic in the back of the boat. He held his course occasionally adjusting it to keep the boat on the correct approach. After about thirty minutes, Jeffery pointed and said, 'You see those boulders on the hills. If you look south back along the shore, you can see that there is some flat land recessed into the escarpment. That's where the village is.' Dominic changed course and headed in that direction. As they drew nearer, he saw there was a beach with huts strung out all along it quite close to the water. Dugout canoes lay all along the shore, but only a few were out on the water. Jeffery guided him towards the south end of the village asking him to reduce speed.

'Now turn the bow to face directly into the beach and drive the boat up onto it. There aren't any rocks here so it won't get damaged.' Dominic followed his instructions, and there was a thud as the bow of the boat mounted the beach. Jeffery carried the anchor up to the bow, threw it onto the beach, and jumped onto the sand, with Dominic following him. No sooner had they set foot on the beach, than ten or more smiling and laughing children surrounded them chattering away, some pulling on Jeffery's clothing. He plunged his hand into his trouser pocket and came out with a handful of sweets which he threw in all directions. Sand kicked up from their bare feet as they scampered off to pick them up.

'Remember to bring some from the warehouse when you come otherwise, they will be disappointed and get up to some mischief on the boat,' Jeffery warned with a laugh. They walked south along the beach for a short way until they came upon a large wooden and thatch dwelling, much larger than many of the others along the way. Four men sat cross-legged in front of an elderly African man with a bush of tightly curled grey hair, sitting on a log stool. He recognised Jeffery with a wave and immediately dismissed the four men who rose and walked away down the beach.

'This is Moses, the village headman. Moses, meet Dominic,' Jeffery said. Dominic looked at the old man and smiled, thinking what an appropriate name he had, with his grey beard. They shook hands and Moses said,

'Pleased to meet you Do…,' then hesitating continued, 'I'll call you Bwana, your name is too hard.' The crooked tooth smile and sparkling eyes were quite engaging. He went into the house and returned with two more stools. When they sat down, Moses lit up a cigarette and puffed enthusiastically on it exhaling a cloud of blue smoke. Jeffery explained that Dominic would be joining him to enable them to transport more fish.

'We need more fish. Now that there are two of us, we can make more trips with the boat,' Jeffery suggested.

'Very difficult to bring in more fish,' Moses replied with deep seriousness. But the eyes twinkled mischievously.

'What's the problem, not enough men, or not enough fish, or not enough dug-outs?' Jeffery asked.

'Not enough money.'

'But I explained that I can't pay more,' Jeffery complained. Moses held his hand to his forehead for a moment and closed his eyes.

'If we have more lamps, I think we can get more fish, but we have no money.'

Putting his hand in front of his mouth and staring away in the distance, Jeffery shook his head, trying to show that this was a problem.

'How many do you need?'

'Ten,' Moses exclaimed.

'Impossible,' Jeffery countered.

'Six,' Moses suggested.

'Four. If you get the volume up, I'll add another two.'

'Good, when can we get them?'

'Dominic will bring them tomorrow when he comes to pick up the next batch of fish.'

'That's good, Bwana will bring them tomorrow,' he said, pointing at Dominic with a crooked finger. He waved for a man who had been standing nearby waiting to approach them.

'This man has something he wants to show you,' Moses explained.

The man took out a small packet from his pocket, opened it and showed them. A collection of stones, each about the size of a fingernail lay in the palm of his hand.

'What are they?' Jeffery asked but had already guessed. The man gave him a questioning look, which Jeffery took to mean he couldn't speak English. He switched to the vernacular and repeated the question.

'Diamonds,' the man replied, but they looked like dirty pieces of quartz.

'Where did you get them?'

'Williamson's Diamond Mine.' There was no way of knowing if that was the truth. He took out a piece of glass and demonstrated that it would scratch it. The two of them continued until the man smiled, nodded, shook Jeffery's hand and went on his way.

'I've offered him a free ride to and from Sumbu with the fish the next time Omar is around. No doubt the stones are stolen, so I'm not interested but Omar may be,' Jeffery said, 'we need to help people here to discourage competition.'

They took their leave and walked along the beach in the direction of the boat. Dominic took in the scene with interest. It was an example of idyllic rural artisanal life. Everyone looked remarkably healthy and clean. Children played happily along the beach, running in and out of the water, sometimes swimming a little way out and then back again. A few older women sat mending nets, spreading them out, looking for holes through which fish could escape. Inland, just behind the dwellings lay cultivated fields of cassava, maize, groundnuts, and some vegetables, bordered by mango trees. Bent at the waist, women were busy with hoes, working in the vegetable gardens. Beyond the cultivated fields was the beginning of the forest. There were many reed mats spread out along the beach on which thousands of kapenta lay drying in the sun, crystals of coarse salt sprinkled over them. Every so often, there was a wood and thatch shelter in which were stored sacks of fish ready for collection.

Jeffery stopped at the boat and retrieved a spring scale with a hook protruding from the bottom. He led Dominic to one of the shelters, took a bag of fish and weighed it, showing him the reading and the simple calculation to arrive at the price.

'Each group of fishermen have their own number, so a label with that number is attached to each of their sacks. Jimmy will come with you tomorrow to handle the labelling and help translate for any fishermen who don't speak English. If we later find there are any problems with the quality of the fish, not fully dried, for example, we insist on replacement bags without charge. It works. We had a few problems at first, but seldom anymore,' Jeffery assured him.

'Tell me about the lamps.' Dominic prompted when they had found a clear place on the beach to sit in the sand.

'Well, I think you already know that the fishermen go out in dugout canoes in groups to manage the nets. At night, they fish using paraffin lamps to attract the fish. You know the ones where you pump up the pressure. They have a silk mantle that gives off a bright white light. It's a good selling item but as you noticed that old rogue Moses has bargained with me to get them for nothing in exchange for the increase in volume. But not to worry, we'll make it up on something else.

'Once it gets dark, you'll see the whole operation in progress or at least you'll see the lights out there. Of course, when there is a clear full moon, the catches fall off quite dramatically.'

Jeffery got up and beckoned him to follow. Both men had removed their tennis shoes, and they cooled their feet walking in the shallow clear water.

'Is the boat secure where it is, what about the tide?' Dominic asked, splashing his feet as they walked along.

'There's no tide to talk about, but the water level does alter by a foot or so during the year. Of more concern is if there is a storm. Then the waves are strong enough to move the boat, but there is no sign of bad weather.'

Walking north along the beach they approached the end of the village where the rocks began, and the land rose sharply out of the water. Nearby two men were hollowing out the trunk of a tree with adzes. 'It's the wood from a Sausage Tree,' Jeffery noted as they passed. Finally, right at the end of the beach, they came upon a man sitting on a log stool chipping away with a chisel on a piece of teak. Behind him on a reed mat were a collection of woodcarvings, human figures, animals, and masks. Jeffery stopped with a greeting and the two of them chatted away in the local dialect while he examined the woodcarvings. After a while, he pointed, one after another, to several carvings, which the carver gathered to one side. When he had collected about half of them, Jeffery took some notes from his wallet and paid for them.

'Omar will sell them to a dealer in Ndola who distributes them to the curio shops in Lusaka, Livingston, and the Victoria Falls. There are few tourists if any around Sumbu,' Jeffery remarked as the carver collected them in a reed basket and ran off to put them in the boat.

When they returned to where they had been sitting on the beach, someone had installed two wooden log stools and brought firewood to make a fire.

'Are we being looked after?' Dominic asked with surprise.

'Of course, they know me well. I never sleep in their homes if I have to stay over. I always sleep on the beach. You don't mind doing the same?'

'Of course not, it'll be nice to sleep under the stars.'

'They'll also prepare us a meal later when the fishermen eat before going out.'

For the remainder of the afternoon, they watched as the fishermen gradually emerged from the dwellings where they had been resting or sleeping, to prepare the dugouts for the night's fishing. They were loading their nets, refuelling lamps and checking paddles. As they were so close to the bottom of the escarpment, the sun set earlier behind it casting a shadow out into the water. Beyond the shadow, flecks of white raised by a light breeze reflected in the sunlight. As time passed, the shadow advanced across the lake into the distance until only the odd cloud was tinged pink by the setting sun. At this latitude, the sun set almost perpendicularly into the horizon, and darkness descended rapidly.

'Go ahead Dominic, light the fire, we need a little light,' Jeffery said with a smile.

'I haven't got any matches,' Dominic replied.

'Well, use this,' Jeffery directed taking the Zippo out of his pocket and tossing it to him.

'So that's where it went! I thought it was still where you found me.'

'Yes, I picked it up on the shore where you last started a fire. I've been waiting for the right moment to return it, but be careful this time,' and they both laughed.

By the time an elderly woman arrived with their meal, the sky was awash with the most brilliant display of stars, even more so than usual with the absence of the moon. Jeffery went back to the boat and returned with a bundle of blankets. One to spread out on the sand as a groundsheet. Another to cover themselves and the third to fashion a pillow. As they sat on their stools consuming a plate of *ubwali*, antelope meat, and gravy, a delicacy in a world where fish was the primary source of protein, they watched as the lamps came on gradually defining the shore. Soon, the lights started moving out into the water until they looked like bright stars dotting the darkness of the lake. Dominic lay on his blanket with his body raised on his elbows, wondering at the peacefulness of the scene. What a contrast to the conflict he had experienced on the other side of the border not that far away. The dugouts and lamps would be in and out of the lake all night. He threw some more wood onto the fire, which crackled alive spewing sparks.

'I'm going to get some sleep,' he said, moving a little way away from the heat of the fire to make up a bed. Jeffery agreed and did the same on the other side of the fire.

Dominic did not fall asleep immediately. He lay there under the blanket running through the task to be undertaken the next day for his trip back to pick up the sacks of kapenta. Jeffery would bring supplies for sale on his journey because it would take some time for Dominic to become familiar with this activity. As he lay there turning this over in his mind, a figure came walking along the beach, heading in their direction. When the figure got closer, now better defined in the flickering light of the fire, he saw that it was a young woman draped in a blanket that covered her from her shoulders to her ankles. She approached Jeffery, where he lay under the blanket and he heard her whispering. As he watched, she let the blanket fall onto the sand at her feet. Completely naked, she stood there in full view illuminated by the light of the fire for a few seconds, before bending down to lift the blanket and crawl into the makeshift bed next to Jeffery. Muffled talk exchanged between them and a giggle, followed by still more muffled talk and more giggles. For a while it became silent, but then he heard her sigh a few times the sound rising from her belly, followed by small rhythmic grunts which continued for some time until with a final sigh she went silent. Dominic had become aroused at the sounds and thought how long it had been since he'd had the company of a woman, but he turned away putting it out of his mind.

CHAPTER 8

As the weeks passed, Jeffery with Dominic's help, managed to increase the volume of fish they brought in from across the lake. A much happier Omar came up more frequently to transport the fish down to the Copper Belt. By this time, Dominic had spent some time analysing their operation to expand it even further. He drew up some budgets and a business plan based on acquiring another larger boat. Intending on using it as a mother boat so they could become directly involved in fishing offshore at Sumbu, without disrupting their current activities along the west coast. He discussed it with Jeffery, who acknowledged that he didn't understand the figures and had no idea how they could afford another boat. Dominic undertook to see what he could do. He phoned Michael Nicholls at the bank and made an appointment.

'Come and see me at twelve, and when we're finished, if you dress appropriately, I'll treat you to lunch at the club,' Michael Nicholls suggested. Colonial clubs set the same dress standards way out here in Africa as you would expect in London.

'Alright, I'll do that. See you at twelve.' Dominic's impression of the bank manager turned out to be right, the man enjoyed his lunches and would record it as a business lunch in his claims, irrespective of whether anything came of the deal or not. You couldn't win them all he would conclude.

Dominic went to the wardrobe in his room and searched through the old man's clothes picking out a suit, shirt and tie. The suit was a satisfactory fit, but the shirt was a little tight around the neck so he would have to leave it loose and hope the tie would conceal the fact. Wearing tennis shoes would not be acceptable, so the best he could do was wear his combat boots, the upper parts hidden by the trouser legs.

While he was going through this trial run with the attire, he heard the old man talking to someone out on the veranda, a voice he did not recognise. From the tone of their voices, there seemed to be some disagreement. The old man's voice was deep and calm, contrasted with the more excitable higher-pitched voice of the other man.

Curious, Dominic changed back into his jeans, T-shirt, and tennis shoes, and went out onto the veranda. Parked outside the house was a large car with a driver sitting idly on the mudguard.

'Can I offer you gentlemen a cup of tea or coffee?' Dominic inquired as an excuse for meeting the visitor.

'I'd like you to meet Max Freeman,' the old man said, 'out here from London.'

Max Freeman looked Dominic up and down as if he were examining something for sale. Portly would be a kind description of the pale, balding man, dressed in an ill-fitting suit with waistcoat and puffing on a cigar. He looked like a derogatory characterisation of a capitalist one could find in a drawing in a satirical magazine. They shook hands and Dominic noticed the heavy gold ring on his left hand.

'A cup of tea if you don't mind,' Max Freeman said.

Back in the kitchen, Dominic made a pot of tea for the two men on the veranda and a cup of coffee for himself. Once he'd delivered the tea, he walked down the steps from the veranda cup in hand and walked around to the back of the house. It was a big overgrown garden at the back, with enough room to lay out drying racks to sun dry fish.

He paced out the size and went back to his room and with a pencil and paper did some calculations to estimate what volume of fish they could dry using a workable rack size. Partway through the calculations, he heard the car start up and drive away. By the time he had finished, it was time to dress up in the suit. Once dressed, he went out onto the veranda to thank the old man for allowing him to use it.

'You look grand,' the old man commented, without asking the occasion.

'Thanks to you sir. I'll be back a little later,' Dominic replied.

He walked from the house to the bank and waited, sitting in the chair outside the manager's door, eye on the clock until it reached twelve. Then he knocked, opened the door and looked in to have Michael Nicholls stand and wave him to the chair in front of his desk.

'Come in and sit down, Mister Harrison,' he said, smiling broadly below his pink cheeks, 'call me Michael, may I call you Dominic?'

'Of course,' Dominic replied.

'How can I help?'

Dominic slid the business plan and budget across the desk. Michael Nicholls picked up his narrow reading glasses, placed them low on his nose, and took his time to read the hand-written document, occasionally nodding to himself. He spent some time with the budget, writing with a pencil on a pad as he went.

'So, you need finance for Jeffery Simpson with this fishing venture?'

'As you can see, we need to purchase another boat, larger than the one we have and we need some working capital,' Dominic explained.

'Well, in principle, we can provide a hire-purchase agreement for the boat and an overdraft to assist with your cash flow requirements. On the positive side, it's a cash business, but there is a high risk for the bank without some collateral. What deposit can you put down on the boat?'

'How much would you require?'

'Fifty-percent,' the bank manager suggested.

'That's pretty heavy,' Dominic complained.

'Well, if you default on the repayments, we have to repossess the boat and dispose of it as soon as we can, probably by auction. Not that many buyers around here so we would need to take it to Mpulungu.'

'Surely a third deposit would be enough.' Michael Nicholls thought this over for a while, shaking his head. Then he said, 'The best I can do is forty-per-cent.'

'What about the overdraft?'

'Can't provide that without collateral,' he said.

Dominic sat there, silently doing some calculations in his notebook. And then he suggested, 'If you can provide Jeffery Simpson with a hire-purchase agreement to cover the cost of the boat and an overdraft for the working capital I'm prepared to sign surety using the deposit I made the other day as collateral. If you look at the budget, you'll see we should be able to pay the monthly interest charges as well as the hire-purchase repayments. What do you think?'

Michael Nicholls took off his glasses, leaned back in his seat, and closed his eyes for a moment twiddling the pencil in his fingers. This is not such a bad deal, he thought.

'You know you're taking quite a risk without taking a share in the business. Do you really want to do that?'

'Yes, I owe him something and want to help.'

'Give me a few days to consider it,' Michael Nicholls said, 'I may have to clear it through head office,' he continued. He knew he had authorised discretion to approve this level of investment. It just gave him an excuse to decline without personally antagonising a client.

'Fine, I'll leave the documents with you for the moment. If you can't assist I'll just have to try elsewhere,' Dominic said.

'Don't worry. It will be fine, I'm sure. Let's go up to the club for lunch.'

'Before we go, I'd like to arrange a transfer of funds from my account in Salisbury to my cheque account here. Can you arrange it?'

Michael Nicholls left his chair, fetched a form from a cabinet against the wall, and returned handing it to Dominic.

'Fill it in and sign it, and I'll do the rest.'

Nestling at the edge of the forest, the club sat a few hundred metres above the lake and from the front there was a hazy view across the lake to the escarpment in the distance. At the rear was a car park from where the club entrance led into the lobby area. An African receptionist stood behind the counter down one side of the lobby and behind him, to the right, another sat at a telephone switchboard with cabled plugs inserted into the numbered plugholes on the face of it. A door, standing open, led into the secretary's office. In the middle of the reception area was a large antique oval table with a glass bowl of flowers in its centre. Continuing straight through the lobby was a passage leading to the veranda at the front of the clubhouse where members could sit at tables and enjoy the view. Double doors leading from the reception formed the entrances to the bar, dining room and lounge. Waiters dressed in white uniforms and caps carried trays from the kitchen down the passage to the dining room and out onto the veranda.

The bar, exclusively for male members, left the women free to use the other facilities. The majority of members frequenting the club were employed by the local colonial civil service. It was reserved for Europeans only and this rule applied to visitors introduced by members.

Michael Nichols signed Dominic in as a visitor at reception and led him into the bar where the few members standing at the counter greeted him. In such a small town, everyone knew the bank manager. He introduced Dominic as a new arrival in

Sumbu intent on starting a business. After the introductions this solicited a few questions which Dominic fielded with a little caution. Nobody seemed to associate him with the fire on the other side of the lake or the circumstances surrounding his arrival. Something he was determined to put as far as possible behind him. Far from feeling alienated by his surroundings, Dominic found it quite relaxing, and the conversation in the bar was jovial with humorous exchanges between the men.

Dominic and Michael Nicholls sipped their drinks and discussed the fishing activities around the lake and the business opportunities this offered. As they talked, the other men in the bar gradually filtered away to take lunch in the dining room, those with wives passing via the lounge to pick them up.

There was a commotion in the reception, and an agitated woman's voice rose over the protestations of a man. From the bar, their voices were clearly heard, and Dominic immediately recognised Michelle's voice.

'Excuse me a minute,' Dominic exclaimed and made a hasty move through the door out into the reception area.

'I'm sorry madam, but you are not permitted in here,' the receptionist shouted.

'Well, I'm here, and I'm not leaving until I'm ready to,' Michelle screamed back at him, at which point he grabbed her arm and attempted to lead her out of the door.

Dominic leapt forward and grabbed the man's other arm firmly and twisted it half-way up his back, causing him to let out a yelp and let go of Michelle's arm.

'She's with me,' Dominic shouted at the man who now backed off in surprise.

'But Sir, she's not allowed in here.'

'She's my guest, and if you know what's good for you, you'll let her come in,' Dominic warned menacingly. He took Michelle, who was by now in tears of anger and guided her gently into the lounge. The remaining wives in the lounge looked up as they came in and sat at the nearest table. The women exchanged whispers amongst themselves, but said nothing, although occasional glances of disapproval passed their way. As if by agreement, they all arose together and left the room, leaving Dominic and Michelle alone.

'Sorry,' Michelle said, 'just let me leave.'

'No, I won't have it,' Dominic replied, calling a waiter over to their table.

'Tea?' he asked her. She hesitated, and when he smiled, she relaxed a little, influenced by how he somehow seemed to be in command of the situation.

'Alright,' she replied.

The waiter went away with their order but was soon back to report that he was unable to serve them. Dominic turned to Michelle and said, 'I'm not going to let them get away with this, please stay right here. Promise me you won't run away. Don't give them the pleasure, promise?'

'But I don't want to make a scene,' she pleaded.

'Don't you want to stand up for your rights?'

'Yes but …'

'Promise me you'll be here when I get back, it'll only take a minute.'

'Promise,' she said.

Dominic walked back out into the reception to find a small crowd of people remonstrating with a tall slim grey-haired man with glasses. Dominic estimated him to be in his mid-fifties.

'It's unacceptable,' a shrill woman's voice proclaimed, and others joined in sharing her objection.

'Alright, please be calm, I'll sort it out,' the tall man urged holding up his hands with his palms forward, 'why not go out onto the veranda until I've done it?'

This seemed to settle them a little, and they trooped off grumbling down the passage in the direction of the veranda. Only one person remained who he recognised as being the source of the problem.

'I'm the club secretary' he growled, 'I suggest you and your girlfriend leave immediately before I call the police.'

'I don't think that would be a good idea. If you do, I will take the lady with me to the dining-room and demand that you serve us lunch.'

'But you're not a member, and in any case, she is...'

'Coloured, non-European, of mixed blood?' Dominic prompted.

'Quite.'

'I may deal with that matter later. In the meantime, if you serve us the tea we ordered, we'll leave without embarrassing you any further.'

'You'll leave within half-an-hour?'

'Yes,' Dominic nodded.

The club secretary summoned a waiter and Dominic returned to their table in the lounge. Although she had overheard the exchange with the club secretary, he found Michelle sitting there quietly composed, radiating her serene beauty. But he'd seen her fiery side now as well. Not just a pretty face.

'Tea's on its way,' he announced with a wry smile as he sat down.

'Thank you. You're quite determined when you get going, aren't you?'

'It upset me the way they treated you.'

'I'm used to it,' she replied.

'But surely you don't have the same racist attitudes in London?'

'No, it's far more subtle because it's illegal,' she explained, 'but it infuriates and embarrasses me from time to time.'

As they enjoyed their tea, Michelle regarded Dominic with new interest. She was surprised at how readily he had leapt to her defence without regard to how it might affect his standing in this closed colonial community. It would hardly enhance his advancement here if that were what he intended. His chances of gaining membership of the club had just taken a great backward step so he had probably alienated himself from the one place he could enjoy some social interaction.

'You know what you have done to yourself looking after me the way you have?' she asked.

'You mean I'm now as popular as a skunk in a perfume factory,' he chuckled.

'That's an apt way of putting it, yes.'

'You're more important to me than the club and its members. I don't really fit in.'

This comment awakened something in Michelle because she had tended to keep him as distant as possible. What did he mean that she was more important than the club and its members? Whatever social acceptance he might have sought from the rest of the colonial community was now dead and buried. Leaving the only real contact he had with other people being Jeffery and her father. On the other hand, he was a mercenary with an unknown background, so perhaps there was good reason to be cautious. She found herself comparing him with Misheck. There was something dangerous and adventurous about Dominic, whereas Misheck tended to be gentle and considerate and possibly in love with her.

'What brought you to the club in the first place?' Dominic asked.

'The doctor was due to see my father this morning to bring us more medication. On his way, he stopped at the club but left to tend to an emergency. He called to let me know he had left the medication at the reception. I still need to collect it.'

'Let's finish our tea and get out of here. We'll pick up the medication on the way out.' Dominic said. As they left the club, Dominic noticed that the same police sergeant that had questioned him at the hospital lingering near the exit door. They exchanged glances, but the policeman showed no sign of recognition. His presence was hardly a coincidence.

In the car park, Dominic offered to drive the Land Rover, but Michelle elected to drive herself. As she went, she watched

Dominic out of the corner of her eye as he lounged back in the seat with his feet resting on the dashboard ledge in front of him. Looking at him, dressed in a suit, he would pass for any businessman found in the City of London. The last thing she would have imagined was that he was a mercenary fighting in the Congo. The suit masked his muscular body with only his tanned face and hands displaying an outdoor rather than city existence. She tried to compare him with any of the men she had met in London, but none came to mind. Was it because he was so unusual that she found him so attractive? Up until today, she hadn't entertained any thoughts about him, but now he had undergone a metamorphosis in her mind transforming himself into an agent for fairness and justice. But was he driven by integrity and honour or some mercenary motives?

'What are you thinking?' Dominic asked as if reading her mind.

'Trying to figure you out,' she replied, looking over at him.

'Not much to tell.'

'I don't believe that. What were you doing over there in the Congo?'

'It's a long story, I don't want to bore you with it,' Dominic countered. Having finally gained the attention of this beautiful girl, the last thing he wanted to do was spoil it with anything from his past she might find distasteful. How could he explain that he was not a professional soldier and why he had joined up?

'I want to know more about you,' she said, disappointment in her voice.

'Fighting in the Congo was not what I wanted. It's something I'm trying to forget. Give me time. When we know each other better, I'll tell you the whole story.'

Michelle didn't press him any further, but she remained curious. Desiring to know her better implied that he wanted to spend time with her. Did she want to spend time with him? She still did not feel comfortable with that idea. But there was something about him that she found attractive. Up to now, she had avoided him based on a preconceived judgement as to what he represented, but now she was not sure she was correct in her assumption. Was he not entitled to the benefit of the doubt?

That evening when they sat down to the table for dinner, it was clear to both Jeffery and his father that something had transpired to break the ice between Michelle and Dominic. The old man took the lead in the conversation by giving them a report on the news he had heard that day on the radio. The war in Vietnam was not going well for the Americans. Mixed reports were arriving on the progress in finding a solution to the conflict over the border.

'The war in the Congo is being conducted and encouraged by mining interests in Belgium and the United Kingdom,' the old man asserted, 'the mineral wealth in Katanga is sufficient to make an independent state viable. Now that Lumumba is gone and the Americans are backing Mobutu they are a little more comfortable. Lumumba was a threat to American interests because he was encouraging the Russians a power they would prefer to keep out of this part of Africa. They believed that Lumumba was a communist. What do you think, Dominic?'

Dominic felt uncomfortable with the direction in which the conversation was progressing. He had no interest in the reasons for the war across the border. He only knew that he had embarked on a mercenary adventure. Who the paymasters were and their reasons for prosecuting the war did not interest him, but perhaps they should. After his experiences there, maybe he should make an effort to find out why they were fighting.

'I was just a soldier there taking orders. I was fighting for a cause but not my own. Something I'd rather forget about,' Dominic lamented.

'You were fighting for money,' Michelle chipped in critically.

'That's true,' Dominic acknowledged, 'I needed employment, and I probably made the wrong choice.' He did not want to say that he had no other choice at the time. Michelle seemed to accept his statement and remained in a friendly mood despite her rebuke. Eventually he would explain, but not until he felt he had her full confidence. Looking at her across the table, he longed to reach out and take her hand, just to feel her touch.

'If Katanga falls into the hands of an anti-western faction and the Russians gain influence in the Congo, they will be better placed to influence the independence movements on this side of the border. If they can introduce communist ideology here, nationalisation of the copper belt mines is a serious possibility. London mining companies and others are financing the war in Katanga to prevent this. The west cannot intervene directly because it was a democratic election. Although the result is not to their liking, they are compelled to accept it.'

Her father, as was his nature, delivered his opinion in such a logical and unbiased way that she always found it difficult to counter. It was her opinion that nationalisation whilst a possibility was not a foregone conclusion. Was a war worth fighting? Was so much death and destruction necessary? On the other hand, if there was a threat of nationalisation did owners not have a right to protect their property? She was certainly against nationalisation as she believed that governments were inept at running any large business.

'Are you trying to justify Dominic's involvement in the war over the border?' Michelle demanded.

'No, I'm not making a judgement only presenting the facts with some opinion as to the reasons and possible outcome. You need to arrive at your own conclusions.'

As usual, he left Michelle feeling frustrated. She couldn't mount a strong challenge because his position was always so philsophical. If she advocated an alternative scenario, he would dispassionately concede the possibility, so she let it drop much to Dominic's relief.

Sensing that the evening's debate had ended, Jeffery, who had been listening quietly on the side-lines took the opportunity to intercede on a different subject.

'I had a visit by two men this afternoon at the Jetty when I came in. They had been waiting for me. It turns out that they are surveyors who need to get up the lake to the point where the border meets the lake. The District Commissioner sent them to us for help. I've agreed we'll take them up there tomorrow without charge. Dominic, they should be at the Jetty tomorrow morning at six for you to take them there.'

'How long did they say they needed to do the work?' Dominic asked.

'Just for the day. They'll bring their own food and water.'

'That's fine we'll just load up fewer bags to make room for them on the return journey.'

Dinner ended at this point, and Dominic hoped that Michelle would retire to the veranda for coffee where he could continue getting to know her, but she announced that she was going to bed. Maybe tomorrow evening, Dominic thought.

CHAPTER 9

Misheck Ozumba reviewed the notes he'd written a few weeks before he had taken Michelle to the north shore of Lake Mweru Wantipa to view the elephants. He'd mounted an operation that resulted in the arrest of four poachers with only warning shots fired. They had outnumbered the poachers two to one, so the simultaneous skyward gunfire from all of them had prompted an immediate surrender. The only problem was that they had found three freshly slaughtered elephants, but the poachers were only carrying a pair of tusks. They confiscated two rifles and ammunition as evidence, and Misheck had taken photographs of the dead elephants with a thirty-five-millimetre camera. Denied bail, the four suspects were at present in the holding cells at the *boma* awaiting a preliminary hearing which would take place that morning. He'd presented all his evidence to the public prosecutor. The penalty for poaching was usually higher than the district court was authorised to pass down so if the evidence passed the scrutiny of the District Commissioner who acted as the magistrate he would refer the case to the high court in Ndola. The prisoners would be transferred to the prison there to await trial.

To mount the operation, he had brought in game-guards from all over the district. Once they had arrested the perpetrators, he returned them to their respective camps. Now, he needed to send someone back to Mweru Wantipa to search for the missing tusks. His best tracker went back and when he returned, reported that he had been unable to locate them. Up to that point, the poachers claimed that an accomplice carried the tusks deep into the Congo. Eventually, the police managed to separate the poachers and interrogate them individually offering a plea bargain to any one of them who could lead them to the location of the tusks. The first one they questioned agreed, and he led them to the location of the tusks a ten-mile walk through savannah woodland towards the Congo border. When they arrived, they found no tusks and the police accused the prisoner of misleading them, but he was adamant that the tusks had been there. He admitted that they had no accomplices who could have carried off the tusks. As no people were living in the area, the suspicion turned to someone in the game department. This raised the question of where and who had hidden the tusks.

The next day the police returned with a tracker and two police officers provisioned to stake out the location of the tusks if they found them. Other than the faint trail moving away from the original cache location, the tracker found another leading away perpendicular from the original route. It was deliberately faint, made by someone who knew how to make his movements almost undetectable. A half a mile away in thick bush they found the tusks but only one pair rather than the four tusks they had expected. Not only did the thick bush hide the tusks, it afforded an ideal stakeout place for the two policemen. They would need to maintain silence by communicating using sign language. The police would patrol the road every morning and evening to pick them up if they were successful or to provide more provisions.

On the second day, well before sunrise Misheck's top tracker arrived at the cache dressed in civilian clothes rather than his game guard uniform. He put up no resistance and surrendered his hunting rifle to the police. He claimed that he was pleased to have finally found the tusks for which he had been searching. He was not wearing his uniform and could offer no plausible reason. To reinforce their suspicions, when the three of them arrived back at the road, they found his personal vehicle concealed in the bush where it would not be visible to any passing road user. They later discovered that he had taken two days leave, so his explanation fell apart. His case would come up the following week, and Misheck was sure they would easily get a conviction.

DC Arthur Cameron resplendent in his white uniform, as usual, sat at his desk preparing for the morning's hearing in respect of the four poachers. The sergeant knocked and came in as instructed, saluted smartly and handed the DC a telex message.

'What have we here?' he asked without looking at it.

'The Salisbury police report on Dominic Harrison.'

'Well, what does it say?'

'He has a criminal record,' the police sergeant exclaimed with some satisfaction.

'We have a trouble-maker?'

'Sir, after the disturbance at the club it would seem so.'

The DC took the message, read it, and laughed. The sergeant was not sure if it was genuine humour or satisfaction that they now had something on him.

'Contact him and ask him to come and see me,' the DC instructed, 'it's time he came and picked up his dog tags.'

At the Mercenary Recruitment Office overlooking Cecil Square in Salisbury, the retired colonel from the British Army summoned his adjutant to his office. There was quite heavy fighting in Katanga as a result of the United Nations 'Operation Morthor', but he was a little too far away, and reports were too infrequent for him to judge if it was succeeding from a military point of view. As a measure, he could only make a judgement on the casualties reported to him for appropriate action. They notified the non-family member identified by the mercenary in writing if it was bad news. Fortunately, casualties were light, and they had only needed to repatriate a few of the mercenaries either dead or requiring hospitalisation.

'What do we have today?' the colonel asked.

'There's one casualty awaiting evacuation from Elizabethville.'

'Is the DC3 ready to depart?'

'We have more supplies arriving tomorrow for shipment.'

'Let's not wait, get the aircraft off today and make sure Mark is the co-pilot then Sally will go at short notice as a medic. Those two are inseparable. I see from the report that he will require an operation so sort out the admission formalities at the General Hospital to avoid any delays when he arrives.'

'Have we finalised the repatriation of Major van der Walt?' the colonel asked.

'His body was air-freighted to Johannesburg last week,' the adjutant confirmed.

'What is the situation with the funds he was carrying?'

'The rebels stripped the Jeep of everything. Our side only found the major's body. In it, there were no firearms and no radio. They had even removed the wheels. It seems he must have been carrying the money and the cashbook with him in his backpack. Presumably, the rebels have taken it. Without the cashbook, we have no way of knowing how much he was carrying.'

'Well, we may have to write it off in our records, but let's wait for the moment, you never know. What's next?'

'Dominic Harrison,' the adjutant replied, consulting the list.

'Ah yes, not often we have an M.I.A. What's the latest?'

'Well, we've paid someone on the rebel side to obtain information with the promise of more if he is released or his body returned. It turns out that our scout jeep opened fire on what they thought was a Congolese unit, but it was from South Kasia. It seems they have escaped the defeat of their province and are now hiding out in Katanga. They and we have a common enemy. An unfortunate misunderstanding, they did not intend to engage us.'

'Have we had any response?'

'They say they haven't got him which is probably true otherwise they would take the money we offered.'

'He escaped, maybe wounded and died in the bush?'

'That's certainly possible.'

'He's still being paid?'

'Yes, and there are no withdrawals from his account so far.'

'Keep an eye on it. He may surface at some time if he's still alive. It'll present a real problem if we can't find him or his body. What's next?'

They continued reviewing the status of their men.

Meanwhile, further north at Sumbu, Dominic Harrison was very much alive waiting for the surveyors at the jetty. Jimmy was busy refilling the two fuel tanks hand pumping the petrol out of a forty-four-gallon drum. The boat would be empty of cargo on the journey up the coast so the surveyors would be quite comfortable on the way out. Coming back they would be a little heavier than usual once they had loaded the fish. Dawn was approaching in a cloudless sky, so there was little colour other than a light brown hazy tinge. Small waves lapped against the wooden columns of the jetty and boats squeaked against the old motor vehicle tyres attached to its sides. A cormorant sat head raised vigilantly at the end of the jetty.

A green coloured long wheelbase Land Rover with a canopy at the rear drew up in the parking area. The sides of the canopy were fitted with metal gauze widows. This allowed the air to circulate through to the interior. At the rear was a roll-down canvas cover with a transparent plastic window.

The two surveyors who stepped out of the vehicle wore the same clothes. Not a uniform but a practicable form of dress for their occupation. *Veldskoen* boots, socks, shorts, shirts, and bush hats all coloured khaki. They both looked about the same age, early twenties, slim, muscular, heavily tanned from working every day outside in the sun. Dominic went forward to meet them.

'You're the surveyors?' Dominic prompted.

'Yes, I'm Eric Sandham,' the blue-eyed one said, 'and this is Tony Cochran.' They shook hands and Eric continued, 'it's generous of you to offer to take us up the lake. We're used to driving everywhere through the bush, but a mass of water this size is a new experience.'

'Up until recently it was the same for me,' Dominic agreed, and continued, 'How far have you come this morning?'

'It's just over an hour's drive from our camp.'

'I don't see any equipment; I was expecting a … what do you call it?'

'Theodolite, yes we use them all the time, but for this work, we don't need one. We only have this bag with some aerial photographs. If you like I'll explain on the way up.'

Jimmy indicated that he had everything ready and organised on the boat, so they clambered aboard with Jimmy taking the tiller as Dominic instructed. That would leave him free to talk to the surveyors. Once they were out on the lake, Dominic handed a metal mug to each of the surveyors and poured them coffee from one of the two thermos-flasks he'd brought along. After which he poured a mug for Jimmy and handed it to him at the back and then one for himself. They sat back, and with the humming of the motor in their ears watched the sunrise.

When they had finished their coffee, Dominic rinsed the mugs by holding them over the side and allowing the water to flush strongly in and over them. Once the sun was up and the light bright enough, Eric Sandham removed a packet from his bag and took out a black and white aerial photograph and passed it to Dominic. It was about nine-by-nine inches in size, and he could see the lake, western coastline, and the land to the west. Studying it more closely, he could see what appeared to be one of the villages along the shore.

'Is this a village?' he asked the surveyor.

'Yes, but the photo scale is unusually small because the aircraft took the exposure from high altitude. Here take this magnifying glass, and you should be able to see individual huts.'

'From what altitude was it taken?'

'Probably between forty and fifty thousand feet,' he replied.

'What on earth flies up there?'

'A Royal Air Force Valiant bomber. Five-four-three squadron so the rumour goes. We've seen a Valiant parked at Salisbury Airport, and there is nothing around this part of the world to bomb.'

'And these are used to make maps?'

'Yes, we need to identify beacons on the photographs where they exist or survey in new ones where required. We use these to position the photos on a blank gridded map and trace the visible detail onto it using special instruments.'

'Sounds quite complex,' Dominic observed.

'Yes, it is a bit.'

'You'll need to tell us where we must take the boat.'

Tony, who had been studying a number of the photos said, 'You know the north-most village along the coast. Well, come close inshore there and proceed north slowly about two hundred yards out into the water parallel to the coast. I'll follow our position by matching what we see on land with what is visible on the photographs. We know approximately where the border beacon is, but it's too small to be visible on the photographs and anyway it's likely to be overgrown, so we need to search that area. I'll tell you when to head for the shore so we can get out.'

Dominic repeated the instructions to Jimmy at the tiller. He nodded and adjusted course slightly to take them in that direction. For the remainder of the trip, Dominic spent some time trying to see the terrain on the photographs in three-dimensions using a folding stereoscope with guidance from Eric Sandham. When he did finally manage to master the technique, the mountains rose out of the water in three dimensions right before his eyes.

When they reached the village, Jimmy guided the boat just offshore with the engine turning over quite slowly whilst Tony Cochran followed their progress on the aerial photographs. Boulders made up the narrow shore, excepting partway along where there was a beautiful small sandy beach edged by palm trees. Although an idyllic place, it was too small to offer space for the development of a village. This section of the shore was deserted other than an African fish eagle perched on a tall tree overlooking the lake. After about twenty minutes, Tony called on Jimmy to stop the boat.

'Somewhere here, the border meets the lake. We need to get ashore and start searching for the beacon.'

'What does it look like?' Dominic asked.

'A truncated pyramid about as high as my hip.'

Jimmy manoeuvred the boat as close to the shore as he could without grounding it on the rocks, holding it steady while Dominic threw out the anchor. Looking over the side, he could see the bottom through the clear water estimating it was about waist high. When he lowered himself over the side, his feet found the rocks with the water up to his hips. After being wet, his tennis shoes dried quickly in the sun but the *veldskoen* boots the surveyors were wearing, though ideal for working in the bush, were hardly suitable for wading through water. They could take them off and wade barefoot over the rocky bottom. This would be extremely uncomfortable and potentially harmful.

'Rather than taking off your boots,' he said to the surveyors, 'I'll piggy-back you to dry ground.' This raised some wry comments, but they agreed and were carried one-by-one onto the rocky shore. Dominic joined them in the search for the beacon. Tony found it after about ten minutes and he walked up and down, looking back and forth from his surroundings to the photograph using a small eight times magnifier. Eventually, he sat down on a rock and started sketching the location of the beacon.

From the border, they headed south back down to the village to buy and load the fish. The surveyors remained on the boat whilst this was in progress, comfortably sitting on a couple of sacks. Moses and Dominic were in conversation on the beach, checking some figures in the notebook. Moses had a great interest in the value of fish loaded, receiving a carbon copy of the hand-written entries. Dominic wondered what commission he got from the fishermen, although he'd never detected any dissatisfaction, so the old rogue was perhaps wise enough to make it relatively small.

On the way back in the boat, the three Rhodesians exchanged personal details: where they had gone to school, which university, and what sports they played. All three had undergone military training because of the compulsory conscription in their country. Eric asked Dominic how he came to be in Sumbu in response to which he explained that he wanted to invest in a fishing business, not mentioning his activities in the Congo and his escape to Sumbu.

'How much longer do you expect to be here?' Dominic asked.

'About eight weeks, moving camp every two weeks or so,' Eric replied.

'How often do you come into Sumbu?'

'Once a week to the post office to send progress reports to our office in Salisbury, but for our shopping, we usually go down to Fort Rosebury every three weeks. There we buy mainly canned food, including condensed milk and some fresh food to enjoy for a few days. We have a crew of *Shona* survey assistants that we bring with us from Salisbury. Their traditional diet consists mainly of meat and *sadza* maize meal every day, but without a refrigerator, we can't keep the meat fresh for long, so we have a permit to hunt in the control area around the edges of the game reserve.'

'What about the local villages?'

'Yes, we get some vegetables and eggs from them. Our *Shona* cook either pays them in cash or exchanges some antelope meat. He's a pretty good cook. We keep a supply of flour and yeast, and he builds an oven at each site to bake bread for us when we run out.'

'You're welcome to take a sack of dry fish for your men free of charge if you like,' Dominic offered.

'That's kind of you, but we've tried, and they won't eat fish, only meat,' he explained opening his bag and removing some sandwiches offering one to Dominic which he declined and then passing one to his companion. Dominic retrieved a sandwich of his own from his pocket, handing one to Jimmy at the back who was leaning back with his eyes closed almost asleep.

Once they had tied up the boat at the jetty at Sumbu, the surveyors bid Dominic and Jimmy farewell and made off in their Land Rover. Jimmy organised some of the labourers to assist in offloading the boat and storing the sacks in the warehouse while Dominic walked up to the house to let Jeffery know they were back.

He would call Michael Nicholls, the bank manager from the house to apologise for abandoning their luncheon.

At the court, the DC sat fulfilling his role as the magistrate in his appointed position with the four accused restrained with handcuffs lined up in the front seats. The men had appointed the shortest of them, one who spoke some English, to represent them. Although there were seats for the public, no one had bothered to come. That was not surprising as there was no publicity or local news to attract them other than the notice posted on a board at the court that nobody bothered to read. There was an air of informality, but two unarmed policemen stood to one side to deal with any disturbance or to take instructions from the DC. On the right side of the court, a man neatly dressed in a dark blue safari jacket acted as prosecutor. A vernacular translator sat to the left of the accused. At the front where the DC and accused could see them were two ivory tusks and two hunting rifles. Misheck sat alone outside the courtroom waiting to be called.

'You have been accused of poaching in the Sumbu National Park in an area on the northern shore of Lake Mweru Wantipa. This is a serious offence, but you will not be asked to plead. The purpose of this hearing is to determine if there is sufficient evidence to refer the case to the High Court in Ndola. Do you understand?'

The representative for the accused addressed this statement to his comrades in the vernacular without referring to the translator. They looked at each other and nodded.

'Yes sir,' the representative confirmed.

'Let's hear the evidence,' the DC prompted addressing the prosecutor, a man that the DC found to be especially pompous with an irritating tendency to the theatrical.

Prosecutor Mills called on one of the policemen to admit Misheck to the court as a witness. The police sergeant swore him in from the witness box to the left of the DC. Mills read out the report that Misheck had written giving the court translator time to repeat it to the accused.

'Is this statement you have provided to the court true in every respect?'

'Yes, it is.'

'Are these the tusks that you confiscated from the accused when they were apprehended?'

'Yes, they are.'

'Are these the rifles they were carrying at the time?'

'Yes.'

Prosecutor Mills advanced to the DC and handed him the photographs that Misheck had taken of the dead elephants.

'Your honour, can we admit these photographs as the third exhibit?' DC Cameron nodded and made a note and examined the photographs.

'Are these photographs of the elephants that you found on the day you apprehended the accused?'

'Yes, they are.'

'Your honour, I have nothing further to ask this witness.'

The DC addressed the representative and asked if he wished to ask the witness any questions, but he declined with a casual shrug.

Next up was the police sergeant who had made the arrest when the poachers arrived in Sumbu. Had he questioned the prisoners after their arrest? Yes, he had, and they admitted that they had shot the elephants and taken the tusks. This elicited another shrug from the representative.

DC Cameron made a few more notes and said, 'The court finds that there is sufficient evidence for the case to be referred to the High Court. No bail has been applied for, nor would it be entertained as the accused are foreigners, and can be expected to attempt to escape across the border. They are to be remanded in custody and transferred to the prison in Ndola.'

The secession of the South Kasai province of the Congo enraged Lumumba who had won a democratic election which covered the whole of the Congo. Situated in Leopoldville on the Congo River in the extreme west of this enormous country presented Lumumba or any leader who attempted to rule over it an enormous challenge. As was the case in many African countries, its colonial masters ignoring tribal and ethnic divisions had drawn up the boundaries. So removed were they by distance and ethnic resentment from the government in Leopoldville that they sought their own independence. In their view, the least acceptable political dispensation was independence under a federal system. Led by Albert Kalonji from their capital Bakwanga, South Kasai Province unilaterally declared independence before the independence of the Congo as a whole.

First Lumumba and later Mobutu operating out of Leopoldville sought to reintegrate the South Kasai State back into the Congo by force of arms. Apart from the political reason for reintegrating the State back into the Congo, there was the additional desire to gain control of the diamond mining wealth that the Leopold Government coveted to create revenues for themselves.

In an attempt to cut off the flow of funds into South Kasai from the sale of diamonds, the Leopold Government strangled the usual lines of commerce through its controlled territory in the west by confiscating the consignments. To counter this, it became imperative for South Kasai to find an alternative route for the diamond trade to the east. This meant routing through Katanga and out to the market through Tanganyika or Northern Rhodesia. Although Katanga had also declared independence and was fighting its own war with Leopoldville they were likely to be less hostile if they discovered a covert operation across their territory as they had a common enemy. To avoid contact with Katangan Gendarmeries and their mercenary supporters, the route would need to navigate past all significant towns and villages. They decided to send a small military contingent dressed in South Kasai uniforms. In the event of capture, it would provide them with official status allowing South Kasai to intervene on their behalf. They were armed but under strict orders to withdraw immediately if they came in sight of either Katangan or Congolese Government forces. At least if an attack on them became inevitable, they would be able to defend themselves. The defence minister explained this plan to Commander Gautier Mwando when summoned to put the operation into effect

Two weeks later, Mwando found himself some way north of Pweto in Katanga just west of the village of Kapulo in the forest at the top of a west-facing escarpment with his officers assembled in a large tent under the trees. A large muscular man with flecks of grey in his thick short hair, he was a product of the Belgian Royal Military Academy in Brussels.

In trying to move his contingent south in Katanga to bring him closer to the southern end of the lake, he had run into Katanga Mercenaries and become involved in a short firefight with one of their scout vehicles. He was not there to become involved in the Katanga war and was about to withdraw when they came under fire. It was an uneven fight because he outnumbered a single jeep with limited firepower. One of the mercenaries died, and the other escaped. They stripped the Jeep of everything they could find, leaving the body of the officer for recovery. He sent two men to follow and catch the escaped mercenary to hold as a hostage, but when they returned two days later, they reported that he was last seen entering the bush heading in the direction of the Northern Rhodesian border.

Later, through a Baluba tribesman acting as an intermediary, the Mercenary Commandos sought the release of the missing man with an offer of payment. But having been unsuccessful in capturing him this was not possible. During the failed negotiations the tribesman revealed that he had overheard that there was a considerable amount of money carried in the Jeep which they presumed was now in Gautier's hands and was therefore lost. As they had removed every single item from the Jeep and found no money, the only explanation was that the escaping mercenary had taken it with him.

Up until now, Gautier Mwando had considered the matter of no further interest, but his scout had returned with some interesting news. He stood with his officers around the table with a map spread out on the surface. The scout stood silently, waiting for the Commander to address him.

'Let's have your report,' he ordered.

'I've found a route to the most northerly village in Northern Rhodesia this side of the lake,' he said pointing to its position on the map, 'from here there is a boat that regularly comes to pick up fish and delivers the catch to here at Sumbu.'

'How far did you get in finding an agent to route the diamonds into the international market?'

'I took the boat through to Sumbu and met an Asian trader who transports goods between Ndola and Sumbu. From Ndola, there are airline services to link to anywhere in the world.'

'The Asian trader's name?'

'His name is Omar.'

'Is he reliable?'

'Well, I handed him the diamonds, told him the selling price, and he came back a week later with the money and bank deposit slip,' he confirmed removing a wad of French francs and pound notes, placing them on the table. 'The only complaint he had was that they want deliveries in much higher quantities.'

'That's something we can build up to once we are sure he is reliable.'

Mwando examined the bank deposit slip issued from the bank in Lichtenstein, made some calculations with a pencil, checking that the portion of the sale remitted in cash reconciled with the commissions and disbursements. When finished, he was satisfied that the plan had worked and he now had enough money to continue with the operation.

'This seems to be in order. Who is the diamond dealer in Ndola?'

'I asked Omar that question, but he said that the dealer asked that his name not be disclosed. He fears a charge of illicit diamond dealing.'

'I suppose that's a reasonable explanation. Is there anything else?'

'We need the headman at the village as one of the links in the chain. His name is Moses.'

'Who operates the boat?'

'Well, there's a problem here. A white man has just arrived in Sumbu and taken the operation over from a local black man who seems to be the boss. According to Moses, he's a mercenary from Katanga.'

'Ah, now that is too much of a coincidence,' the commander exclaimed, 'did you meet this man?'

'Yes, just for a few moments. I discussed the diamonds with the black man, I think his name is Jeffery, but he wasn't interested. But the next day the white man took me to Sumbu to meet Omar.'

'Did you get the white man's name?'

'No, Moses only referred to him as Bwana. He couldn't remember his name.'

Gautier turned to one of his lieutenants and ordered, 'Bring me that backpack we found in the mercenary's jeep.'

Taking a passport out of the backpack, he held it forward with the owner's photograph on display.

'Is this the white man you met in the village?'

'Yes, it is,' the scout confirmed after studying it carefully.

'Good, do you have anything else to report?'

'No, that's all.'

'Thank you, well done. You're dismissed,' the commander said.

The scout left the tent, and the commander sat down and invited his officers to do the same.

'Well, we seem to have found a conduit for the diamonds, but we have a problem. We can't trust a European in the chain until we're outside the British controlled countries. To make it worse he's a mercenary and the one that escaped us after the fire-fight.'

'You want to get to him for the money,' one of his officers suggested.

'That a secondary issue,' he snapped, 'we just can't have him in the chain, it's too dangerous.'

Mwando leaned back in his chair, took out a cigarette and lit it using a match, then scratched the back of his head. There was only one course of action, and that was to eliminate the mercenary. They would have to make payments to the individuals in the chain since to expose their activities by offering the European money to support them had too high a probability of failure. Black people tended to be more reliable: one they were anti the government; two they tended to be poorer and in need of money.

'How do we get rid of this mercenary?' he asked. The officers shifted uncomfortably in their chairs, looking at each other for suggestions. 'Well!' he prompted irritably.

'We need to infiltrate an operative into Sumbu,' one of his lieutenants suggested, 'it's a long way from here so he would need to drive down to Pweto, cross the border into Northern Rhodesia and drive east along this road to Sumbu.' He traced the route on the map with his finger. 'He'd have to find a point to cross the border at night to bypass the border post.' The officers nodded in approval.

'Alright, that sounds like a reasonable plan but remember he has to get back again. If we had a pistol with a silencer that would be ideal, but we don't. He'll need to use a knife and carry a pistol as back up. If he does it in the late afternoon, he would have time to drive all night and back over the border in the early morning. If he lets off any gunshots, it will greatly reduce his chances of escape. What else?'

'He must speak good English,' someone suggested.

'Good. What else?' Nobody had anything to offer.

'Find a right-hand drive Land Rover from somewhere. If we go over in a left-hand drive jeep, he'll stick out like a sore thumb. Also, make sure you install false number plates in the style they use over the border. That's all. You're dismissed but send Jules Ntaganda to see me he's the ideal man for the job.'

When Jules arrived, Gautier Mwando spent half an hour briefing him on his mission.

'What about the money that the mercenary has?' Jules asked when the briefing ended.

'Don't concentrate on the money, we want this man eliminated. If you find the money, bring it back here.'

As he left the tent, Jules smiled to himself. If he found the money, it would change his life. If he kept it, the commander would never know one way or the other.

CHAPTER 10

Over the next few days, Dominic spent the evenings sitting on the veranda with Michelle and her father. Jeffery joined them for dinner most evenings but was often absent attending meetings of a yet undisclosed nature. Michelle inquired, but Jeffery made some vague reference to business opportunities without elaborating. After dinner, out on the veranda, Michelle and her father competed for which station should be selected, she preferred music and her father the news and political or business debates. By the time her father was ready to retire, so was Michelle, so there was limited opportunity to engage her in a personal discussion. He had often wondered what Michelle did in her spare time as she was away from the house each day for most of the morning often extending into the afternoon. It turned out that she was temporarily teaching English at a nearby mission school as a charitable contribution.

Eventually, one evening, the old man retired early, and Michelle took the opportunity to tune the radio to a music station.

'What music do you like?' she asked.

'I'm a jazz fan, not traditional but cool like Miles Davis, but I also like opera.'

'That's quite a contrast,' she remarked. Here was a man she had initially thought of as a racist based on where he came from, and now, she found he liked jazz, especially a black trumpet player. 'What about rock-and-roll?'

'Quite like Elvis Presley.'

'Let's find some jazz,' she suggested turning the tuning dial over some stations.

'You'll need to find Voice of America,' he said. She tried but couldn't find it so left it on some unknown station that seemed to have a variety of music.

'You really were gallant the other day at the club. Nobody has ever been so protective before. Why did you do that?'

'I told you. Because I like you, but I wasn't sure you liked me. I'm still not sure.'

'Well, I must admit, at first I didn't, but that has changed. You stood up for me in a situation where any other white man here would most likely have left me to be humiliated. That makes me comfortable in your company. It means I could go anywhere with you without you being embarrassed. Yes, of course, I like you,' she said emotionally tears welling up in her eyes.

After all the coolness he had experienced from her, Dominic felt suddenly overwhelmed by this display of emotion. He didn't just like her; she captivated him. Whilst alone, she dominated his thoughts. Not only was she beautiful, but intelligent, serene, and as he had observed had a fiery determination when provoked.

'Michelle, I don't know what the future will bring. I only know that I want to be near to you.'

Michelle smiled at him warmly and said, 'Just wait here a moment I'll be right back.' After a moment, she returned with two glasses of sherry, and when seated raised her glass in his direction and without a word took a sip; a silent toast which he reciprocated with the same gesture. They sat in silence, gazing out over the starlit lake listening to the music on the radio. After a while, a haunting melody came from the radio, Percy Faith orchestra playing the theme from the film 'A Summer Place'.

'I love this piece of music,' Michelle murmured, 'dance with me.'

Dominic stood up and offered her his hand, which she took, allowing him to lead her out onto the front of the veranda. It was the first physical contact between them. Dominic drew her close to him. Her cheek rested on his shoulder, while his nestled against her hair. A faint fragrance of apple blossom enveloped him. As they danced slowly in time to the music, he could feel the firm and supple movements of her body against his. He locked this experience into his memory and replayed it later when he lay in bed before falling asleep.

That same evening Jeffery was at a clandestine meeting at a house on the outskirts of Sumbu organised by the United National Independence Party (UNIP). They invited him to meet some of the officials of the party who had travelled up from Lusaka, visiting and appointing activists. They were recruiting members to assist in the planning of a campaign of disobedience. This campaign had several objectives; first to accelerate the independence of the country; second to ensure that UNIP and its leader Kenneth Kaunda would eclipse all other contenders to take over as the new government after elections. In preliminary discussions with UNIP, Jeffery became Jeffery Mazabuka his mother's surname in preference to Simpson which name presupposed that he was a European. He also made a generous contribution to the party, which held him in good stead.

Apart from the delegation from Lusaka, included were three other local men identified as activists expected to further their purposes in the Sumbu area. The delegation's representative introducing himself and addressed the four men.

'Welcome and good evening. It's encouraging that you have chosen to join us and are now members of UNIP. The secretary will issue you with your membership cards at the end of our meeting.

'We are here under the direction of the leadership of UNIP. Join us in taking our independence from the British. Unlike Harry Nkumbula and the ANC, we are not patiently waiting for the British to grant us independence; it's our country and our right to govern it. This is Zambia, not Northern Rhodesia. How will our people respect us if we do not demand and, if necessary, fight for what is justly our right? We demand an amendment to the constitution that gives us full political rights and leads to an all-inclusive election where we take our rightful place in parliament and ultimately as the government. Another challenge, which will come later, is how we reduce European control of the economy.

'We need to put pressure on the British Government by mounting a civil disobedience campaign which is to be non-violent but vigorous. This campaign is to consist of pickets, boycotts, rallies, and other actions, which we will announce from time to time.

'A further task we would encourage you to undertake is to recruit as many people as possible as card-carrying members of the party. There will be an election, and UNIP must be prepared. To lose is unthinkable.

'To formalise you as a branch of UNIP in this area, it is with pleasure that I announce the appointment of Jeffery Mazabuka as our representative and spokesman in this area. I ask that you give him your full support. I now ask Jeffery to say a few words.'

Jeffery knew that they intended to appoint him and even though he protested that he was still young and had no experience in politics, they insisted. We need young men because one of our problems has been that the old politicians are too soft. Energy and determination are more important to us than experience. We believe you have these attributes.

'Gentlemen,' Jeffery began, 'Your confidence humbles me, but with your encouragement and support I'm sure that we can succeed. Ours is a noble cause, which I hope I can serve with honour. Thank you very much.'

There was a small burst of applause, during which each of the delegates and newly appointed members came forward to shake his hand. Jeffery hoped that he had done the right thing. Change was coming, and he was positioning himself for the future.

Max Freeman walked the short distance from his home to Kensington High Street and hailed a cab. As they drove towards London's West End past the Royal Albert Hall, Max reviewed his visit to Northern Rhodesia and his meeting with Harold Simpson in Sumbu. It had not gone as he had hoped, and Simpson remained obdurate. Max had made him an offer for the mining licence his family trust held, but the old man had declined. He had given him a falsified and pessimistic report on the geological composition of the ore body established from the drilling undertaken by Postlewhite on their concession in the south. The generous offer exceeded reasonable expectations expected from a professional appraisal. Simpson's rejection came as a surprise. It left him to return to London empty-handed, and his failure proved an embarrassment when reporting it to the board. He was not finished yet and was determined he would secure the Simpson mining licence one way or another. He knew that the old man was ill and might die at any time, which might make it easier. His son and daughter might find the offer to their liking, particularly as they had little knowledge of mining or geology.

The taxi passed through Hyde Park and along Piccadilly, car lights reflecting off the wet road in the darkness, tyres hissing as they went. The driver turned into a side street and negotiated the one-way streets until they arrived outside the Club. He paid the driver and followed under the doorman's umbrella up the steps through the double doors into the lobby.

Membership of the Club past and present represented a cross-section of British aristocracy a class which he could claim no lineage. Nevertheless, he was a successful businessman of recognised standing, and through membership sought the company of those with political power and influence. The club had occupied the grand seventeenth-century building since the latter part of the nineteenth century. Originally, members of the officer class, who had seen military service, formed the club. Portraits of great British generals, politicians and other men of note adorned the luncheon, dining, and smoking rooms. Max had invited an investment banker he'd met recently to dinner, in order to discuss the mining opportunity that had presented itself in Northern Rhodesia. When he entered the lobby, he found his guest waiting in a leather club chair.

'Bernard, good to see you,' he said, shaking the man's hand. Bernard Argent was a tall, slim man with fair hair, impeccably dressed in a dark suit, wire-rimmed glasses resting on his nose behind which were a pair of penetrating blue eyes. He was the antithesis of Max Freeman. 'Let me sign you in,' Max continued, walking to a small desk on which a large visitors book lay open. Once signed in he led Bernard Argent through to the bar.

'What will you have?' Max asked.

'Gin and tonic will be fine.'

Max ordered two gin and tonics, which they took to one of the small round tables in the bar and sat down. They made some small talk until Bernard Argent decided it was time to find out what was on Max's mind.

'You have a proposition for me?' he enquired.

'Yes, it's about the exploration we're busy with in Northern Rhodesia. The drilling has revealed an ore body with rich veins of gold. Our preliminary economic study shows that we can achieve a high yield with better than average profits. We're looking for investors to take shares in a new company to finance the development of the mine.'

'What percentage of shares can you justify for your mining licence and investment so far?'

'Well, we would hope to hold controlling interest from the outset, so not less than fifty-one per cent,' Max suggested.

'And how much do you hope to raise for the balance?'

'We estimate about fifteen million pounds, subject to confirmation. This figure includes the value of the adjoining concession, which I'm busy working to acquire.'

'As you know, we are interested in investments in mining. What you will need to let me have is a business plan and the drilling results for our analysts to evaluate.'

Although not a geologist, Max proceeded to describe the main features of the deposit and its potential yields based on what he had gathered from internal reports from the field.

The waiter brought the menu through to the bar for them to place their orders for dinner, and Max, ordered a bottle of claret, after inquiring if it would be acceptable to Bernard. They ordered two more gin-and-tonics, which they consumed in the bar before making their way through to the dining room. Max had made sure that they had a table by the window where they could look out over the park garden in the middle of the square. Although it was dark outside, the street lighting illuminated the square, so the view of the park belied the fact that they were in the middle of London. After placing serviettes on their laps and presenting the bottle of claret for Max to approve, it was poured and presented again for Max to taste and accept. A trolley arrived on which lay a silver carving platter surmounted by a silver dome, which, when removed, revealed a leg of roast lamb, the chef's recommendation for the evening. The waiter placed generous carvings on the preheated plates, followed by another waiter who served vegetables and gravy. During the meal, Bernard pondered the proposition while Max expounded on the balance of payments and growth problems in the British economy and the unsuccessful efforts of the conservative government of Harold Macmillan to correct it.

'There are a number of risks in your proposition which are going to be picked up by our analysts. You'll need to have answers. How will you secure the adjoining mining licence? Second and of more concern, how do you intend to manage the political uncertainty in Northern Rhodesia?' Bernard Argent took a sip of his wine and waited.

'Yes, we are aware of that. Northern Rhodesia will gain independence, and there is an election coming. From all accounts, there is no doubt that UNIP will win the election, so we are already in negotiations with some of their leaders. With their assistance, we intend to secure the investment in the new mine. It will provide employment for more of their people so they are supportive and need to show once they are in power that they can improve the economy. We will have at least one of their nominated representatives on the board of the new company, and there will be inducements to ensure things go our way. There is one key European civil servant, whose co-operation we need to work with UNIP and ourselves, to facilitate the deal. Once the new government comes to power, he will be out of a job. We intend to make him a lucrative offer here in London, providing he assists us in engineering my plan. The Simpson's mining licence or, more correctly, that of his family trust is due for renewal in a few months. The Ministry of Mines will reject the renewal application. They will revoke the licence, arguing that for an extended period it has been held without further exploration or development. We will immediately apply for and secure the licence. Previously, we had made an offer, which I delivered personally, to Simpson in Northern Rhodesia. He declined our offer. That will turn out to be a disastrous miscalculation for I now intend to acquire it for just the cost of the annual renewal.'

Max Freeman leaned back in his chair with an air of satisfaction, smiling at Bernard Argent believing he had recruited him as a co-conspirator. Bernard Argent had seen it all before and knew that the history of mining was replete with the shrewdest and most ruthless and successful adventurers to have walked the earth. Time would tell if Max Freeman was to join this illustrious gallery of rogues.

Bernard Argent declined the pudding and Max followed suit asking the waiter to have their coffee served in the smoking room. They finished their evening sitting in leather club chairs, puffing on cigars. An entirely successful evening, Max concluded.

After breakfast, the following morning, when Dominic was out on the lake and Jeffery was working on his accounts, Michelle joined her father on the veranda. As usual, her father had the radio tuned to the BBC Overseas Service, listening with his eyes closed, his second cup of tea going cold on the table. When she sat down, he opened his eyes and unusually switched off the radio.

'Jeffery told me what happened at the club the other day.'

'Very embarrassing and infuriating,' Michelle growled, 'Dominic was wonderful.'

'Yes, I understand he was. What do you intend to do about it?'

'What do you mean?'

'I mean about the incident. I'm not sure that they had a legal right to refuse you entry. Recently a law was passed outlawing racial discrimination.'

'Is that a fact' she exclaimed, with an indignant tone to her voice.

'Well, I heard it on the news, so you would need to check it out.'

'The secretary implied that my race was a reason for denying me access. But of course, I'm not a member and was not signed in as a guest, so they have another argument.'

'I'm not sure they have.'

'But a club is not a public place,' Michelle pointed out, 'it's for private members.'

'I was around when they built the place, and the Provincial Authorities gave the members permission to build the clubhouse on land that forms part of the National Park. The land on which the clubhouse stands is indistinguishable from that of the National Park. They pay no lease or rental for the land the club occupies because it has no boundaries of its own. As far as I'm concerned that makes the club a public place.' He looked at Michelle speculatively.

'Well, that's even more interesting. If you are right and if they thought I was troublesome before, now I have news for them,' she exclaimed, 'they haven't seen me when I'm really angry.'

The old man smiled slightly.

She stood up and walked to the top of the steps that led down from the veranda and looked out over the lake, deep in thought. Where could she confirm the existence and promulgation of the racial discrimination law? Surely, the court would have such information. Yes, it should be in the government gazette. She turned to her father,

'When did you hear about the racial law amendment?' she asked him.

'I can't remember, but it was some time ago.'

'Thanks, father, I'll find it.'

She took the Land Rover and drove to the *boma*. It took her a while, but eventually, she found herself in an archive where amongst other records copies of the government gazette were stored. Covered in the dust as a testament to the lack of interest over the years, she found them neatly filed on a bookshelf, correctly ordered. Working from the most recent issue backwards, referring to the index in each one, she soon found the relevant amendment to the act. *Ordinance No. 32 of 1960 of Northern Rhodesia. Outlawing racial discrimination.* Without anything to make a copy, she read it through a few times committing the significant clauses to memory.

CHAPTER 11

A week later, DC Arthur Cameron was in his office, running through the reports that had come in from all corners of his district. The hospital was again requesting more funds for drugs and medication. A bus had crashed for no apparent reason on a straight section of road in the south causing six injuries but no fatalities. A troublesome hippo had again entered a village on the edge of the lake trampling crops and terrorising the inhabitants. The police restored order one night in a local tavern, after a brawl broke out, initially over a woman. Hail had caused crop damage in the east. There were further reports but little of any consequence.

Halfway through the morning, the sergeant had requested an audience with him. He had had to wait until the DC had completed a phone call to his wife in England, where she had travelled to be present at their daughter Jane's entry to take up studies at Cambridge University. When the sergeant entered, and after his customary salute, he said, 'There are problems on the road to the club.'

'And what might they be?' the DC asked.

'A group of about ten men have set up a roadblock outside the club. They are preventing anyone other than workers, from entring.'

'How extraordinary, have the police been notified.'

'Yes, they are there, but there is no attempt to prevent them from continuing their activities,' the sergeant complained.

'Is there some discontent or other reason for this illegal action?'

'There is a rumour Sir.'

'Come on, sergeant, out with it, what's going on?'

'It's operation Cha-cha-cha, a disobedience campaign organised by UNIP.'

'Are the men armed in any way?'

'No, it's quite peaceful.'

'Alright, thank you, leave it with me.'

The DC waited until the sergeant had left the room, then put a call through to the Ministry of Native Affairs in Lusaka. Once he got through to the security section and identified himself, the director gave him a situation report. Some incidents of civil disobedience had broken out across the country, but no reports of any serious violence had been received. The Ministry was advising all districts not to intervene unless there was a threat to public safety. Authorities were asking the Police in particular to exercise utmost restraint. He rang the chief of police and advised him that on no account should they interfere, or otherwise attempt to remove the roadblock. They will tire of it in due time, he suggested, and in the meantime, members would need to be patient.

Later in the afternoon, he received a phone call from the club secretary.

'I'm sure you are aware that we have a problem here at the club,' he stated dryly.

'Yes, what's the latest, are they still there?'

'The situation is unchanged on the road since this morning, but there has been a development. I have here Miss Simpson, and she has a proposition that may resolve the problem, or so she says. But she wishes to speak to you in person.'

He remembered that she and Dominic Harrison were involved in an altercation at the club a week or so ago. He was not convinced that the club secretary had handled the situation particularly well.

'Alright I'm prepared to listen to what she has to say, ask her to come in now and I'll give her half-an-hour of my time.'

While he waited, he consulted his diary to see what was coming up before the court. Among others, there was a hearing regarding the game guard arrested for removing elephant tusks from a poacher's cache. The same poachers that had been sent through to Ndola for trial in the high court. He would wait to see what evidence the police could produce and what case the prosecutor could assemble.

When Michelle arrived and entered the DC's office, he saw an extraordinarily beautiful girl coming through the door. Hesitating for a moment as he admired her, he quickly regained his composure, stood, shook her hand as she said, 'Sir, I'm Michelle Simpson.'

'Yes, we've not met, but of course, I knew you were coming, please sit down.'

Once she settled down, he continued, 'How can I help you?'

'I have some grievances concerning the club.'

'Yes, I expected that might be the case. I'm aware that there was some unpleasantness at the club the other day.'

'It was unpleasant, but not only that, it was illegal.' The DC looked at her curiously, and with renewed interest. It was not often that someone presumed to make judgements on what was and was not legal, that was usually his prerogative.

'Tell me more,' he encouraged her, sitting back in his chair in a gesture that suggested he was quite prepared to listen patiently to what she had to say.

'The other day at the club, I overheard the secretary say that my presence in the clubhouse was not acceptable because of my race. I have a witness to corroborate my statement. Sadly, that did not surprise me since that has been the case for many years. This implies that the club will deny me entry even as the guest of a member. You will be aware that Ordinance No. 32 of 1960 outlaws racial discrimination?'

'Yes, you are correct,' the DC confirmed, this young woman has done her homework he thought.

'But that is not all. It has come to my notice that I had a right to be in the club because it's a public place.'

'How do you reason that?' the DC asked.

'Well, the club house stands on state land. It is not private property, so the members cannot conclude that they have the right to deny entry to anyone.' She paused here to give the DC time to consider what she had said, not sure if she had presented her case convincingly or not. She could see that he was giving himself time to consider the pros and cons of her argument.

'You pose a sound argument. Without consulting the relevant acts, I can't immediately comment. But I suspect that even if I did, I would discover that there would be an element of ambiguity as is often the case. You have every right to lodge your complaint with the police in which case I would need to decide if anyone had committed a criminal act. Most likely, I would need to refer this to the high court. You would then be required to be ready to spend time in the court in Ndola.'

'I have a question. Ignoring all the legal rights I may or may not have, do you think I'm morally entitled to some satisfaction?'

'Yes, I do, I think your treatment was unnecessarily, inappropriate and regrettable. Are you behind the protest at the roadblock?'

'No, I'm not, but I took advantage of it to confront the club secretary. The protest is independent of my personal dissatisfaction, but if it's any help, I believe I can bring influence to bear to have it abandoned, but there are conditions.'

'Let's hear them,' the DC said, with a smile just evident at the edges of his mouth and the corners of his eyes. Did she imagine it, or was he actually enjoying her argument?

'First, it's time that a non-white person was voted and approved as a member of the club. It seems to me that the members must surely be aware that this is inevitable anyway.'

'And second?' the DC asked.

'That I am permitted to propose a member.'

'What about yourself?'

'No, I have no reason to use the club, but there is someone who would find it gratifying. Try to imagine this. You are a senior game ranger in the park and amongst your duties are to take visitors on game drives to view the animals. These tourists receive temporary membership of the club, as there are no other facilities of an acceptable standard. At lunchtime, the tourists return to the club for lunch before another game viewing trip in the afternoon. The senior game ranger is unable to join the tourists for lunch in the club, and they carry refreshments out for him to eat in the car park. You must agree that this is most demeaning, in fact quite ridiculous. His name is Misheck Ozumba.'

'So, what you're suggesting is that if the club changes its rules and admits Mr Ozumba you can arrange for the removal of the demonstration and road-block.'

'Yes.'

'And you undertake not to proceed with any legal action?'

'Yes, as long as the club gradually introduces a few suitable non-white members. You'll be surprised at how few will be interested.'

'Miss Simpson, you have a most persuasive manner. Leave it with me, and I'll see what I can do. It's in the hands of the members and management committee. Perhaps I can be as persuasive as you,' he chuckled.

'I have your word, and I trust you. I will use my influence to have the road-block removed by tomorrow evening.'

Now just how does she have such influence the DC wondered? Well, Jeffery had told her that it would only be a one-day event, but the DC was not to know that.

About an hour later, Dominic Harrison arrived at the *Boma* on the chance that the DC was available in response to his request to collect his dog tags.

Having walked from the house, he proceeded up the white stone edged driveway within its well-manicured lawns. The gardens contained beds of cannas and geraniums, displayed poinsettia and frangipani bushes and a large tree into which a bougainvillaea had clambered right to the very top, interspersing the branches with red flowers.

Some gardeners dressed in prison uniforms were tending the flower beds under the watchful eye of a policeman armed with a single barrel shotgun. As he passed, he heard a voice call his name.

'You survived,' the voice remarked, 'I didn't believe you would make it.' Dominic turned, and to his surprise, Daniel was squatting on his haunches loosening soil in a flowerbed.

'My God, Daniel, what are you doing here?,' Dominic called, noticing that although he was working with the prisoners, he wore different coloured overalls than the others.

'I'm in a bit of trouble,' he said, but before he could question him further, the policeman arrived at his side and ushered Dominic away. 'Sorry sir, but you're not allowed to speak to the prisoners.'

'The public prosecutor will give you the story,' Daniel called out as Dominic continued his walk towards the Boma, leaving the policeman to his duties.

When Dominic got to the DC's office, he discovered that he had already departed for the afternoon, so he made his way to the courthouse in search of the public prosecutor. He found Prosecutor Mills in his office dressed in his dark blue safari jacket, as was his preference.

'Do you have an appointment,' Mills asked, looking officiously at his diary, 'I'm very busy you know.'

'Sorry, no, I don't, but it won't take much of your time.'

'Does it concern one of the cases?'

'Yes, it does. Daniel Ngosa,' Dominic offered.

'You have evidence that can help me with a prosecution?' You know that we've successfully obtained an extension of his detention to give us more time to gather evidence?'

'No, quite the contrary,' Dominic answered, 'I intended to represent him depending on the charges. I need to understand the charges and what evidence you have.' From his own experience, he knew that the public prosecutor was obliged to disclose the charges and evidence to him if he took on the case.

'Has he appointed you?' Mills asked.

'He asked me to speak to you to understand the charges,' Dominic replied. Not strictly an appointment but near enough he thought.

Mills thumbed through some folders until he found the correct one and handed it to Dominic.

'I don't have a copy for you, but you are welcome to sit here and read through it and make notes if you wish, but do not remove it from my office.'

'Could I trouble you for some blank paper and a pencil?' Dominic asked having come unprepared. Mills looked at him contemptuously, removed some paper from his desk drawer, and handed it to Dominic followed by a pencil. He's incompetent Mills thought. Dominic sat quietly reading the report and charges.

When he ran into Daniel in the forest, he had assumed that he was a poacher; that is what Dominic expected the charge would be and the reason Daniel was now in detention. But it appeared more a charge of theft or dealing in contraband goods. He had removed tusks from the poacher's cache, and as Dominic knew, had carried them into the Congo, with an accomplice who was probably the Congolese link in disposing of the ivory. Dominic found himself a potential witness, but since he owed his life to Daniel's generosity out there in the forest, there was no way he would be able to bring himself to testify. If he undertook to defend him, on the other hand, he would not need to compromise Daniel's defence. But what defence could there be? He scanned through the report once again searching for some loophole or misconception he could use. The report referred to the location of the cache as being near the Congo border. How near? Was there a fence or visible line identifying the boundary?

'Mister Mills,' he said deferentially, 'is it possible to show me the location of the cache of tusks on the map?' Mills looked up irritably from some document he was reading and stared at Dominic for a few seconds.

'We've marked it approximately up there on that map on the wall, but as you can see, there are no features on the map to which we can relate the position of the cache with absolute accuracy.'

'The report says that it's near the border. How has this been determined?'

'I don't see that it's relevant, but we know that the border is about twelve miles from the road and the cache is estimated to be about ten miles.'

'But how did you measure the ten miles?'

'Based on how long it takes to walk there.'

Dominic didn't press the matter, but he realised that this question was important. If the cache was located on the Congo side of the border, it was out of the jurisdiction of the Northern Rhodesian courts.

'When is the hearing due to take place?,' he asked.

'This coming Tuesday,' was the reply.

He left Prosecutor Mills moodily muttering to himself and made his way back through the garden the way he had come. When he passed by where Daniel was working, he called out, 'Hang in there. I'm going to try to get you off. Can't promise anything but I'll try.' Daniel smiled and gave him a wave.

Instead of walking directly back to the house, Dominic went down to the jetty where he found Jeffery and Jimmy unloading a consignment of supplies from Omar's truck. Omar was sitting on the mudguard of the truck making some entries in his notebook looking skyward occasionally thinking and returning to the notebook. When he saw Dominic, he stopped his writing and slipped off the mudguard with a smile of greeting. They were soon in conversation, or more precisely, Omar did most of the talking. The weather was exceptionally hot that late afternoon. He had just heard that his wife was expecting their fourth child. The road up to Sumbu was still in need of repair. Sadly, he needed a new truck. Would they ever build a bridge over the Luapula River to replace the ferry pontoon at the border with the Congo?

'Driving in today, did you notice a camp anywhere along the road?' Dominic asked him.

'Oh yes, it's not more than two miles out, on the bank of the stream. If you drive from here, it's near the first bridge. If you look up the stream as you cross the bridge, you can't miss it.'

'It's quite late, are you going to stay over tonight in Sumbu?'

'No, as soon as the fish are loaded, I'll drive back to the Copperbelt. If I drive all night, I will arrive at the border when the Chembe border post is about ready to open. Once through I'll cross the Luapula on the ferry pontoon into the Congo. Driving on the right-hand side of the road, it takes about an hour to cross the pedicle strip. After crossing the border into Zambia, it's another two hours to Ndola and home.'

'That's quite a journey,' Dominic remarked, 'would you mind dropping me off at the camp when you leave.'

'Happily,' Omar replied, 'pity you don't want a lift to the Copperbelt, I could use the company.'

Dominic made his way to the warehouse to plan the next few days with Jeffery. The moon was full, and the volume of fish landed at the villages had been tapering off, so it was better to curtail their visits up the coast until conditions improved. That meant either a waning moon or heavy cloud. This late afternoon, the sky was clear, not a cloud in the sky. They decided to take a break for a few days, and Dominic told him where he was going and that he might be late for dinner.

Once, Jeffery and Omar, had had the fish loaded and completed their commercial transactions, Dominic got into the truck and they drove away. Dust rose behind them as they climbed out of Sumbu, with the lowering angle of the sun streaming in on the driver's side. It was not that far, and Dominic intended to walk back to the house after he had met with the surveyors. When Omar stopped the truck, the cloud of dust followed and enveloped them. He waved Omar farewell, wished him a safe journey, and made his way along the track that followed the stream and led to the camp.

There were four tents with fly sheets arranged in pairs with a further two frames covered with tarpaulins. One of the tents contained two iron-folding beds made up with pillows, sheets, and blankets, with a paraffin pressure lamp on an upturned box between them. A mosquito net hung over each of the beds, not only to protect the sleeper from mosquitoes but also to discourage scorpions, spiders, and even snakes from trying to share the sleeping arrangements. Another tent served as a bathroom and contained two galvanised iron baths, and incongruently some meat strung up to dry to make *biltong*. All the tents had tarpaulin groundsheets and flaps that closed to discourage smaller wild animals from entering the tents uninvited. The other more rudimentary tents were for the survey assistants and camp cook who was busy preparing food on two fires next to which was a pile of firewood.

Relaxing nearby the four survey assistants were engaged in an animated discussion laughing and prodding at the fire in which they appeared to be roasting some meat.

Washing was hanging on some lines strung out between trees a short way away, and another fire was heating water in two twenty-gallon drums. Parked on the far side of the camp were two Land Rovers next to two forty-four-gallon drums of petrol. Two trailers with tarpaulin covers, probably used during camp relocations, stood nearby held horizontal on stands.

In the third tent, the two surveyors were working at a wooden folding table seated on canvas and wooden folding chairs. On the table were two large books, a few soft cover files, graph paper, and pencils. Eric Sandham was winding the handle of a mechanical calculator, which made a strange grinding sound and an occasional ring, much like a tuning fork.

'Dominic. What a pleasant surprise. What brings you here?' Eric Sandham asked.

'I thought I'd come and see what you were up to, and make sure you were making good progress.'

'It's going well. We should be able to move to another camp further south by the end of next week. Can we offer you a cup of coffee?'

He summoned the cook, and coffee followed some ten minutes later on a tray with china cups and saucers, a jug of condensed milk and bowl of sugar. He placed the tray on a second table outside in the shade of the trees. The three of them sat around the table drinking coffee while Dominic explained why he had come and whether the two surveyors might be able to determine which side of the border the cache was. Tony Cochran fetched a map from the office tent and spread it out on the table for Dominic to indicate the location as best he could from his memory of its position on the map in the office of the prosecutor.

When he'd done that, he laid out aerial photographs covering the area next to the map. Whereas the map showed little detail in the area of interest, the photographs were highly detailed, revealing clumps of trees, *dambos* and small streams.

'It shouldn't be a problem if someone can lead us to the location. I can follow our progress on the photos as we proceed until I identify the position of the cache when we arrive there.

Looking at this terrain, we should be able to drive cross-country in the Land Rover,' Cochran said.

'I'd really appreciate it if you could do this for me,' Dominic appealed, looking speculatively at both men.

'Of course, we'll help you, after all, you saved us a major overland expedition to the beacon in the north,' Sandham interjected.

'When will be the best time?'

'Well, we rest our assistants on Sunday, so that would be the best day if you can manage it. It will also give us time to transfer the borderline onto the photographs.'

'All right, I'll come by at seven in the morning on Sunday and bring a guide with me. If for any reason I can't make it, I'll come out again one evening to let you know.'

While these discussions were in progress, Michelle drove up in the Land Rover, turned the vehicle around to face the way out, and switched off the engine to wait for Dominic. He bid the two men farewell, walked over to the vehicle, and got in.

'Well this is a surprise, you've come to pick me up,' he offered her as a greeting.

'It's a pleasure,' she said with a broad smile that caused his heart to beat faster. A familiar fragrance greeted him as he entered the cab. On the short drive back to the house, he found that she was in high spirits, chatting away happily about nothing in particular. Whatever it was that had invoked these high spirits he didn't mind. It was just so pleasant to be in her company and share in her mood.

That evening as they sat down to dinner, her mood became quite infectious, and he was able to make his own contribution by telling Jeffery that they had been successful and had raised the funds from the bank that they needed to expand the fishing operation. Jeffery was delighted and kept repeating, 'Amazing, absolutely amazing.'

The old man called George to his side and whispered something in his ear at which he departed for a few minutes and returned with a bottle of champagne and four glasses.

'I've been keeping this for a moment to celebrate,' he said, holding the bottle aloft, 'this is it.' He opened the bottle, which popped and foamed on the tablecloth, then handed it to George to dispense.

'George, you better join us, pour yourself a glass, and we'll propose a toast,' the old man insisted.

They toasted to continued success and speculated on what their next step should be, particularly the acquisition of a larger boat. An atmosphere of excitement flowed over them throughout the meal. Dominic couldn't help remembering and comparing how different this night was to when he first arrived. Each of them had their own personal celebration. Michelle was happy with the events earlier in the day, and Jeffery had already achieved his first political success. For Dominic, just to have Michelle nearby was always a celebration.

At some point during dinner, a second bottle of champagne appeared, the celebration continued after they had finished eating and George had cleared the table. Jeffery excused himself, announcing that he had to attend a meeting and, the old man decided after the few glasses of champagne, it was time to retire. Not to the veranda as usual but to bed. Dominic and Michelle left the table and moved out onto the veranda. After a while, George came out and asked if he should make tea or coffee, but Michelle insisted that he should go home as they had kept him a bit later than usual.

'There's somewhere I want to take you,' Michelle said, 'it's about a half-mile walk from here, and it's such a beautiful evening. I'll take a basket so we can make coffee when we get there.' Dominic waited while she went away coming back a little while later with a basket and a blanket. She took the radio off the table and put it into the basket with a small paraffin stove, coffee percolator, packet of coffee and sugar, a small bottle of milk, two mugs and a spoon. Michelle led the way off the veranda, turning right and towards the shore. She carried the blanket and Dominic the basket.

'If we walk east along the shore, we're soon in the National Park, so there are no inhabitants. There's no path, so we have to work our way over the rocks and through some reeds for a while, but we soon come to a beach where it's easy to walk,' Michelle informed him. It struck him at how confident she was walking at night into this wilderness something she learned in her childhood. He was used to it by training, but he admired her courage and adventurousness, she just seemed to adjust so naturally to any circumstances. Nobody else in his experience had so captured his attention and imagination.

They were soon on the beach, and she kept on walking for a while leading him onward. Eventually, she stopped and said, 'This looks like a good spot, just lay out the blanket there.' A little way from the water, the sand sloped towards it so they could lie there looking out over the lake with their heads elevated above their feet. They lay on the blanket next to each other with the light of the full moon reflecting off the water and the waves swishing gently on the sand. Night had not brought down the temperature, and he noticed tiny droplets of perspiration had formed on her upper lip.

She removed the radio from the basket and switched it on. It crackled as she tuned through some stations until she found one playing music. Having removed her sandals, she ran barefoot down to the water with the coffee percolator and filled it. Dominic left her to do everything noticing that she was enjoying herself. When she got back, she took out the small paraffin stove and made to light it.

'Damn it,' she cursed, 'I've forgotten to bring the matches.' Dominic reached in his pocket and handed her the Zippo cigarette lighter.

'Oh great,' she exclaimed, 'that's a saviour, but what are you doing with a cigarette lighter? You don't smoke.'

'No, but I'm very attached to it, it saved my life way over there on the shore when the hyenas were about to attack me.'

'Well, it's saved us again,' she said, kissing the Zippo and raising it to the sky in a kind of salute. 'Thank you for saving Dominic; otherwise, I wouldn't be with him tonight.'

Lying there on the blanket together, looking up at the stars, Michelle felt at peace with the world. Her being back here in Africa after London was a contrast challenging to comprehend. How could you possibly compare the wild beauty here to the magnificence of London? But even more exciting was being with one of the two men that she felt closest to. She knew that Misheck was in love with her, but what about Dominic. In any event, while attracted to both men, was she in love with either of them. How did she reconcile the racial differences? If she chose one in preference to the other, how did her racial situation influence her choice?

As the coffee percolator bubbled away, Bobby Rydell's voice soared into Volare, and she felt Dominic take her hand. She squeezed it gently without looking at him, concerned she might show some emotion that arose in her subconsciously. She withdrew her hand to pour the coffee, and during this time, Dominic had not said a word, and she wondered what was going through his head. There was the glimmer of a smile and a far-away look on his face. Was he here with her or somewhere in his past life?

'Are you happy?' she asked, sipping her coffee.

'More so than usual,' he replied.

'But what about your home? You've been away so long, and we are not your family, yet you have been so generous.'

'You must remember that Jeffery saved my life, and I will always remember that. Also, you took me in when I was recuperating. I told you before, and I mean it. As long as I'm close to you, I am happy.'

'But I won't be here forever, at some time I need to go back to London. I have a job there and whilst it's wonderful to be with my father and Jeffery again, there is no long-term future for me here.'

'I've tried not to think about that,' Dominic replied.

'Come on,' she exclaimed happily changing the mood, 'let's not get gloomy, let's go for a swim and enjoy ourselves whilst we can.' She leapt up, pulling the cotton dress over her head and ran down to the edge of the water where she turned to face him. So surprised was he at her sudden impetuousness that he lay there rooted for a few seconds during which time he marvelled at the beauty. In no time, he found himself naked and running down to the water to join her as she waded out laughing and splashing water ahead of her.

At first, the water seemed cold but soon his body adjusted until it had no temperature at all, just a smoothness against his skin.

Michelle swam out just far enough until she couldn't stand and then swam back towards where Dominic was standing up to his waist in the water. When she found her footing again, she waded towards him until they stood face to face. She threw her arms around his neck, and kissed him passionately holding it as he responded, his hands travelling down her back pulling her tightly against him. She felt a rising pleasure that threatened to sweep her away out of control.

'Wow, I've really excited you,' she exclaimed, pulling away and giggling.

'You're seriously naughty,' he gasped relaxing so she could escape and run out of the water and up the beach to where they had been sitting. When she got there, she turned towards him.

'Come on, get out of the water,' she called mischievously. He hesitated but then abandoned any modesty that might have restrained him and ran out of the water.

She watched unashamedly at first but turned away and pulled her dress over her head.

'I'll have to be very careful with you,' she laughed, 'you're an animal.'

During their walk back to the house, Dominic explained, how there was a game guard charged with dealing in contraband ivory and how it would be necessary to establish whether the cache was in Northern Rhodesia or the Congo. This was necessary for Misheck's case against him to succeed. If Misheck could accompany him and the surveyors to the site of the cache on Sunday, they could resolve the matter. She was sure that Misheck would be pleased to assist, and Dominic was sure he would too if only to please Michelle. He had to admit that he had no antagonism against Misheck other than an element of jealousy.

Later, when they were back at the house, Dominic sat out on the veranda long after she had retired savouring the moments they had shared on the beach and in the water.

CHAPTER 12

Preliminary talks were taking place in London between representatives of UNIP and officials at the Colonial Office to pave the way for more formal negotiations expected to lead to a new constitution for Northern Rhodesia. A delicate matter conducted without general knowledge or any publicity. But Max Freeman, through his insider contacts, had become aware of the meetings and recognised that there was an opportunity to initiate his plan for taking over the Simpson mining licence.

The British team were awaiting the results of a commission report to ensure that any decisions taken regarding independence were properly motivated. As far as the European settlers in Northern Rhodesia were concerned, they expected the protection of a qualified vote as a minority in any new constitution. UNIP, on the other hand, wanted an immediate, unconditional announcement that there was an early commitment to independence. Whilst UNIP felt that there should be only one voter's roll they appreciated that there was a danger that if they pressed this too hard at the outset, an agreement would be difficult to achieve, and a war of independence might follow, something they were keen to avoid. Better to accept a transitional constitution that would ensure UNIP majority-black representation, from which base they could influence the future and a rapid move to independence.

Initially, the concept under discussion was to have two qualified electoral rolls determined by the income and property owned by the voter, but this resulted in disagreement on the division of the racial composition of the constituencies. Neither side had the authority, nor was it advisable to commit to the finer points until they had reported to their leaders and official talks resumed.

During this period, Max Freeman had the Chairman call an extraordinary meeting of the board of Postlewhite International Mining to discuss their strategy for working with UNIP to acquire the Simpson mining rights. The venue was the company's boardroom at their offices on Lombard Street, with the time set for nine in the morning.

The dark-suited men assembled before the appointed time, helped themselves to tea or coffee and biscuits, talking earnestly amongst themselves about the great opportunity that presented itself to the company. They had been extraordinarily fortunate to acquire a licence to mine what from the reports was proving to be a rich gold ore deposit. With the current price of gold at thirty-five dollars per ounce, the initial estimates of the mining costs left an attractive return for investors. Yes, there were risks, but the price of gold had remained stable for the past ten years, and there seemed no reason to expect that it would fall soon; the main concern was political, and it appeared that there might be a way of mitigating this risk.

Once they sat around the highly-polished mahogany boardroom table, with a surprisingly young woman clutching pencil and notepad, ready to take minutes, the chairman called the meeting to order, and after completing the statutory formalities invited Max Freeman to address the other directors.

'Good morning Mister Chairman, gentlemen,' Max started, 'I have a proposal that I would like to present to the board, but before doing so would like to give you some idea of what is going on here in London and how it might present an opportunity for us. Not far from here at the Colonial Office in

King Charles Street, talks are taking place between officials of the United Independence Party of Northern Rhodesia and our government. I would ask that you keep this privileged information confidential as it is not common knowledge. The exact agenda and purpose of these talks are unknown. But I think you will agree that it is reasonable to assume that they concern the process which is to lead to the independence of Northern Rhodesia. We can anticipate this as being part of the government's decolonisation policy led by the Secretary of State for the Colonies. For us, what is more important is that right now, here in London, are some senior officials of what is likely to be the future government of Northern Rhodesia. These people have influence even though they are not yet in power. Now is the time to associate ourselves with their cause. They are likely to be in power for much of the early years of mining on our project. We need their support to secure the Simpson mining rights. What I propose is that we contact one of the senior members of their delegation and offer to assist them by contributing financially to their political activities.'

Max Freeman stopped at that point and looked around the table at his co-directors.

'Mister Chairman,' Mark Atherton, their operations director began, 'I have a concern that I believe we should consider very carefully. Most of the mines in Northern Rhodesian spread along the so-called Copperbelt, which is close to the Congo border. There is a war in progress there just the other side of the border in the Katanga Province funded by Belgian and other mining interests intent on supporting Moise Tshombe in his determination to effect the secession of the province from the rest of the Congo. Despite the principle of the International Community to recognise the borders established by the European colonies, there is no guarantee that this conflict and the movers behind it might not seek to lay claim to the Copperbelt and attempt to annex it to form part of Katanga. In the present circumstances, is this an acceptable risk?'

'You certainly have a point, but there are several reasons to be optimistic that this will not happen, or if it did that it would not succeed. First, it's unlikely that the British government would not act to counter any attempt of the sort you suggest. Secondly, although it would create some general disruption if conflict were to break out, the deposit we're considering is remote from the Copperbelt so would not be so easily included in such an annexation. Thirdly, as we would be extracting the gold on site, we would be insulated from any disruption of the transport system unlike what might happen with the export of raw copper using the railways west through the Congo and Angola. We could even airfreight the gold out from the mine by building a small landing strip.'

This seemed to satisfy Mark Atherton's concerns, and Max Freeman waited for further questions, which he was sure, would come.

'You went to Northern Rhodesia to buy the Simpson licence, and as we know, you failed to secure it. Without that licence, anything else we discuss here is academic. How do you plan to get your hands on that licence? And how confident are you that you can pull this off?' Frank Osborne was a no-nonsense experienced executive with sharp insight and a high level of scepticism. Max Freeman felt his cheeks flush at the obvious slight but suppressed the temptation to retaliate choosing with some effort to retain his composure.

'I'm confident that the strategy which I'll now outline will be successful. I have a contact in the Department of Mining and Geology in Lusaka who will prevent the renewal of the Simpson licence on the grounds that no further exploration or mining development has taken place since the licence was issued.'

'And why would he do that?' Frank Osborne asked.

'Many of the present civil servants in Northern Rhodesia are concerned about their futures, and quite rightly so. With independence, native Northern Rhodesians will replace them. On my last visit there, on my way back from the meeting with

Simpson, I made contact with someone in the department who is in a position to have the Simpson licence revoked for the reasons I've explained. In exchange for this, I have offered him employment in our company here in London.'

'Are there legal grounds to support the revocation of the licence?'

'No, there could well be an objection, but this is where we need political support from someone in UNIP. Their challenge will not only be to work behind the scenes to ensure that the licence is revoked but to ensure that it is awarded to us as the adjacent licence holder. If we plan it correctly, the ministry will reject and revoke the Simpson's application for renewal at the latest possible moment, leaving little time for an objection. The whole matter will be *fait accompli* before the Simpsons can react.'

'You seem to have thought it through, but I must warn you that if anything goes wrong causing embarrassment to the company or exposing the company to any legal charges, you will be called to account,' Osborne exclaimed.

'And if I succeed?' Max Freeman asked sarcastically.

'We'll deal with that bridge when we cross it,' the Chairman interjected to defuse the situation.

'What about the employment of our man in Lusaka?' one of the directors asked.

'That's not a problem,' the Chairman replied, 'staff employment levels fluctuate within our normal operations, so we don't need to pass a resolution for that. He turned to Max Freeman and asked, 'How do you intend to make contact with the member of the delegation?'

'Well, I have a contact I'd rather not name who would be prepared to arrange a meeting.'

'Can we have it here in this room?'

'I don't see why not, but perhaps we only need one other director and yourself so that we can arrange it at short notice.' Max Freeman suggested.

'Are we agreed on that?' the Chairman asked, looking around the room. It was agreed and left to the Chairman's discretion to select the second director to attend the meeting.

'Now we get to the important point,' the financial director exclaimed, 'what do we have in mind as an amount we intend to pay?' Max Freeman had already given this some thought.

'I suggest we make a payment every quarter,' he announced, 'that way it leaves us the option of asking for favours before each payment. At this point, we can discuss with them an annual amount.'

The Chairman looked at the financial director and asked, 'Have we got a surplus in one of the budgets?'

'Yes, I can consolidate a figure from several presently approved expense items.' He opened his file and paused for a moment as he looked at the figures. 'The maximum I can find is about one hundred thousand pounds.'

'Perhaps we should make it eighty thousand pounds per annum subject to renewal at the end of December each year. If we see no benefit, we can discontinue it at that time. We can then make payments of twenty thousand per quarter.' Max looked around the table at the other directors, eliciting a nod from each of them excepting Osborne, who glared at him contemptuously.

'Where do you expect we'll need to make payments, here in London or Lusaka?' the financial director asked.

'I expect it will be here in London and probably to more than one account. It's likely to benefit a number of individuals if you know what I mean.'

Looking at each other around the table, they acknowledged that they understood what Max meant.

'Can I take it that we have a resolution that is to read:

"It was resolved that, eighty thousand pounds is to be paid to the United Independence Party of Northern Rhodesia as a contribution to their political campaigns, to be paid in four instalments and to be reviewed at the end of each financial year," proposer Max Freeman. Do I have someone to second it?'

They voted in favour of the resolution, once the seconder raised his hand. The young woman noted it by scribbling in her notepad.

Max Freeman left the meeting satisfied that he had achieved his objective despite the irritating scepticism of Frank Osborne; when it came to pessimism, he was definitely of the 'glass half empty' type. When he arrived back in his office, he made a phone call to his contact to arrange to meet the member of the delegation.

When told that they were staying at the Langham Hotel at 1 Portland Place, one of the premier hotels in London, Max wondered who else was funding UNIP if not the British Government. This thought made him feel more confident as it must surely mean that he was not the only one that recognised the future importance of UNIP for doing business in Northern Rhodesia.

Having advised his contact that the board had approved the funds for UNIP, he received congratulations and a promise that he would call back with a day and time for the meeting at Postlewhite International Mining offices.

At five o'clock the next afternoon, a chauffeur-driven Bentley arrived outside the Langham Hotel, and Max Freeman alighted from the vehicle when the hotel doorman opened it. He entered the lobby, went directly to the front desk, and asked the concierge to notify Mister Jacob Gomani that he, Max Freeman, was waiting in reception.

After a short wait, Jacob Gomani came out of the lift and walked directly towards Max at reception. He was a dapper, well-dressed man with flecks of grey in his beard and an amiable smile displaying a set of even white teeth. His eyes had a twinkle to them that belied an obvious toughness that Max recognised hiding beneath this outward display of warmth.

'Very pleased to meet you Mister Freeman,' Gomani said, extending his hand and giving Max a firm shake.

'Likewise,' Max replied trying not too successfully to match the man's natural charisma, 'I have the car waiting outside, if you're ready to leave, we can talk in the car.'

During the journey back to the office, not knowing what to talk about he was happy to discover that Jacob Gomani was quite garrulous.

'What a wonderful city you have the privilege of living in. You know, Africa still has a lot to learn and a long way to go. Here history is evident everywhere whereas in our part of the world buildings of any substance mainly originate in this century. If you go to Southern Rhodesia, you can visit the Great Zimbabwe ruins. You colonialists suggest that Africans did not build it. Even suggesting it was Arab slave traders or even the Queen of Sheba.'

He laughed at this mischievously. 'But on the other hand, God has seen fit to provide us with the most extraordinary natural wonders. The Zambezi River and the Victoria Falls, we say *Mosi-oa-Tunya* or "the smoke that thunders." But your doctor Livingston named it after his Queen. Perhaps we will rename it in the future. A good idea, don't you think?'

But Max just smiled and nodded his head. He didn't care what they called it as long as he could get what he wanted. 'Then there are the lakes, much bigger than anything you have here. Beautiful and majestic wild animals, not just badgers, foxes and hedgehogs,' he laughed again teasing. 'We may not have an ocean, but to the north, we share Lake Tanganyika the second deepest fresh-water lake in the world. I must admit though that you colonialists did bring us one important gift. You brought us the English language. We have so many different dialects in Northern Rhodesia it would be difficult to build an administration if we had so many languages competing to become the *lingua franca*.' And so it continued, until they pulled up outside the building in Lombard Street.

When they arrived at the company's boardroom, the chairman and financial director were already in discussion on some other subject, which they abandoned as their visitor entered the room. Max Freeman made the introductions and offered their guest tea or coffee which was delivered shortly afterwards together with a plate of biscuits by the young woman with the shorthand skills. She left almost immediately prewarned that no minutes were to be taken at the meeting to preserve utmost discretion.

'Mister Gomani, it's a pleasure to welcome you to our offices and we appreciate your taking time out from your busy schedule to attend this meeting,' the chairman said in a somewhat deferentially diplomatic tone. 'As you may know, Postlewhite International Mining is one of the world's largest mining companies, and we have a mining concession in your country which we intend to exploit by raising capital here on the London Stock Exchange. Not only will this venture provide a return to the investors but, more importantly, it will provide tax revenues for the Northern Rhodesian Government and employment for the people in your country. It is our opinion that UNIP, whom we understand you represent, will form the new government of Northern Rhodesia in the not too distant future. Naturally, for such a venture to succeed, we need to work closely with the government. In this case, not the incumbents, but their replacements. We are anxious to commence with the development of the mine as soon as possible. Rather than waiting for UNIP to assume power, we feel we need to work with UNIP from the outset and even assist it in its political efforts in the form of funding. Our meeting today is to find out if you would be interested in assisting us with such a venture.'

A relaxed Jacob Gomani seemed to have a constant smile, so it wasn't easy to know by looking at him if this had had any impact on him or not. Perhaps he was accustomed to offers of funding for his political party. If he wasn't, there was no air of excitement to betray the fact.

'Mister Chairman,' he replied formally, 'I thank you for your warm welcome, and may I say that it's a pleasure to be here to meet you and your directors. And yes, of course, we are interested in investors who wish to contribute to the development of our country. Furthermore, we welcome offers of funding for our party. As you will understand, we represent the poorer people in our country, so funding is always difficult. The trade unions are a potential source of funding, but there is still considerable white settler influence, so this also presents some problems. If I may ask, what was the amount of funding you had in mind?'

'Well, we have board approval to offer eighty thousand pounds per annum. This is, of course, subject to our making good progress with the mining venture. We have to be able to reassure investors that the project is a sound investment. That is where we need your help.'

'That's an exceptionally generous offer,' Gomani exclaimed, 'and we will assist you as best we can. There is an element of inertia in the present administration due to political uncertainty. We can exert our influence behind the scenes if we are discreet.'

'There is one important issue that we believe you may be able to assist us with to initiate our venture. Max, can you please explain to Mister Gomani what we need to get things going.'

Max Freeman described the plan in detail, and the reason they needed to take over the Simpson mining licence. He also gave him the name of the official in the department of mining and geology who was able to engineer this providing he had the necessary support. If Gomani declined to go through with the plan, he was exposing his contact to retribution. As far as Max was concerned, he was expendable.

'I see that you have formulated a quite ingenious scheme,' Jacob Gomani observed stroking his beard. 'Leave it with me, and I'll see what I can do. I'm leaving to go back to Lusaka the day after tomorrow. I'm sure your kind offer of financial support will be favourably received.'

'We can deposit twenty thousand pounds almost immediately if you can provide us with banking details,' the chairman offered.

'Excellent, but there is no immediate rush, we will send someone here soon to make the arrangements.'

'Well that's it then,' the chairman said, 'this is my card if you need to contact me,'

Once the meeting broke up, Max Freeman offered to take Jacob Gomani to dinner, which he accepted. They would talk further over their meal, and by the end, Max made sure that Gomani would use him as his contact even although he had the chairman's business card.

Not far away in Dorking, Surrey, at the premises of one of Britain's most successful pharmaceutical companies, Clive Francis director of research, was under pressure to accelerate the development of their latest drug known as project 'Wounded Knee.' No significant breakthroughs had come since the departure of his brightest researcher who was away on compassionate leave somewhere in Africa and he felt sure that she would have been able to resolve some of the problems that were confounding the team. She had a most intuitive analytical mind that seemed to enable her to untangle the most complex interrelationships between various chemical compositions. He needed her back and fast; otherwise, he risked compromising his reputation and that of his team. Although she had left her methodical research well documented, the next step was not clear to any of them. It would emerge somehow from her insight and almost magical ability to discover the extraordinary.

When he called a meeting to review their progress, he found this was, however, not a shared opinion.

'I see no reason why we should need Michelle Simpson back,' Graham Samuels asserted, 'it needs for one of us to take over the leadership of the team and improve the coordination of the tasks.'

'And who do you suggest should play that role?' Clive Francis asked knowing what the answer was likely to be.

'Well, I'm prepared to take over providing Michelle Simpson works under my supervision if and when she returns.'

Clive Francis gave this some thought. He was not convinced that Samuels was the right man for the job, but without Michelle, he had left the team leaderless for too long. He was leaving himself open to criticism from management if he allowed this situation to continue, and the delays became intolerable. Better to let Samuels take responsibility for coordination and credit if he was successful. Michelle would be disappointed, but he could do no more until she was back.

'All right, if you feel you can improve our progress I'll agree, but keep me up-to-date, and let me know of any particular problems.'

'I assure you that progress will improve,' Samuels said.

'Another thing, we need to present a paper on some aspect of our development on project "Heartburn", the patent is in an advanced state of registration so will become common knowledge fairly soon so someone may as well get some recognition before the event. It must only be a part of the overall formulation and procedures. Make sure it's a personal contribution. Who is prepared to present a paper at the Royal Society Conference?'

'Well, if I am to lead the team, I guess it should be me,' Samuels suggested.

'Very well, I'll leave it to you. All right team, let's get back to work, and we'll see how things are going same time same place next week.'

Although he had agreed that Samuels take over the coordination of the team, he was not convinced that he could pull it off. He went back to his office and called in his administrative assistant.

'Where is Michelle Simpson?' he asked her. 'I know that she went to visit her sick father somewhere in Africa.'

'In Northern Rhodesia,' she replied.

'Where the hell is that?' he exclaimed.

'Central Africa, you'll need to look at the map, it's landlocked.'

'Do we have her address?'

'Yes, she gave it to me before she left.'

'Good, I need to write her a letter and get it off as soon as possible, how long do you think it will take to get there?'

'Oh, probably take two weeks or so.'

'My God, that long! I better get it off right away.'

That same day, he posted the letter to the address of the post office in Sumbu.

CHAPTER 13

On Sunday as agreed, two Land Rovers laboured their way in low gear cross-country in the direction of the Congo border. In the lead vehicle were Dominic and Misheck who knew the way and in the following one the two surveyors, one driving and the other following their route on the photography. Now and again, the following vehicle would stop. One of the surveyors would get out and look around, to and from the photography. On the bonnet of the lead vehicle sat a game guard tasked with looking out for stumps hidden in the long grass.

As they drove, at Dominic's prompting, Misheck described some of the problems he faced in his operations.

'This park is so remote that it cannot be considered a tourist destination. Most foreign tourists come to see the Victoria Falls and then visit the nearest game viewing area, which is the Kafue National Park just a two-hour drive away. We are starved of tourists because it is a two-day drive to get here from Victoria Falls. My task here is one of preservation and protection of the animals. As you know from our reason for being on this trip, it is difficult for us to achieve our goals. We need more game guards and vehicles, but there are limited funds, and without generating income from tourism, our argument is persuasively weak. The war on the other side of the border is not helping. The present events are distracting their administration and game preservation is low on their priorities. Also, our police are just too thinly spread to expect there to be any patrols along the border.'

Dominic was sympathetic and felt a little guilty that he was trying to defend someone who had not been helping improve the situation by encouraging the ivory trade. Still, on the other hand, he felt some obligation to help Daniel.

Eventually, Misheck asked the question that Dominic had been anticipating.

'How do you come to be interested in Daniel?'

'I met him purely by chance, but it's more a case of looking for the truth. If the cache were on this side of the border, the prosecutor would have a strong argument to pursue prosecution, but if they referred the case to the high court and the cache was in fact in the Congo, they would throw it out as no offence was committed in Northern Rhodesia,'

Dominic made this point as truthfully as he could but evaded offering more details. His mind turned to Michelle and the competition for her affections. He did not doubt that Misheck was a serious contender and Dominic could not think of any reason why he wouldn't be a suitable partner.

'Are you married?' Dominic asked even although the man driving did not wear a ring.

'No, I'm not. There's no shortage of women out here, but it's difficult to find one suitable as a bride.'

'Yes, I'm sure it is,' Dominic replied, noticing that he deliberately refrained from mentioning Michelle. This conversation terminated abruptly, and nothing further was said on the subject.

Continuing cross-country with Misheck concentrating on the driving; they were making good time, although they were slowing now as they had entered some woodland, which caused them to zigzag. Dominic checked the mileometer, which showed that they had travelled more than eleven miles. On that basis, he figured they must be nearing the border. He looked speculatively at Misheck for some remark as to how close they were, but he was engrossed in his driving. A short while later there was hooting from the surveyor's Land Rover. Misheck stopped, and they all got out of their vehicles. Eric Sandham walked forward to where they had stopped.

'We've just crossed the border,' he announced, 'is it much further?'

'Probably about another mile,' Misheck responded, 'looks like it must be in the Congo.'

'Yes, but let's keep going so that we can positively identify the site on the photographs.'

As Misheck had estimated about a mile further on, he stopped, got out of the vehicle, and pointed out the site. Tony Cochran wandered around the area with the photographs walking back some two hundred yards and forward again picking up and identifying the patterns of the trees on the emulsion of the prints. Using a grease pencil, he made a small circle on the photograph to mark the spot.

'Eric, please check and confirm I've picked the right spot,' he said, handing the photographs to him. Eric went through a similar procedure but walked off in a different direction until returning. With the photograph placed on the bonnet of the vehicle, they gathered around and inspected it, and Eric confirmed that it was the correct location.

'It's definitely on the Congo side of the border, we've just entered without going through immigration formalities,' he laughed, 'what do we do now?'

'Either way, we were going to require you to sign an affidavit regarding the location of the cache. It's Sunday, so there is nothing we can do about it now. Can you come through to the *boma* tomorrow sometime? I'll have a commissioner of oaths available to hear your statement and for you to sign it in his presence. Preferably tomorrow afternoon,' Dominic suggested.'

'Will four o'clock be alright?'

'Yes, that's fine, but don't forget to bring the photograph with you. And thanks for your help. We would not have had certainty otherwise.'

On the way back to Sumbu, Misheck seemed unusually subdued, and Dominic could appreciate how frustrating it must be for him to see someone escape punishment for what he had done.

'You know that he's going to get off?' Dominic said.

'Yes, and it's hardly justice is it. How am I supposed to run my operation when someone can get away with something like this?'

'Fire him!'

'What?'

'Fire him. He deserves it.'

'But you know he will not survive without a job. In prison, he would be clothed and fed no matter how poorly that might be.'

'If you don't fire him, he will have escaped the consequences of his actions. He doesn't deserve that. It also gives your other employees a bad impression.'

'I can't bring myself to do it.'

'Let me take responsibility for his future,' Dominic offered.

'You'd do that?'

'Yes.'

'Why would you do that, he's nothing to you?'

'Let's just say that I owe it to you and him. He needs to atone, and I'll try my best to see that he does. Let's just leave it at that.'

The rest of the journey back to Sumbu passed in a more relaxed and light-hearted atmosphere.

Early the next morning, when the *boma* had not yet come to life, Dominic set out across the lake in the cool predawn light. He'd left it for Jeffery to make an appointment for him to see the DC that afternoon to report to him as instructed. Later, once Dominic had completed his trip, Jeffery came down to take over with the news that the DC would see him at two-thirty. It gave him just enough time to walk to the *boma*. Entering by the same route as he'd previously used, there was no sign of the convict gardeners or Daniel. He entered the court building and made his way to the DC's office where he waited in the anteroom. Apart from the coat of arms of Northern Rhodesia on the wall, there was a photograph of the Queen and the Governor-General in full ceremonial dress, a reminder that the British Crown still exercised power here even if its tenure was now in question. Filing cabinets lining the walls, and desks occupied by several clerks shuffling documents and files, confirmed this as an administration office of some importance. After a while, a buzzer sounded on the desk of a police sergeant at work nearby, who immediately rose and beckoned to Dominic, and opened the door to let him into the DC's office.

DC Arthur Cameron was sitting as usual at his desk, impressive in his official uniform but not quite as intimidating as Dominic expected. Or did his relaxed warm smile hide some more sinister personal characteristic?

'Mister Harrison, please sit down. Thank you for coming in,' he said. Dominic did as he instructed and waited patiently whilst the DC read some papers on his desk. Then he looked up and studied Dominic closely for a few seconds as if trying to evaluate him based on his appearance.

'Have you fully recovered from your gunshot wound?' he asked.

'Yes, Sir, I have.'

'You have arrived in Sumbu in rather disturbing circumstances, and I need to ask you some questions. I have a rather enthusiastic sergeant who has been pointing out to me several offences that you may have committed. If you were not European, by now, he would have had you in detention. Do you have your passport with you?'

'I think you probably know from the sergeant's report that I was in the Congo. I have a Rhodesian passport but lost it among other personal possessions during an engagement near Pweto over the border.'

'Alright, the first thing you need to do is have a new passport issued. Right now, you have entered Northern Rhodesia without immigration formalities. Officially, there is no record of you being here. Once you have it, bring it here, fill in the appropriate forms, and we'll forward this information to the immigration department in Lusaka. That's point number one. You undertake to do this?'

'Yes, I'll apply through the home office in Salisbury.'

'Point number two is the sergeant's opinion that he should charge you with arson for starting a huge fire that raged up the western escarpment and to God knows where in the Congo. Of course, as the sergeant points out, you cannot prove that the reason for causing the fire was to ward off some hyena. Nevertheless, from independent reports from the hospital, I am satisfied that had you not started the fire, your presence would have passed unnoticed and you would have died there on the shore. I consider your action to be justified.' The DC turned a page in the sergeant's report and pondered for a moment.

'You are a mercenary?'

'I was a mercenary.' Dominic corrected him.

'We have no reports about any military action near Pweto, and neither are we likely to. Mr Simpson found you in a military uniform with a bullet wound in your side, so it's reasonable to assume that your statement is correct. There have been no reports at that time of any gunfights here in Northern Rhodesia, so I'll accept your explanation.'

'Thank you, Sir,' Dominic responded.

'Do you have a weapon?' This question caught Dominic off-guard, the nine-millimetre pistol was still in the drawer next to his bed. Although he had no ammunition for it, for some reason, he had a disturbing feeling that the day might come when he would need it. If he declared it, the DC would definitely confiscate it.

'Yes, I had an FN rifle which I carried with me on my march to get here, but I abandoned it under a culvert in the Congo. It made me too conspicuous.'

The DC made a note in the file, which Dominic now realised, was one especially for him. If he had doubted that there was interest in his presence here in Northern Rhodesia, the next statement put that to rest.

'You have a criminal record?' By now, Dominic realised that he had attracted their attention and they probably had a report to confirm that he had.

'Yes, I have.'

'Mister Harrison, I am astonished at this report I have in front of me. Why didn't you appeal?'

'At the time, I didn't have the money to appoint a lawyer to lodge an appeal.'

'Well, you should have tried to find a lawyer to take the case *pro bono* this judgement against you was excessively severe. I've no doubt you would have won an appeal.' DC Cameron leaned back in his chair, relaxed and smiled again after his quite serious demeanour during the questioning. Dominic felt like a schoolboy just disciplined by a paternal headmaster.

'One other thing Mister Harrison, you've been stirring up trouble at the club.'

'Yes, but I …' but before Dominic continued, the DC laughed out loud, cutting him short.

'Jolly good thing too,' he remarked now reduced to a chuckle, 'but Miss Simpson continued your good work and has caused a total change of attitude at the club, and not a moment too soon. It needed to be done.'

'What do you mean?' Dominic asked.

'She didn't tell you? I thought you would know being resident in the Simpson household. She's a brilliant girl and not without courage, either.' He related the whole story, obviously enjoying the retelling of it. Dominic was astounded, right under his nose, and he had not even noticed.

'Here's the good news though they had a committee meeting last night and they have met all of Miss Simpson's conditions. Visitors and members no longer need to be white, and Misheck Ozumba is a member with immediate effect. As an act of contrition, they have waived his entrance fees and subscription for the first year. Please pass this news on to Miss Simpson with my compliments.'

'I'll certainly do that, she will be delighted,' Dominic said, still shaking his head in amazement.

DC Arthur Cameron took the dog tags out of his drawer and handed them to Dominic.

'I think you came for these, but I hope you have no reason to wear them again.' He said handing them over, which Dominic took as an act that was to terminate their meeting.

'Before I go, there is one other matter I would like to raise if I may.' Dominic proceeded to explain the circumstances surrounding the case against Daniel Ngosa and the evidence that the surveyors had produced regarding the geographical location of the cache.

'I knew those surveyors were here, but I would never have believed that they would have been of any immediate use,' the DC remarked. He pressed the button on his desk, and a few moments later, the sergeant appeared saluting smartly as was his habit.

'A surveyor will be coming in at half-past-four to complete an affidavit regarding the Daniel Ngosa case. Make sure you're here to record his statement and have him sign it in your presence. It seems that the ivory cache was in the Congo outside our jurisdiction. Please ask Prosecutor Mills to come through to my office immediately.'

Before Mills arrived, the DC said, 'It's up to Mills to decide if he wants us to proceed, but with this latest evidence it will be difficult for his case to hold water.' He took out a file from his desk drawer to review what had transpired with the case thus far. Mills entered the room, glared at Dominic and seated himself without invitation.

'Is there some problem?' Mills asked, looking back and forth between the two men.

'Not really,' the DC replied, 'it's just the Ngosa case. Mister Harrison here arranged for a surveyor to go to the ivory cache site. He's coming through later this afternoon to sign an affidavit proving that the cache was located in the Congo outside our jurisdiction. Do you still have a case?'

'Well, that certainly complicates matters.'

'Has Daniel Ngosa committed an offence inside our borders?'

Prosecutor Mills muttered under his breath and drummed his fingers on the desk for a moment's thought to the DC's obvious irritation.

'I'll have to rule out theft. Dealing in contraband has taken place in the Congo. We don't have any evidence that he has received any money although I'm sure he has. He didn't bring anything into the country. He didn't use any of the game department's property. The only remaining offence is illegally crossing the border without following immigration regulations.'

'Come on Mister Mills, you and I know that people are moving back and forth across the border all the time to visit relatives, gather wild fruit whatever. The British and the Belgians agreed to a line on the map without recognising any ethnic boundaries. There's no fence or even a cut line to mark the border, and there isn't a border post for miles. Admittedly, there are no villages either side where Ngosa crossed the border. But the principle is the same. If we turn a blind eye to people moving between villages across the border, how can we now charge Ngosa when it's an accepted practice? If it were a European, however, that would be another matter because there is no common ethnicity.'

Dominic sat listening and watching as Mills squirmed in his seat. Pragmatism was to prevail; he could feel it.

'Very well, I have no case, at least not in your court,' Mills exclaimed sourly.

'Not in any court Mister Mills. Not in any court.'

When Mills had left the office, DC Cameron turned again to Dominic.

'Mr Harrison, you have a knack of popping up and influencing events, so far for the better. Just be cautious that it remains that way. I have the distinct impression that you have a propensity for adventure. I hope if we meet again, it will be for the right reason.'

'Thank you, Sir, I'll try my best to behave,' Dominic promised with a smile. He left the office with a growing respect for DC Cameron.

That evening at the house, when they were all at the table for dinner, Dominic related what had happened at the DC's office earlier in the afternoon. Of course, they were aware that he and Misheck had visited the site of the ivory cache with the surveyors and they had proved it to be in the Congo. Once the affidavit was in the hands of Prosecutor Mills, Daniel's release in the morning, now seemed inevitable.

'I'm keen that we offer Daniel a job,' Dominic said, looking directly at Jeffery, 'now that the loan is approved, we need to move quickly to get the operation going. I believe we can use him.'

'Are you sure we can trust him?' Jeffery responded.

'There is certainly a question mark about that, but I'm prepared to take responsibility for him.'

'Alright, let's give him a try, but if things don't work out, he will have to go.'

'That's fair enough,' Dominic agreed.

'I know that Misheck will appreciate that,' Michelle added. So, she knew what he and Misheck had agreed, Dominic thought.

'There's something else he's going to appreciate.'

'Oh, and what's that,' Michelle asked, raising her eyebrows.

'I think you know,' Dominic said mysteriously.

'Is it what I think it is?' Michelle asked excitedly.

'Well, what were you expecting?'

'Is it good news?'

'The DC asked me to tell you that the club lifted racial restrictions last night and they approved Misheck as a member.'

'Hooray, great,' she exclaimed banging her fist on the table, 'I can't believe it.'

'How did you do it?' Dominic asked with admiration.

'Oh, just my natural charm,' she explained.

'Not to mention a great deal of cunning,' Dominic said. The old man who had been sitting quietly at the head of the table turned to him and said, 'Since you've arrived here, we seem to have reasons to celebrate. I'd suggest a repeat of the other evening, but we're right out of champagne. Let's have another glass of sherry.'

CHAPTER 14

As the days passed, Dominic put his mind to planning their expanded fishing operation. Other than trying to find a larger boat, there was the drying and salting of the fish to consider. To fully commercialise their present modest operation presented two choices. They could purchase a fully self-contained kapenta rig which would allow them to bring in large catches that they could store, after adding salt, into baskets on board, or they could acquire a mother-boat without its own net but supported by fishing canoes. When Dominic put together his business plan, he concluded that they would not have enough money to buy a rig, so they needed a suitable mother-boat.

There were enough local fishermen with canoes who would welcome the improved income they could earn by being able to offload fish on the water. They could operate further out than usual where catches were likely to improve. This would save them time by avoiding successive trips to the shore to offload there. Later, if this expansion of their operations proved successful, they could reconsider and invest in a fully equipped rig.

In discussions with Jeffery, they made plans for Jimmy to continue with the current western shore operation while Dominic and Jeffery would spend more time developing the new one. Daniel had now joined them after Dominic had laid down some strict rules by which he intended to monitor him.

He seemed suitably contrite and thankful that he remained employed, so Dominic felt confident that he would behave. While Dominic and Jeffery would focus their efforts on the new boat, Daniel was to be responsible, with assistance from the casual labourers, for the construction of the drying racks.

At this point, the old man, despite his deteriorating health, proved most helpful as he had once visited a fish sun-drying unit in Mpulungu. With his help they refined Dominic's original design with drawings based on the standard sizes of wooden sections and other materials. When he finished the design, they placed orders with Omar for materials and tools. He made some special trips, with the labourers stacking the wood to one side of the house each time he arrived.

When the clearing began, in preparation for the construction of the drying racks, they left an undisturbed area between the clearing and the house to act as a buffer to reduce the smell of drying fish. During the day, the wind tended to come in off the lake, so they hoped it would not be too much of a problem.

'We need to go to Mpulungu to look at boats,' Jeffery said once the clearing was underway.

'By road,' Dominic suggested.

'No, it's a long journey by road because there are mountains and rivers between here and Mpulungu. It would take us all day. By boat, it's about two-and-a-half hours. If we leave early, we can get there by nine in the morning. That should give us time to look around and if we get lucky, buy a boat. Mpulungu is the only place we'll get one, so we'll have to choose from what's available.'

'I'll bring the cheque book along then.'

'Good, but we need some cash as well to buy fuel when we get there and to pay for accommodation if we need to stay over. Also, we need to take extra drums of fuel and a tow rope. I'll get Jimmy to prepare the boat for us. I've checked the weather, and it should be clear for the next few days. I'll phone Ian

Campbell if he is available, and arrange for him to meet us. He's the boat sales agent there.'

Early the next morning, Dominic and Jeffery set off for Mpulungu. There were a few clouds about but nothing that looked as if it might build-up to a storm. Jeffery took the tiller and headed on a north-easterly direction parallel to the shore just a couple of miles out into the lake. The sun rose, and they had to shield their eyes to look ahead although there was no other craft in sight, so the chances of a collision were about zero. After about forty minutes, they rounded a small peninsula quite close inshore, and Jeffery steered the boat on a south-easterly course. A couple of crocodiles were visible sunning themselves on some rocks as they passed by.

'Do you get many crocodile attacks on the lake?' Dominic asked, remembering how Michelle had run into the water that night without a care.

'No, not often, there are many large fish in the lake, so that keeps them well fed. Of course, in the rivers one has to be careful because they prey on animals that come down to drink, including humans. The odd old crocodile that is no longer fast enough to catch fish may occasionally pose a problem.'

When they had rounded the peninsula Jeffery pointed out Kasaba Bay with its large and beautiful white sandy beach. 'A nice place to spend the day,' he remarked. Dominic took over the tiller, and Jeffery moved up to the front lounging with his back to the bow compartment. As they continued southeast down the coast, mountains rose out of the lake. Wooded and indented by shadow-defined streams like the creases on some ancient face. They stopped for a while to switch fuel tanks filling the empty one from one of the drums. Before they started again, Jeffery took the flask out of the bow compartment and poured them both a cup of coffee.

Setting off again, they continued in the direction of Sachi, a village on the shore further down the coast. Before they got there, Jeffery took over once more, turning the boat due east and into the low elevation of the sun, pulling the peak of his cap low to aid his vision. In the distance, the haze of the early morning obscured Mpulungu but Jeffery instinctively knew the direction to navigate. Half an hour later, a little after nine, they made their approach towards some fishing boats moored close to the shore, flanked on each side by numerous canoes.

Once they were ashore, Ian Campbell walked down to meet them carrying a file under his arm. He appeared to be in his mid-thirties, tanned, short and stocky, with a dark goatee beard and a Panama hat. He politely removed his hat to shake hands revealing a smooth bald shaven head. Noticing the tattoos on his arms, Dominic concluded that at some time he had been in either the merchant or the Royal Navy.

'Good timing,' he said with a Scottish accent, 'I've only just got here.'

'Well with the seventy-five horsepower Evinrude motor and an unloaded boat we can maintain a good speed,' Jeffery responded.

'That's a useful boat and outboard motor combination, do you want to trade the boat in on another?' Campbell asked hopefully.

'No, it's not for sale, as I said, we need another larger boat.'

'About twenty-foot?'

'Nearer thirty would be more suitable,' Jeffery said, looking around at the boats moored nearby.

'Nothing for sale here, but if we drive over to the north side there are a couple there, I have on file.'

'What sort of prices are we looking at?' Dominic asked.

'Around about seven-fifty,' came the reply.

They drove to the north side of Mpulungu in Campbell's Ford Zephyr with all the windows open, through the village with its modest houses and huts, until they came to an area where there were a few warehouses.

'Up to now, the fishing here has been mainly artisanal but a few commercial fisheries are starting up,' Campbell explained gesturing towards the warehouses. 'You can see the rows of drying racks over there.'

They got out of the car and walked towards some boats moored nearby.

'Of course, being daytime they're all in, so you can see what they are using here,' he continued.

They viewed a few of the boats he had on his list, one was far too big, and another was the right size but in poor condition. The last thing Dominic wanted was to start with refurbishment and repairs. They were determined to get going as soon as they could.

'Tell you what lads, I have an almost new launch that the bank has repossessed. A failed company involved in tourism owned it,' Campbell suggested, 'but they're asking much more than I mentioned, they want nine-fifty.'

'What are the specifications?' Jeffery asked.

'Twenty-nine-foot wooden hull, good working space aft and a small cabin forward. A hardtop covers the aft section.'

'What about the engine?'

'It's an inboard Kelvin sixty horsepower.'

'We're not looking for speed so that might be suitable. Let's take a look.'

'It's just a short walk from here. I'll just fetch the keys from the car in case you want to take it for a test run.'

They walked along the shore in front of the warehouses past more boats and canoes until they came to a bright blue and white launch fitted out with seats in the covered area; probably intended for use by tourists for pleasure cruises. Campbell got on first, went forward, unlocked the cabin and retrieved a spanner. He came aft, opened the engine hatch, and connected the battery. The way he worked gave the impression that he was probably a marine engineer. He then invited them both into the cabin and gave some instructions regarding the controls.

'All right captain,' he urged Jeffery, 'let's see you take this lassie for a ride.'

Jeffery fired up the engine, which came to life with a low rumbling sound. He pushed the throttle forward, and the boat moved smoothly out into the lake. The weight and stability compared to their present craft were immediately apparent. Jeffery called Dominic into the cabin out of earshot of Ian Campbell.

'What do you think,' Jeffery asked him.

'It seems fine, right at the start there was a small amount of water that was released by the bilge pump, but it's probably been standing in its mooring for weeks now. No problem there.'

'All we need to do is remove the seats, and we're in business,' Jeffery remarked, 'but what about the price?'

'Let's discuss it with Campbell.'

They all went back to Campbell's so-called office, a room full of marine spare parts, with a desk as an after-thought. He put a call through to the bank and offered them eight-hundred pounds, which they rejected. Eventually, they settled for eight-hundred and seventy-five. Dominic made out the cheque and it was not yet midday.

Campbell made out the bill of sale. Dominic and Jeffery took possession of the keys, operating manual, and other boat documents. Campbell drove them back to the boat, 'Blue Vista' by name, to board their new acquisition. Having bid Campbell farewell, they prepared Blue Vista for its first short journey around the Mpulungu peninsula to pick up their other boat. Before they could leave, they had to purchase two drums of diesel for their new boat.

They hitched up the smaller boat with the tow cable and set off on the return journey. They had no idea of how fast the new boat would go, but after a while, they were able to work out that it would take an extra forty-five minutes towing its charge.

When Michelle arrived back at the house at lunchtime following a busy morning teaching the children at the mission school., there was a letter waiting for her on the coffee table in the lounge. Jeffery must have left it there for her after he picked up the mail from the post office. Her father was not out on the veranda but she could hear the radio coming from his room. He was probably on his bed, resting. She would make him a sandwich and some tea for lunch but if he were sleeping, she would not disturb him. From the return address on the back of the envelope, she knew that the letter was from Clive Francis and had been half expecting it. She had been remiss in not communicating with him earlier but her father's health although not good, was not deteriorating rapidly, so what was there to report. Waiting for someone in your family to die was trying but had moments when one could enjoy their company and share some memories. She opened the letter and read it.

Miss Michelle Simpson
Poste Restante,
SUMBU.
Northern Rhodesia.

Dear Michelle,
I trust this letter finds you well and coping with the concerning matter of your father's health. I'm sure that he really appreciates your being there.
Here, the research and development of the new drug has not been progressing at all well since you left and your colleagues have been unable to bring it finality. I have been considering involving the university thinking that they might be able to find a solution, but management have vetoed that idea because it would complicate the patenting of the new drug. As you can imagine, I'm under great pressure to resolve this problem.
I know that I'm imposing on you at a difficult time, but could you return here to London for a short while to assist us. We would of course pay the expenses for your flight back here and return to Northern Rhodesia thereafter.

Yours sincerely,
Clive Francis

It was much as she expected excepting that she had thought that the team would be able to cope without her. All the research notes were on file, so something unexpected must have happened. What had she overlooked? Her mind started tracing back through her memory of the research, but she forced herself to put it aside; otherwise, it would consume her to the exclusion of everything else. She had a single-mindedness of purpose and an uninterrupted application of her mind to analysis every waking moment. Even her subconscious mind when sleeping had resulted in success in solving some complex problems. But once she started, she became obsessed and now was not the time for that. Instead, she should wait until she was back there before allowing her mind to devote itself to the issues at hand to the exclusion of all else.

From this last thought, she realised that she had now decided to return as Clive Francis was suggesting. How would this affect her father? She felt torn between her personal interests and the wellbeing of her father.

Putting the letter in her pocket, she went through to the kitchen and made herself and her father a sandwich. Before making tea, she went through to his room and knocked. 'I'll meet you out on the veranda,' his voice announced through the door. From back in the kitchen, while she made the tea, she heard the radio move through the house and out front. She put everything on a tray and carried it out to join him on the veranda. Once seated, she glanced in his direction, examining him closely, without speaking. She could see that he had become visibly frail and thin, his cheekbones protruded, and his cheeks were hollow. Despite this, he looked remarkably relaxed and contented. Rather than tell him what she intended to do, she handed him the letter to read, and he turned down the radio.

'Michelle, you need to go back, they need you,' he said.

'But you do too, how can I just up and leave,' she sighed gloomily.

'There's nothing more you can do for me. I'm just happy that you came. And remember me as I was. Promise me you won't come back when I die. Just carry on with your life.'

'I can't bear the thought of you not being here,' she said, tears rolling down her cheeks. Somehow, she suppressed the sob that was lingering in her throat.

'I'll always be here in spirit and always love you,' he said, looking directly into her eyes and smiling. It was too much for her. She had to get away.

'I have to get back to the school. I'll be back later,' she managed to blurt out and ran off the veranda and towards the Land Rover. Once in the cab, she let out a wail as her body convulsed in grief.

Back on the veranda, the old man experienced a feeling of relief. He had let her go, and that made him happy. The memories of her as a child and young girl flooded back as he leaned back in his chair, smiling in satisfaction. How lucky he had been.

He turned up the radio again and listened for a while until the news came on. United Nations General Assembly had voted U Thant as their new Secretary-General. Criticism continued regarding the detonation by the Soviet Union of a 58-megaton hydrogen bomb. An armistice had come into effect between the Katanga rebels and the UN forces.

When Dominic and Jeffery arrived back at the jetty in Sumbu, Jimmy had been waiting patiently for their arrival all day. They would return with either two boats or one. At first, he didn't recognise them, but as the smaller boat appeared from behind, he ran out onto the jetty to catch the rope and secure it to a mooring post. Jeffery hauled the smaller boat up to their stern and stepped on board to retrieve its mooring rope. When Jimmy had secured both boats, he climbed on board Blue Vista and looked admiringly around.

'We've even got seats,' he exclaimed sitting on one with an expansive gesture.

'Don't get too excited about that,' Jeffery said, 'our first task tomorrow is to remove them all. Make sure that you bring the tools down first thing in the morning.'

'Omar delivered another load of wood and other items this morning, and Daniel has taken some of it up to the house,' Jimmy told them.

Back at the house, Dominic went to the back to check on the progress, only to find Daniel struggling to drill the holes needed in the wood sections to take the bolts. The African teak was hard, and it was taking a long time to drill each hole with the hand drill.

'Hold on Daniel, stop drilling, I'll be back in a minute,' Dominic said.

He went back to the warehouse, searched around until he found a power drill, some cabling and a fifteen-amp plug. If he rigged up a cable from the house and kept all electrical items in it switched off, there should be enough power from the generator to drive the drill. He would show Daniel how to start the generator.

By late afternoon, the drill was working, reducing the time taken to drill a hole. They decided to resume the erection of the fish drying frames in the morning.

When Michelle arrived back from the school, Jeffery immediately insisted that the four of them walk down to the jetty to view the new boat before dinner. He supported his father as they made their way down, occasionally stopping to allow him to rest.

'Wow,' Michelle exclaimed, putting her hands on her hips, 'now that's what I call a boat.'

'Not only looks good,' Jeffery added, 'it goes like a dream.'

'It certainly looks to be in good condition,' the old man observed, 'and big enough for purpose.'

Later during dinner, much of the discussion revolved around the new boat and their plans for its use. But there was a cause for concern.

'You know that the rains are coming soon now and that affects the drying. It will require careful planning, particularly coordinating with Omar. We should start building up a reserve in the warehouse but need to be careful of beetle infestation.'

'What about a drying unit?' Dominic asked. 'We would need a power unit as well so the cost would increase, but the selling price must increase if the demand exceeds supply. Have you found this to be the case in the past?'

'Yes, every season,'

As they paused to consider this idea, Michelle seized the moment to make her announcement.

'I'm leaving soon to go back to England,' she said quietly. Dominic and Jeffery stopped eating and looked at her with surprise. The old man intervened on her behalf in case there was an objection from Jeffery.

'She needs to get back. A letter has arrived from her company. She's been away long enough and there's no reason for her to stay longer,' the old man announced. Jeffery opened his mouth as if to complain but quickly closed it tight. How could he suggest that she should stay until their father died? It would sound so callous.

Dominic had known that the day would come. It was so sudden and he had hoped to spend more time with her. Did they have a relationship or not? What did he expect; she had a life back in England, so this was just a break to her, like a small holiday romance, soon forgotten. Somehow, he felt disappointed that she had not mentioned it to him first rather than making her announcement in front of them all.

'We're all going to miss you,' Dominic said, making it inclusive rather than personal.

'I'll miss you all terribly too,' she replied, 'but I do have to go. I'll remember my visit here always, especially my trips to see the game and some of the countryside. Part of me will always be here, no matter what happens.' She paused as tears welled up in her eyes again. 'There's one last thing I'd like to do.'

'What is that?' Jeffery asked.

'Well, I've been all over the park but have never explored the lakeshore.'

'Let's remedy that. How would you like to take a trip on the new boat?' Jeffery offered.

'That would be wonderful,' she said.

'Dominic, would you mind taking Michelle around the lake?'

Dominic smiled and replied in the affirmative. Would he mind? He was over the moon. Anything for a few last hours in her company.

CHAPTER 15

The next day, Jimmy removed all the seats from Blue Vista and made a place for their storage in the warehouse. They took up a lot of space, but what was to become of them he had no idea. Without the seats in the boat, a large working area remained that would be more than adequate for their needs. Whereas the Evinrude on the smaller boat ran on petrol, the Kelvin in the new boat used diesel.

Jeffery came down with the Land Rover. They drove through to the fuel depot and bought two forty-four-gallon drums of diesel and a new hand pump to use exclusively with that fuel. Blue Vista had a large fuel tank, which gave it a much greater range compared to their smaller boat. Jimmy thought it was a pity they would be using it mainly for nearby offshore operations, rather than up in the north around the villages because he would then be able to make at least two trips there and back without refuelling. Nevertheless, he was happy that Jeffery had entrusted him with the small boat operations.

Dominic estimated that if they followed the shoreline from Sumbu to the northern-most village and back, it would take more than a day, so he and Michelle planned to spend one night on the boat in the north before returning. Dominic loaded the boat with two mattresses; bedding; towels; toiletries; plates; glasses and cutlery; two folding camp chairs; a paraffin lamp and stove; a can of paraffin and other items he felt they would need. Michelle went off in the Land Rover to buy food and drink.

By nine o'clock, they were out on the water traversing close into the shoreline working in a westerly direction, eventually heading north. Michelle seemed remarkably quiet, not her usual ebullient self. Perhaps it was because she was leaving her father, Dominic reasoned, but she became almost morose, and he got the feeling that she was avoiding looking at him and even talking. Her demeanour was much like the days when he first arrived in Sumbu. But if his company was causing her discomfort, why had she agreed to go on this trip. After enduring half an hour of this icy atmosphere, he turned the boat away from the shore heading out into deeper water and cut the engine leaving the boat to drift rising and falling on the gentle swell.

'You're very quiet,' he remarked. Michelle looked at him with her brow furrowed in a scowl, shaking her head from side to side with her eyes closed, looking miserable.

'Who are you?' she snarled.

'What do you mean,' he asked becoming serious himself.

'You have a criminal record,' she blurted.

'Where did you hear that?'

'So, it's true. You don't deny it?'

'Yes, it's true, but I can explain. First, tell me who told you.'

'When I went to do the shopping just before we left, I bumped into Misheck. He got it from the sergeant at the *boma*,' she said. Dominic thought about this for a few moments and was furious with Misheck. But he couldn't blame him. Michelle deserved to know, and he had failed to tell her.

'Well,' she demanded still scowling intensely.

'I made a silly mistake,' he said, 'one weekend in Salisbury after a rugby match, I was drinking in the club bar with some supporters of the visiting team. They were from out of town, and I didn't know them, but we got rather drunk and were in very high spirits. When the time came for them to leave, I asked them to drop me off at my flat before they drove home. On the way there, we passed the local fire station and parked outside was a gleaming red fire engine. Our driver stopped and told us that there were too many of us in his car, and three of us should get out and use the fire engine instead. It was a joke. But three of us got out, and he drove off. One of the guys got into the cab and started the engine. I climbed up on top of the fire engine with the other guy, and off we went. Well, as you can imagine, it wasn't long before we had a police car in pursuit.' He hesitated for a moment and looked askance at Michelle to see her expression. Something in her had softened and there was just the glimmer of a smile at the edges of her lips. 'Eventually, the driver yelled that he was going to stop and we should make a run for it. He jammed on the brakes and as he did, I lost my grip and fell to ground winded and slightly concussed. The other two got away and the police arrested me.'

'You took a joy ride in a fire-engine?' Michelle exclaimed in astonishment.

'Yes, it was a joy ride, a silly prank,' Dominic asserted.

'What happened after that?' Michelle asked, trying to suppress a giggle with her hand over her mouth.

'After that, things got serious. They took me to the police station and wanted to know who the other men were, but of course, I didn't have a clue. They particularly wanted to know the name of the driver. It happened on a Saturday, so they held me in jail until Monday morning when they dragged me up before a magistrate who handles all the minor offences that occur over a weekend. You know, drunkenness, public disturbance, that sort of thing. These offences attract fines and short sentences. When my case came up, the magistrate was particularly agitated that the police had not apprehended the driver of the fire engine. The police only charged me with assisting in the theft of a vehicle.'

'What on earth would one do with a stolen fire engine?' Michelle exclaimed.

'Exactly, using a vehicle without the owner's consent was a far more appropriate charge, and the magistrate quashed the assisting a theft charge. At that point, I thought I would get off. But because the police believed that I was deliberately hiding the identity of the driver, they had a second charge of defeating the ends of justice. That was how I ended up serving two months of a three-month sentence.'

'But that's dreadful,' Michelle said, putting a hand on his arm.
'Yes, I thought that too up until the time I came to Sumbu.'
'How do you mean?' she asked.

'Well, when I came out of jail, I found that I had lost my job and when I came to look for another one I discovered that it's difficult if you have a criminal record. After some weeks of trying, I was running out of money, so I needed to do something quickly. I learned that there was a recruitment drive going on in town to employ mercenaries to serve in the Congo. They were looking for men who had actual combat experience, whereas I had only been through military training. As an accountant, they decided that I might be able to help them in a non-combat role to assist with the payroll and act as a driver for one of the officers. That's how I ended up in the Congo.'

'But what good did that do?' she asked.

'If none of what I have told you happened, I would never have met you. Being with you has brought me more pleasure than anything I have ever experienced. I wouldn't turn back the clock no matter how things turn out in the future.' Dominic left her side and moved back into the wheelhouse of the boat to prevent his emotions from getting out of control. He wanted to say more, but he was not sure how Michelle felt about him. As he stood there in the wheelhouse looking out to the horizon, he felt her arms encircle his chest and her head against his back.

'I'm so sorry I judged you so harshly,' she whispered, 'let's enjoy the rest of our trip. We have so little time left together.'

Dominic's spirits rose now she knew about his past and why he was fighting in the Congo. Her response, in the end, had restored their relationship to what it had been the day before.

As they traversed the shoreline, Michelle enjoyed the view looking back at the land after spending so much time looking out over the lake. As they gradually turned north, the escarpment rose sharply out of the rocky shoreline, covered in forest and undisturbed by human habitation. The fauna and flora occupying the area survived in a time capsule spanning back perhaps thousands of years. If they were to stop now and go ashore to walk in the forest, they would probably be the only humans to have ever set foot there. This evoked a magnificent feeling of isolation, hiding her from the eyes of the world, yet somehow embracing her.

Further along, she noticed that the fire had scarred the face of the escarpment black and grey. It showed no signs of life. Between the branches devoid of leaves, the bare earth was visible despite the wispy branches of the undergrowth.

'Is this where you started the fire?' Michelle asked.

'Yes, I don't know exactly where, but the wind was blowing slightly from the north so it will be a little further on nearer where we see the unburned vegetation.'

'It's devastated,' she remarked in a shocked tone.

'Surprisingly, it will all recover when the rains come. Remember there are often fires here caused by lightning, so the forest has survived successive fires for millennia.'

Further on still, as they were approaching the pristine forest again, he said, 'It must be about here.' Michelle looked at the rocks along the shore and noticed a rock that was larger than all the others were.

'That's Zippo Rock,' she said, pointing to it. Dominic laughed. 'No one will know.'

'Oh, but we know, and that's enough,' she responded.

As they progressed, Michelle took out the flask, poured them both a cup of coffee and continued to admire the wild beauty of the shore. Before they saw the fish eagle, they heard its cry, and as they passed it took flight its powerful wings flapping in a lazy slow motion.

Around midday, they arrived offshore from the main village that he and Jeffery visited almost daily. Dominic cut the motor, and they drifted watching the women on the beach tending the drying fish and the fields at the back of the village.

'There are only a few men in sight. Don't they work?' Michelle asked.

'Yes, fishing all night. They appear in the late afternoon to prepare the dugouts.'

A dugout canoe left the beach coming in their direction, and as it approached, they saw that there were three young boys and a girl paddling energetically. When they arrived, laughing alongside they called out in the vernacular, and Michelle laughed and replied. Dominic knew what was coming even although he couldn't understand a word. Michelle went into one of the baskets, took out two oranges, and with a knife cut them in half, passing them down to the children. More dugouts were launching from the beach filled with children.

'I've really started something now,' Michelle cried, 'we better go, there's not enough for all of them.' Dominic laughed, but started the motor and turned the boat around and out into the lake at full speed to discourage any thoughts they might have of pursuit.

'Where do we go now?' Michelle asked.

'I know a little beach just further up. I've never landed there but saw it when I took the surveyors to the border beacon. We can have lunch there.'

'Then I need to cool the wine,' she announced.

'You found wine?' he said with surprise.

'Yes, at the store this morning. It's a Portuguese white wine called Lagosta. Probably gets here via Angola.' She emptied the rest of the oranges from the net bag. Inserted the bottle and hooked the bag around a hitch. Then lowered it so that it dragged in the water.

'You've done this before,' he teased her.

'No, I haven't,' she exclaimed with mock indignation.

When they arrived at the small beach, Dominic stopped the boat a little way offshore and threw out the anchor. He was afraid to go in too close in case they ran aground on the sand in the shallow water where the boat would be too heavy for the two of them to push out again. If they became marooned Jeffery would soon come looking for them, but that would be hugely embarrassing. The water was so clear that he could see the bottom, and it was easy to judge the depth.

Michelle carved the brown bread into slices, buttered them and made ham and tomato sandwiches.

'Of course, you know what I've done,' Dominic exclaimed, 'I forgot to bring a corkscrew.'

'How could you do such a thing?' She said playfully, 'just push the cork into the bottle.' Dominic hauled the bottle back on board and did as she suggested spilling only a few drops but leaving a few pieces of cork floating in the bottle.

They ate their lunch on the deck sitting on the camp chairs in the shade of the cover, protected from the overhead sun. It was the hottest time of the year, just before the rains. Dominic poured the wine into two tumblers.

After they had finished the sandwiches, Dominic poured them each a second glass of wine. While they sat there sipping the wine, a troop of monkeys came swinging down out of the forest. They ran down to the water to drink. As they went, some of the juveniles pulled each other's tails and leapt into the air.

Michelle could feel herself relaxing, whether due to the wine or the surroundings she wasn't sure, perhaps both. They were so isolated from the rest of the world here on this remote beach, with only nature around them, all of society's norms seemed out of place. Her inhibitions melted like ice cream in the sun. She became consumed by her surroundings, lost in this fantasyland far from anywhere. She wanted to touch it, feel it, and become part of it.

Michelle drained her glass and then stripped off her clothes and threw them into the cabin.

'It's so hot,' she complained, 'let's swim to the beach to cool off.'

Totally naked, she dived into the water. Dominic removed all his clothes and followed behind her. It was so hot that the water felt quite cold and refreshing. Michelle got to the shore first, turned and waited to for him to reach her the water beading on her skin. As he came out of the water, she took his hand and led him down the beach towards some overhanging trees that creating a shady pattern on the sand. Once they were under the trees, she turned to face him, threw her arms around his neck, and kissed him passionately with her mouth slightly open. This time he could not restrain himself pulling her fiercely against him becoming fully aroused his heart beating rapidly as her kiss deprived him of air.

Afterwards, lying on their backs basking in the afterglow, she ran her fingers over his chest. Then down to the well-defined muscles of his stomach.

'You are sensational,' he breathed, looking into her eyes and kissing her on the forehead.

They lay quietly there in the shade of the trees for a long time looking out across the lake that remained deserted of any sign of human life. Total isolation.

'Tell me about London and what you do there?' Dominic requested.

'It's difficult to describe compared to where we are now. Whereas here, at this moment I'm experiencing and observing a peaceful natural beauty. London is vibrant and magnificent. You've never been there?'

'No, I haven't,' he admitted, 'I've never been out of Africa, in fact not even north of the equator. But tell me what you do there.'

'I studied medicine at the University in London, and when I graduated, I joined a large pharmaceutical company in Surrey as a researcher. I also lecture at the University quite regularly, so I have an apartment in Earls Court where I've lived since starting my studies. When I joined the company, I thought of moving to Dorking to be closer to work but decided that because I was to lecture, I might as well stay put. I love living in London anyway, so it wasn't much of a decision. It does mean though that I must catch a train from Waterloo station to get to Dorking, but it's not too bad because first thing in the morning most people are coming into London not out. I can always get a seat, and I manage to work for an hour during the journey.'

'And what kind of research do you do?'

'It's mainly the development of new drugs. I work in a team with other researchers, but I spend most of my time working alone. It's difficult for women to build a career out there competing with men and I have the additional disadvantage, which is my colour. I love research because they only judge me on merit and I'm paid the same as the men, in fact, more than some of them. But what about you? That's enough about me. You're always so reluctant to talk about yourself.'

'Well, now that you've accepted what a vicious and mercenary criminal I am,' he said with an ironic smile, 'it's made it a lot easier.'

'Stop teasing me,' she exclaimed, giving him a playful smack on the chest, 'if you'd told me everything earlier it would have made it easier for me. You've been so generous in helping Jeffery and standing up for me. You gave me the confidence to fight back myself.'

'Well, the rest of my story is quite ordinary.'

'There's nothing ordinary about you but carry on.'

'I studied accountancy and business economics at Rhodes University in South Africa, and when I graduated, I returned to Salisbury and worked for an accounting firm. My sister Julia went to the Agriculture College in Salisbury. She's now married with two children and she and her husband live on the family tobacco and maize farm in Banket in the north-west of Southern Rhodesia. Richard, her husband is a mechanic who specialises in repairing and maintaining agricultural equipment. He came to the farm from time to time to attend to the equipment and that's how they met. My parents are less active now and due to retire soon, then Julia and Richard will take over. The rest you pretty much know.'

'Have you been in touch with your parents since you've been here?'

'No, they are rather disappointed in me right now. As far as they are concerned, they think I'm still fighting in the Congo. I want to make something of myself before I contact them again.'

'But you must let your mother know you're alright. She'll be worrying every day. Promise me you'll write to her.'

'All right I will, at least I can tell her I'm now a fisherman.'

'You're more than that, but she'll be happy with anything other than a mercenary.'

She leaned over, kissed him got up, and ran down to the water.

'Come on,' she cried, 'you need to get rid of all that sand.'

He ran down and joined her in the water, washing away the sand that had clung to his body.

Back on the boat, they dried themselves off with towels, she vigorously rubbing her hair, leaving it fanned out to dry in the sun. They dressed, and Dominic lit the paraffin stove to make coffee while she lowered another bottle of wine into the water to cool, ready for them to enjoy later as the sun went down. As they sat in the camp chairs sipping the coffee, he saw that although she was smiling, tears were running down her cheeks.

'Who am I?' she said.

'What do you mean?'

'I'm not sure you would understand,' she replied and changed the subject.

CHAPTER 16

Misheck made a booking for dinner for three at the club on the Thursday evening before Michelle was to leave to wish her farewell. He had wanted to spend it alone with Michelle, but she had pointed out that they would never have been able to consider such a farewell had Dominic not challenged the club on her behalf in the first place. She did not try to include Jeffery because she knew he would not go to the club on principle. Michelle bought a new dress after much searching in the village, and some deft needlework which made it more fashionable. The transformation from shorts, T-shirt, and sandals was a revelation. High heels altered her posture, and when she walked, she seemed to glide along. Dominic entered the old man's cupboard again to don a dark suit and tie.

When they arrived at the club, a waiter received them graciously and ushered them to the lounge where they found Misheck waiting at one of the tables. Heads turned, and there were some whispers from other tables in the lounge, but this time there was no objection-inspired evacuation as had happened on the previous occasion. They ordered drinks, and when they arrived, Misheck proposed a toast.

'To the lady who made this possible,' he said, 'to Michelle, we'll miss her.'

'To Michelle,' Dominic added.

'And to you both for making my stay here so enjoyable,' Michelle answered. After they had taken the first sips of their drinks, she addressed Misheck and asked, 'how are you enjoying being a member of the club?'

'Still a bit strange being the only black face amongst all these whites but they've made a real effort to make me feel welcome. After they made me a member, they invited me to come in and meet the committee. We met in the bar and it was quite surprising, because they were soon asking me all kinds of questions about the game reserve, so I was quite the centre of attention. Perhaps they felt obliged to due to the circumstances of my joining. Time will tell.'

'Misheck, having started this, I'm expecting you to become a committee member. Who knows, maybe sometime in the future you will become chairman,' Michelle said.

'Well, that sounds a bit ambitious.'

'Don't say that. We need to fight for a bigger share in everything,' Michelle encouraged him.

The waiter arrived with three menus and left them to make their selections. Whilst they were scanning through them, the DC came in, neatly dressed in a suit and tie looking quite elegant compared to the military strictness of his usual uniform. Each table greeted him warmly with invitations to join them. The visitors to the club represented whatever pretensions there were to a privileged society in this part of the world. And if anyone was at the top of that society, it was Arthur Cameron, District Commissioner. He graciously declined each invitation and took his reserved table in the corner. He'd barely sat down when he noticed the party of three sitting with the club's new, one and only, black member. Without hesitation, he came over and Dominic and Misheck stood up to greet him.

'Good evening Miss Simpson, Mister Harrison and of course, welcome to Misheck,' he said in his usual formal manner.

'May I join you?' the DC asked, 'I'm inviting you to be my guests for dinner this evening if I'm not intruding.'

'That would be an honour,' said Michelle responding, realising that he was deliberately contriving this piece of theatre for the benefit of the members and their guests in the room. His voice was loud enough for all to hear.

'Excellent,' he said, 'I have an ulterior motive. You see, my wife is away in England for a while, so I come here frequently for dinner and it's good to have company.'

'I'll call the waiter to bring you a menu,' Dominic suggested.

'Not necessary,' he laughed, 'I know the darned thing by heart. For now, I'll just order a gin and tonic.'

The convivial influence of Arthur Cameron dispelled any doubt about the social acceptability of the three of them.

Over dinner, Arthur Cameron discussed the changes he had experienced in Africa during his time in the colonial service and his vision of the future.

'Northern Rhodesia will become independent in the near future just as Nigeria has recently. The real problem in giving the colonies independence is going to be the European settler population. As you have experienced, racism is and will remain a problem for a long time irrespective of legislation to eliminate it. As a minority, it is understandable that they will seek some protection in any new constitution. The real challenge for Africa is the choice between democratic and authoritarian systems of government. Even if democratic constitutions are encouraged and adopted at independence, there is no guarantee that governments cannot successively amend them until the judiciary is compromised and an authoritarian regime gains power. They could then retain it by patronage using the army and the police.'

'You make it sound as if things are very much in the balance and could go either way,' Dominic remarked.

'You're quite right. Just across the border in the Congo, there is considerable concern about the future. The sudden departure of the Belgians without overseeing a transition from colonial rule to democracy has left a vacuum. The West and the Russians are trying to occupy this space politically. Mobutu has taken over from Lumumba, who before he died, was an intellectual and had legitimately won a democratic election. He aligned himself with the Russians, not so much to adopt communism as his political preference, but to counter European attempts to secure the considerable resources in the country, by intrigue or force. The West supports Mobutu to prevent communist ideology taking root in the Congo. If that happens, they would have a foothold and try to influence the course of events here in Northern Rhodesia. It's a dangerous game. And yes, it could go either way.'

'What will you do when independence comes?' Michelle asked.

'Oh, you know, I will go back to where I came from, England. Under a new constitution, my present area of jurisdiction will become one or more constituencies and the political parties will contest them and end up with a member of parliament. A district council with a Chairman will administer it. I will be redundant.'

'I, for one, will be sorry to see you go,' Michelle said, 'thank you for what you did to help me.'

'Think nothing of it. It was the least I could do. But now, that's enough about me, tell me about yourselves.'

It turned out to be an enjoyable dinner, and when they had finished their coffee, the DC put the bill on his account and apologised for immediately leaving saying he had some work to do at home before retiring. Realising that Misheck had arranged the evening to say his personal farewell to Michelle, Dominic suggested that he drive back to the house in the Land Rover if Misheck could drop Michelle off later.

Driving back in the dark, he wondered what future he had here or in Southern Rhodesia, taking cognisance of Arthur Cameron's alternative scenarios. He was one of the settler minorities. What would happen if independence were to come to Southern Rhodesia? Would communist ideology expand throughout central Africa? How would things turn out for his family on the farm? It could go either way.

When he arrived at the house, it was in darkness. He parked the Land Rover and climbed the steps up onto the veranda and was about to enter the house when the old man's voice penetrated the silence of the evening.

'You're home by yourself,' he noted.

'Yes, I left Michelle and Misheck to say their last goodbyes.'

'There's something I need to discuss with you,' he said, 'but first can you go and start the generator again to give us some light. I asked Jeffery to turn it off when he left for his meeting.'

Dominic went around to the back of the house and fumbling in the darkness found the starting cord and with a few pulls had the motor purring. When he got back to the veranda, the light was on, and the old man had pulled the table away from the wall and arranged it with two chairs on either side. On the table were some documents and a map. Dominic sat politely waiting whilst the old man sat reading through one of the documents.

'Excuse me for asking such a personal question, but are you in love with Michelle?' For a moment, Dominic was quite stunned and thought carefully before answering. He hadn't told her so should he tell her father? But it was the truth.

'Yes,' he said, 'but I'm not sure she loves me.'

'That doesn't surprise me … no don't get me wrong, I don't mean there's anything wrong with you, quite the contrary, it's Michelle. You know, she seems to be quite ambivalent when it comes to these matters and I worry she'll never get married. But that's a matter between you both and not what I wanted to discuss. Do you know anything about mining?'

'Not much, only what I've learned auditing mines in Southern Rhodesia and that's mainly financial.'

'You might find that experience quite useful in the future. As you know, I'm a geologist. When I retired from the exploration company, I had to sign a restraint agreement, which prevented me from conducting any geological studies in any of the areas where I had worked or where they had claims. Anyway, I had retired here, and there is little of mining geological interest in the area. Or so I thought. I didn't go about looking for anything. Two years ago, when I was still well and energetic, I was hunting in the control area at the edge of the game reserve when I stumbled over an interesting outcrop of rocks. It was entirely unexpected and pure chance. I had a game guard with me, which is a requirement to ensure that I didn't harm any protected species. It takes two men to hunt if you are on foot. We would carry the animal secured on a pole cut from a tree supported on each man's shoulder. I showed absolutely no interest in the rocks whilst in the company of the game guard, although I was dying to have a cursory look. Although I returned from that day's hunting empty-handed, I couldn't wait to get back there.

'The next day I returned alone but this time prepared to take samples. By the time I had finished, I had a bag so heavy I could only just manage to carry it back to the vehicle. I'd driven cross-country following the tracks of the previous day to as close as possible to the site.

'I took the samples down to a laboratory in Ndola and stayed a few days waiting for the results. As I expected the one seam was rich in gold. I went to the geological department to apply for a mining and exploration licence for a large area I had defined by latitude and longitude on the map. This process takes time, so I returned here and waited for them to contact me. When they did, they had divided the area into north and south concessions and gave me the choice of which one I wanted. I took the northern area where I knew the outcrop was, and the Postlewhite International Mining Company took up the southern area.

'The licence that was issued to me is in the name of the Simpson Family Trust. I knew by then that my health was failing, and I wanted to ensure that it remained in the family after my death. A lot more needs to be done to prove that the ore body is viable for mining. Perhaps some geochemical and geophysical surveys but that would require finance and bringing in investors. I intended to work to achieve this, but as you can see, I'm no longer in any condition to continue. Recently I had a visit from Max Freeman of Postlewhite who gave me some results from their drilling in the southern area and made an offer for the northern area licence. But when I looked at the drilling results, I became suspicious. They just don't make sense compared to the results from the outcrop. I'm convinced that someone has fraudulently contrived to make the deposit appear of much less value than is the case.

'I've come to know you quite well in a fairly short time, and your generosity in helping Jeffery with the financing of the fishing operation and of being so protective of Michelle is much appreciated. Well, neither of them is in a position to devote time to follow up and further the opportunity that this licence represents. The question is, would you be prepared to do it?'

Dominic had been listening very carefully trying to picture in his mind where this was leading, but he had not expected this.

'Well, Sir, it's an interesting challenge, but I'm not sure I'm up to it.'

'I disagree. From what I've observed you have the propensity to put your mind to just about anything where business is concerned, and this is more of a business challenge than anything else,' the old man exclaimed, 'and there is the important matter of trust. From your behaviour so far, I am confident I can rely on you.'

From the way the old man put it, Dominic could tell he wasn't going to take no for an answer. Anyway, how could he not offer to help?

'How do you propose we go about this?' Dominic asked.

'Well, I'm not expecting you to do this for nothing and if you succeed there should be a suitable reward. Not only that, there needs to be a motivation for you to see it as an exciting challenge. I propose we make you a beneficiary entitled to twenty per cent of the trust. You already deserve that from the finance you've raised for the fishing operation. That also falls under the trust. If the three of you work together, I'm sure that in the future you can succeed, but the mining opportunity is largely in your hands. Jeffery can carry on with the fishing.'

'Sir, that's a most generous offer, and I'll do whatever I can to realise what you have started.'

'It won't be easy. There are many tough characters out there in the mining industry, and Max Freeman is one of them. You have to out-think them, and I believe you have the intellect to do that, but you also need the stamina to stay the course. You're young enough to do that.' He rolled out the map on the table, pointing to a small square box inked in red.

'The large square rectangle in black is the extent of the northern concession area; this in green is the southern area. The small red box indicates where the outcrop is situated. You are now the only other person who knows where the outcrop is. Here is the original geological report from the lab. This document here is the licence. It's due for renewal fairly soon so make sure that you do this on time or we could lose it. This document you need to sign. It's accepting to serve as a trustee of the trust, and this is a resolution which has been signed by me, Jeffery and Michelle adding you as a beneficiary.'

'From a business perspective, what would be your next move,' Dominic asked hesitantly.

'We already have this offer for the licence from a company that has undertaken drilling. They are sufficiently encouraged by the results of the drilling to want the northern concession as well. As I've said, the offer is too low because the results from the outcrop, contradict the report they gave me, but how much more it is worth is difficult to say. At the moment, there is no way that we can get access to the drilling results, but the moment they try to raise funding from investors on the London Stock Exchange, they will be required to release the information. That will immediately add value to our licence. If we are patient and just wait, we should be able to sell it to

Postlewhite at a much higher price, or find another mining company as a partner, or list a company of our own.'

'So, in fact, it's a waiting game.'

'Yes, once you have the results, you'll have a better idea of the value. There is no way I can advise any further than that. You're on your own.'

Dominic accepted this statement with some trepidation, but he would certainly make a fight of it. The old man picked up one last set of documents and handed them to Dominic.

'These are the latest financial accounts for the trust that I'm sure you will understand better than I do.' He collected all the documents and handed them to Dominic together with the map. Shaking his hand, he said, 'I wish you the very best of luck and good fortune. Good night.'

Back in his room, Dominic undressed and got into bed but didn't fall asleep immediately but lay there running through in his mind what had just happened to him. He felt a mixture of excitement and apprehension. Where would this new venture lead him? An hour after he had fallen asleep, just before midnight he awoke hearing Misheck's Land Rover arrive in front of the house. A short while later, he heard the vehicle leave followed by Michelle's quiet footsteps on the floorboards as she made her way to her room. She was carrying the high-heeled shoes.

CHAPTER 17

It was that season when the rains came. Michelle was back in London. In the end, her departure was low key. She wouldn't countenance any situation that might play with her emotions. Early in the morning before the day of her flight, Jeffery drove away from the house with Michelle and her luggage headed for Ndola where she would catch a connecting flight to London. Dominic heard the vehicle leave as he lay in bed trying to visualise her; the beautiful firm athletic body; intelligent sparkling eyes and even toothed smile. An apple blossom fragrance returned from his memory, lingering in the air. Neither he nor Michelle had suggested that they should write to each other. Nor had there been any suggestion about when they might meet again. It left him with an empty feeling, and he wondered how Michelle felt. During the days before her departure, there was an air of sadness about her. Not surprising as she was leaving her father and might not see him again, so Dominic could not determine what she felt about their relationship. Was the intimacy they shared just a passing spontaneous, passionate impulse or something much deeper? He had considered confronting her openly with his feelings for her. Still, he decided against it afraid that the emotional upheaval of leaving her father was not the right time to reveal his own feelings.

With the overcast and wet weather, the fish drying process at the villages slowed considerably and the volume of fish they brought in to Sumbu declined. Omar reduced the number of visits to give them time to accumulate a load. Now the completed racks were in use, Jeffery and Daniel concentrated on the mother boat operations in Blue Vista supported by a team of dugout canoe fishermen living in the Sumbu area. The volume of fish soon increased to the point where the drying racks could not cope due to increased drying times caused by the wet weather. Dominic realised that they needed a mechanical dryer with trays and heating provided by diesel burners. Acquiring and bringing the machine into operation required his devoted attention.

In Salisbury at the mercenary recruitment centre, the adjutant had reported to the colonel that there were now withdrawals from the bank account of Dominic Harrison, which proved that he had survived the attack. The colonel amended his status as an MIA and suspended further payments into the account. The withdrawals emanated from a bank in the small town of Sumbu, on the southern shore of Lake Tanganyika in Northern Rhodesia. To record Dominic's change of address, the adjutant contacted the bank in Sumbu to see if the manager there would be prepared to provide them with the details. Once he received the new address, the colonel would send him an official letter, the contents of which he was still trying to decide.

Even further away, in Dorking in England, Clive Francis was at last sleeping a little easier each night. His star researcher was back, and they were now making progress again after being in the doldrums for some time. In her absence, Samuels had put pressure on him to hand the leadership of the unit to him rather than retaining Michelle in that position whilst she was away. He argued that if Clive Francis appointed him, he would find someone equally talented as Michelle. But Clive Francis knew that his main objection to her was that she was female and even more irritating was that she earned more than him. How, Samuels reasoned, could that be acceptable when he was a breadwinner, and she had no dependents. How Samuels knew what she earned or if he was just making an assumption and waiting for him to deny it, Francis did not know. Salaries were, of course, confidential and if someone had broken the company's rules of confidentiality, it was an offence serious enough to lead to dismissal. In the end, persuaded, Francis reluctantly appointed Samuels to Michelle's former position. The good news was that Michelle, with her sharp intellect gradually solved the problems they were experiencing. They disappeared like a dissolving pill.

For Michelle herself, she had returned from her African visit, inspired by her experience. Not directed to her work as a researcher but to the realisation, brought on by Dominic's actions at the club that she could fight for any rights she felt were denied her.

Through her lectures at the university, she came into contact again with students supporting the Anti-Apartheid Movement, which had as its objective pressure to change the racial policies of South Africa. Earlier there had been a massacre at Sharpville where police had shot and killed sixty-nine unarmed black protesters. Encouraged initially by Dominic, she now felt a duty to fight on behalf of other racially oppressed people. With this awakening political awareness, she joined the movement.

Reminiscing about Sumbu, her main concern was the health of her father, but she had prepared herself for the bad news that she knew was bound to come. As far as Dominic and Misheck were concerned, there remained confusion in her mind. On the evening they had dinner at the club after Dominic had left and returned to the house, Misheck had declared his love for her and proposed marriage. It caught her by surprise. She had strong feelings for both him and Dominic, but she was not ready for marriage and was not even sure if she ever would be.

Turning down Misheck had been difficult, and he asked her outright if it was because of his race. It had hurt her that he could even think that was the reason, and she remonstrated with him vigorously to the contrary. With Dominic, it was different. She was as attracted to him as she was to Misheck, but Dominic had not taken the initiative in their intimacy, she had, but he had not made any proposals regarding their future, nor expressed his love for her. In the last few days before she left, this incident had changed her attitude to Dominic, almost as if to show to herself that her feelings for them were the same. Somehow, in choosing a partner, she needed to do it with her eyes closed. Weighing up the attributes of the two men would lead her nowhere as they were so different. What did her heart say? It alternated with each beat.

Dust followed Jules Ntanganda's Land Rover rising to settle in the surrounding trees as he drove on the road towards Pweto. As they had planned, he was driving a right-hand-drive vehicle, was armed with a knife and pistol secreted behind the driver's seat and was motivated with deadly intent and a measure of avarice. When the time came to cross into Northern Rhodesia, there was a pair of false number plates with installation tools stored behind the seat with the weapons. In the one pocket of the trousers of his civilian clothes, there was a roll of Belgian Francs and in the other Northern Rhodesian Pounds. When he arrived in Pweto, he would stay overnight to ascertain where he could find the route to the unofficial border crossing. Hopefully, he could leave in the early hours while it was still dark, make the crossing just after sunrise so that he could negotiate the rough track the other side of the border in daylight.

When he arrived at Pweto in the early evening, he first refuelled the vehicle and then went looking for a tavern. Being out of the close control of the Commander and his officers was an escape into civilian life and some of the pleasant diversions it afforded. Just about everything in the bar was constructed of wood, not the highly polished variety found in major western cities but rough and rustic the knots of the wood protruding here and there. Wooden stools along the bar were heavy and without any padding on the seats. Loud music blasted from a record player behind the bar, sometimes with a repetitive click, as a scratch on the vinyl contributed its own rhythm. Sleeves of long-playing records were standing upright in a wire rack, and the barman would change to a new one every half hour-or-so. The air was thick with cigarette smoke, and there was a slight smell of stale beer.

He squeezed through the people at the bar and caught the barman's eye ordering a beer. When he paid, he withdrew the roll of francs from his right pocket peeling away a note and waited for the change. The barman walked down to the end of the bar and spoke briefly to two girls with heavy makeup, wearing tight jeans and equally tight T-shirts. When the barman came back, he gave Jules his change.

Lucy joined Jules Ntanganda at the bar, leaning provocatively against him using her usual pickup line in French, 'Are you lonely?' She asked, taking his hand in hers.

'Well, I'm here all alone so yes I guess I am.'

'Will you buy me a drink,' she suggested, to which Jules responded by calling the barman and ordering the absinthe that she claimed was her favourite drink. The most expensive he noticed referring to the costs displayed on the wall. After they had had a few drinks, he suggested that they have something to eat, which Lucy seized as a rare opportunity to have a meal bought for her.

'Move off this table,' Lucy screeched at two men who were sitting drinking, 'We want to eat. You can drink at the bar.' Her hands were on her hips as Lucy assumed the pose universally recognised as 'or else there will be trouble.'

The two men smiled and followed her instructions. Who were they to interfere with the business of a working girl. Jules and

Lucy sat down at the table and ordered chicken and sweet corn, which turned out to be the special and only dish available.

Waiting for the meal to arrive they engaged in meaningless conversation, he avoiding her inquisitiveness. The less she knew about him, the better and the false name he used to introduce himself a further obfuscation.

After a while, he said, 'I need to get across the border. I've left my passport behind, is there any way I can get over without going through the border post?'

'But that's easy,' she replied, 'there are any number of ways you can walk over from here.'

'No, I need to drive over.'

'Ah, that's a little more difficult. There is a track a few kilometres north of here, but it's not used very often. If we can come to some arrangement, I'll show you.'

'How much if I stay with you tonight?' he asked.

'The whole night?'

'Yes.'

'Twenty francs and I'll show you the route as well.'

They had a few more drinks and left slightly drunk. As they drove north away from Pweto, she leaned forward in her seat looking out on his side of the road in the headlights. After a while, she said, 'We've gone too far, turn back.' He did as she directed and drove slowly back for a minute. 'Here,' she said, 'you see that track you go in there and just follow it.'

'How do I know when I've crossed the border?'

'When I first started in this business, I thought I could protect my reputation by only having clients the other side of the border. It's a few years ago now, but in those days, there was a beacon of stones next to the track.'

Jules made a mental note of the access to the track and set the trip meter to measure the distance to wherever she was going to take him for the night.

Lucy had a simple rectangular thatched dwelling constructed with wooden uprights, sealed with reeds clad with clay, and painted cream. He parked the Land Rover outside and switched off the lights. There were other dwellings nearby but not that close that there was no privacy. Inside it was quite large and well furnished with a brass double bed appropriate for her profession. After she fired up the paraffin pressure lamp, they both undressed and slipped between the blankets.

In the morning before sunrise, he took a cold shower, dressed and without waking her left a further five francs and went out closing the door as quietly as he could. Checking the trip meter, he reset it to zero and drove back towards the entrance of the track until the required distance displayed. He turned onto the track and advanced slowly into the bush. A couple of times he lost the track as it had become so overgrown and had to reverse in the dark leaning out the window with the torch. As he progressed, he noticed that the small streams had loose stone drifts to aid the crossing of a vehicle. Gradually he went deeper into the bush in the direction of the border until he came to a dry river with steep banks. In the headlights of the Land Rover, he could see there was a makeshift wooden bridge. Taking the torch, he got out and shone it over the bridge, examining it as best he could in the darkness, but in the dark, he could only inspect the entrance. The torch was too weak for him to see the rest of it. There were large tree trunks as uprights with branches secured with rope as beams. His main concern was the strength of the rope, which looked severely weathered. He decided to wait in the cab dozing, waiting for the light to improve.

He awoke with the light streaming in through the windscreen and looked at his watch to find that he had slept a little longer than he wanted. Inspecting the bridge by climbing down into the dry bed of the river and looking up from below he could see gaps in the cross members forming the surface he was to drive on, but nothing that looked insurmountable. The ropes securing the structure appeared to be sound, although old and frayed. Returning to the Land Rover, he engaged the four-wheel drive and extra-low gears and manoeuvred the vehicle onto the bridge. He made good progress until towards the end where the vertical supports on the left side had sunk at some time deeper into the sand of the river, causing the surface to slope quite severely to the left. There was no way back because it would be difficult to reverse without someone else to assist with directions. He could do nothing else but keep going with the Land Rover leaning sharply to the left causing him to cling to the steering wheel to prevent him slipping out of the seat. The creaking sound from the bridge and expanding springs on the right side of the vehicle, filled his ears and his heart with foreboding.

If it toppled now, he would die or be injured before he had even started his mission in earnest. With the lowest gear engaged, it moved forward inch by inch without his foot on the pedal. Somehow, he no longer controlled his future. Leaning his body heavily to the right as if he could somehow counteract the leaning of the Land Rover, he found it straightening and climbing out off the bridge. Putting his foot on the accelerator, it gained firm ground again. He was soaked in sweat even though it was still early and not yet hot.

After that, although it was laborious driving along the rough track at least, he did not encounter any further dangers. It did, however, disturb him that he would need to return by the same route and survive the bridge again. When he passed the beacon of stones that Lucy had mentioned into Northern Rhodesia, he found that the track was just as bad. There was still twelve kilometres to go before he would come to a gravel-surfaced road. He took a break to change the number plates and set off on his way again.

He arrived in Sumbu in the afternoon and once again sought out a tavern. Using prostitutes as a source of accommodation avoided him having to register himself formally, which hopefully would disguise his visit. Sylvia turned out more modestly attired than Lucy with quite conservative makeup. She would pass for a pretty office worker at the *boma,* and he could pose as a visiting relative. He arranged to book her for three nights, reasoning that he could extend his stay if necessary.

The next morning, he made his way down to the Jetty and joined a group of casual labourers loitering near the warehouses. He suppressed the temptation to ask if they had seen a white man working the boats. He made little conversation at all concerned that his accent might attract attention. Midway through the morning, a boat driven by a black man arrived loaded with hessian bags filled with dry kapenta, and he volunteered to assist with the unloading. Whilst stacking the bags in the warehouse, a white man arrived and engaged the boat driver in conversation. From the passport photo he had studied, he knew he had found his man.

He spent the rest of the day following his target at a safe distance. Watching the house, he noticed that a woman servant came during the day, and what he took to be a cook came in the afternoon. Another black man came and went going into the house for extended periods. From these observations, he concluded that two men were living in the house, one white and one black. Late in the afternoon, the two men entered the house and did not come out again excepting when one of them emerged to start a generator and switch on the lights. The woman servant had left early in the afternoon, but even later, the cook came out to start a fire under the boiler and disappeared back into the house.

It was now dark, and his surveillance of the house continued even though he was hungry and thirsty. At about nine at night the cook left and a short while afterwards the black man came out and turned off the generator leaving the house in darkness. If he were to enter the house to carry out his mission, it would have to be no earlier than ten-thirty at night, and ideally, the white man needed to be alone. Alternatively, he might catch the white man outside if he came out to turn off the generator.

Whichever the case, he would need to be here each evening from about six until the opportunity presented itself.

Back at the tavern, he drank two beers in quick succession ordered some food, which arrived despite the late hour. Sylvia declined the food offer having eaten earlier but settled for a brandy and coke. There was no need to rise early the next morning because his plan now was nocturnal in nature. He and Sylvia stayed until the tavern closed and then walked back to her modest house.

In the morning, they arose quite late, and Sylvia agreed that he could stay all day but should keep out of the way from lunchtime when she might come back with one or two clients. As compensation, he was to do some shopping for what she needed for the house.

The third evening after Jules arrived in Sumbu, Dominic, Jeffery and the old man dined at the usual time. They reviewed progress on the fishing operation as had become customary, as Michelle was no longer there. The first tests on the drier were proving to be problematic due to the requirement to calibrate the machine speed using the humidity and temperature measurements. It was a trial-and-error procedure, taking time to perfect. Dominic was taking measurements and drawing charts to obtain optimal settings for the machine. Jeffery and Daniel, who now needed to work at night, had gradually coordinated the team of dugout fishermen and the basket exchange system for bringing the fish on board. In a week or so Jeffery felt, Daniel by then sufficiently trained, could work alone with the assistants on board.

After dinner, Jeffery excused himself and left in the Land Rover to attend another of his meetings. George tidied up the kitchen and left just before nine. When Dominic went through to his bedroom to work on his charts, the old man went out and sat on the veranda as usual. Hidden in the dark at the back of the house, Jules saw the black man drive away in his vehicle the headlights initially giving him a better view of the house. He held the pistol in his right hand and fingered the dagger from time to time to confirm it was still in the scabbard attached to his belt. In his left hand, he held the torch, which he would need when the lights went off.

At about nine-thirty, Dominic heard the old man leave the veranda and go to his room. He continued working for another half an hour and then went outside to turn off the generator. Jules felt his pulse quicken as he saw Dominic coming round the side of the house. Moving as fast and silently as a cat, he positioned himself in the shadows close to the generator. From here, he could surprise the white man and kill him silently with the dagger, but he had other business before he did that. As the engine died, he leapt out coming up behind Dominic cocking the pistol and as he pressed it into his back, locking an arm around his neck.

'Don't move or I'll kill you,' he growled in Dominic's ear. Dominic having heard the pistol cock had no doubt he was serious.

'What do you want?' he asked as calmly as he could without struggling so as not to aggravate the situation further. His mind was racing, taking in everything around him.

'Where is the money?' the man whispered in his ear all the while keeping him in a fierce almost choking neck lock, pressing the gun hard against his back.

'What money?'

'The money you brought out of the Congo when you came here,' he hissed. Dominic thought, 'the money is safely deposited in the bank where else would it be.' But he realised that this man perceived the world a little differently. In his world, it would be under the mattress or hidden somewhere in his house. If he could get him into the darkness of the house, where his assailant would be on unfamiliar ground, he might have a chance.

'In the house,' he rasped.

'Lead the way,' the man ordered, but the grip on him relaxed slightly as he shuffled towards the corner of the house and around to the kitchen door. 'Don't make a sound.'

Inside the house, the assailant switched on the torch and Dominic led him into his bedroom. He manoeuvred to the bedside cabinet and opened the drawer removing his wallet. At the rear of the drawer was his pistol. He regretted not having ordered the ammunition he intended to. Omar would have been happy to source it in Ndola. What made it worse was he had been evasive with the DC to retain it. What good was that now?

'Open the wallet,' the man snarled. Dominic realised that the man had the gun in his right hand pressed into his back and the left around his neck holding the torch whereas he himself had both arms free.

'Is that all?' The man asked, 'where's the rest?'

'In the bank.'

'Make out a cheque,' the man demanded. It was then that Dominic realised that not only was this man not too bright but worse, he intended to kill for the money. If he made out the cheque, the only way the man could cash it was if Dominic wasn't around. Furthermore, it was absurd. Did he seriously believe that Dominic would make out a cheque that would pass the teller's scrutiny?

'How much would you like?' Dominic asked with barely disguised facetiousness. The man hesitated.

'Put down all you have.'

'The cheque book is in the other room,' Dominic said. He needed to get his hands on something he could use as a weapon, and there was nothing here in the bedroom. They moved together with Dominic leading into the dining room the man's torch scanning about briefly illuminating the table and dresser.

'The cheque book's in the dresser drawer,' Dominic said. It was just a brief moment when the man was distracted. Dominic had become deliberately relaxed, which encouraged the man gradually to weaken the neck lock. He broke free, reached out for the candelabra in the middle of the dining room table, and swung it around, striking him, just as he fired. As the candelabra struck him on the left side, the torch went flying clattering to the floor. Dominic took advantage of the dark and dived over the table. He slid over its polished surface and off the other side down onto the floor. Another shot went off, gouging into the surface of the table where Dominic had just fallen away. The torch came on again, illuminating the man for an instant. Followed immediately by another shot, but this time a sharp crack, that he recognised as that of a high-velocity rifle. In the darkness, he didn't see the man fall, but the torch searched out and found the man lying there.

'Quickly,' the old man cried, 'get out there and turn on the generator. I'll keep an eye on this bastard.'

When Dominic returned to the dining room, the old man was sitting calmly on a chair, the rifle butt on the floor and the barrel pointing to the ceiling. Sprawled to one side on his back was the man's body, a patch of dark blood spreading gradually on the front of his shirt.'

'He won't bleed much, the old man remarked impassively, 'it was a heart shot.'

'So, he's dead?' Dominic asked. The old man looked at him with an incredulous expression.

'Well I didn't check his pulse, but I assure you his heart has stopped. Do you know him?'

'I've never seen him before in my life,' Dominic said, 'he wanted money.'

'That dagger in his belt is a military issue,' the old man said, 'I better call the police although with all the shooting they'll probably be here any moment.'

CHAPTER 18

In the days that followed the shooting, the police pursued the case energetically, collecting as much evidence as possible, with the encouragement of the DC, who felt it necessary to conduct an inquest. On the night of the incident, initial police reports based on statements taken from nearby residents confirmed they heard two shots followed by a different sharper shot. All indications led to the opinion that Harold Simpson had shot the unknown man in self-defence after he opened fire on his intended robbery victim. There were also two spent cartridges from the pistol and a gouge in the dining room table. The motive appeared to be robbery to obtain money.

The post-mortem revealed that the man had died instantly with a shot to the heart. Apart from an injury to his left arm, he appeared to be in good health. At the morgue, police took fingerprints and forwarded them to Lusaka to the central fingerprinting unit. They retained a second set at the police headquarters in Sumbu. The dead man's fingerprints matched those found in the abandoned Land Rover near the crime-scene. Nothing was found on his person or in the vehicle to reveal his identity. But a set of Congo number plates discovered behind the driver's seat led to the suspicion that the vehicle was from over the border. A phone call to the central vehicle-licensing department in Lusaka revealed that the number-plates on the vehicle were for a different type of vehicle registered in Broken

Hill. It seemed that the authorities in the Congo would be able to confirm its origin despite there being no evidence from the Northern Rhodesian border post that the vehicle had ever entered the country.

The dead man's military issue boots compared to those used across the border in the Congo, so there was reason to believe that he originated there. Studying the dagger and scabbard did not provide any further link to the Congo, but confirmed that when entering the house, he was prepared to use deadly force if necessary.

Eventually, the police visited some of the taverns in the town and found a barman who recognised the dead man's photograph. This led them to Sylvia, who acknowledged that the man had stayed with her but had left one evening and never returned. Fortunately, he had paid her in advance. She handed over a small bag containing his possessions, revealing more substantial evidence that tended to confirm his origins. His toothpaste and shaving cream were consistent with those brands popular in the Congo. They now also had a good idea of the date that he arrived in Sumbu.

The police delivered photographs of the dead man and the vehicle he had been driving, the Congo number plates, a death certificate, and copies of his fingerprints to the Congo immigration authorities at the Pweto border post.

At his forest camp west of the village of Kapulo, Commander Gautier Mwando received news that the white man was no longer operating the boat between the village and Sumbu. Gautier's diamond runner recruited the man known only as Jimmy, who now managed the boat, to carry the rough diamonds from the village to Sumbu. Omar, their link on the Sumbu-Ndola leg, then transported the consignment to a diamond-buying agent in Ndola. It seemed that his tactical operation had succeeded, and he resolved to send a report to this effect to his superiors in the South Kasai Government.

Jules Ntanganda failed to return, and the Commander considered the possible reasons. He had been captured or killed. Or he had been able to recover some of the money and gone AWOL on one or other side of the border. Perhaps he would find out what had happened in time, but his immediate objective was to accelerate the transfer of diamonds and money back and forth along the conduit.

During this period, Dominic kept in touch with the police and was pleased that they were arriving at the correct conclusions. The dead man had made it clear that he knew that Dominic had escaped from the Congo with a fair sum of money and from his accent; there was no doubt in his mind that the man was from there. He felt sure that by the time the inquest took place, there would be sufficient evidence to reach a conclusion without him disclosing what he knew. It concerned him that if one individual knew about the money, there might be others with similar motivation to get their hands on it. He belatedly ordered the 9-millimetre ammunition he needed for the Walther P38 pistol, and Omar brought two boxes through from Ndola. After that, he shoved it into the waist-band of his trousers without his shirt tucked in whenever he went out at night even when he went to switch off the generator. The rest of the time, he kept it in the drawer of the cabinet next to his bed.

To Dominic's surprise, the old man carried on as usual, as if nothing had happened, not showing any interest whatsoever. He was more interested in the international news and the progress on the fishing operation. After many tests and plotting of graphs, Dominic had finally mastered the drying machine. By taking measurements and consulting the graphs, it became easier to make the correct settings. Daniel trained his brother Felix, who was then employed to take over the drying process.

It was with great surprise that Dominic learned that Misheck had suddenly got married quietly and without ceremony at the church, without guests. The priest presided over the short ceremony with two of Misheck's co-workers as witnesses. The bride was a pretty clerk Dominic had noticed working at the bank. What had brought this on so suddenly was a mystery to Dominic.

A month after the shooting, Dominic noticed that the old man was not eating. Jeffery wanted to take him to the hospital, but he refused saying that it would be no good, as the doctors couldn't help him. This time Jeffery decided not to contact his sister with the news, as it would only upset her, and she was not able to help. The old man became gradually weaker, struggling to walk, which he did now with the aid of a walking stick. At dinnertime, he would sit with them at the table taking a sherry and a glass of water but nothing else, afterwards rising painfully and shuffling out onto the veranda. If Jeffery or Dominic tried to assist him, he would gruffly push them aside. During the day he spent all his time out on the veranda listening to the radio retiring around midnight. Even with the painkillers, Dominic was not sure that he slept.

One evening, when Jeffery had gone to a meeting, Dominic joined him out on the veranda, and they sat together watching the lightning snaking down into the lake and listening to the rumbles that followed a while later. The light breeze coming off the lake was cool after the heat of the day.

'My will is in the drawer of the cabinet next to the bed,' he said quietly. Dominic remained silent, and he continued, 'I find it difficult to raise this with Jeffery.'

'Is there anything you want me to do?' Dominic asked.

'I've made you executor, sorry I should have asked, but it's quite simple because all my assets are already in the trust. You are better qualified to handle this than Jeffery and Michelle is away. I wouldn't want to trouble her with it anyway. I've asked to be buried in the mission cemetery next to my wife.'

'I'll see that it's handled according to your wishes,' Dominic promised.

'Also, keep an eye on Jeffery and Michelle for me. Always give them an honest opinion.'

'I don't think you need to worry about them too much, to your credit they have been well brought up and exercise good judgement in their affairs. But yes, I will always give them my honest opinion.'

'Thank you, Dominic. That brings me peace of mind.'

Dominic went to the kitchen and made them both a cup of coffee which they sat drinking. At eleven, Dominic turned-in leaving the old man to his memories.

The next time that Jeffery went out after dinner to a meeting, Dominic retired to his room to work on revising the budget. After about half-an-hour, a shot echoed through the house coming from the direction of the veranda. His first thought was that another intruder was after the money. He leapt up, taking two strides across the room to retrieve the pistol from the drawer of the cabinet next to the bed. When he opened it, he saw that the pistol was gone. Who could have taken it? In case an intruder was intent on entering the house from the veranda, he ran through to the kitchen, and out into the darkness. Next he turned down the side of the house leading to the front. He stood at the corner trying to hear if there were any sounds of movement, the pounding of his heart drumming in his ears. But there was no movement. Vaulting over the wooden railing onto the veranda, he saw the old man slumped in his chair, his upper body lying on the table. Blood was dripping from the table, forming a pool on the floor. The pistol was lying in the blood seeping from the wound in the old man's head where it rested on the surface of the table. Dominic lifted the old man's limp arm feeling for a pulse in his wrist, then pressed his ear to his chest, listening for a heartbeat. All he could hear was the whistling of the cicadas.

CHAPTER 19

Back in the research team in Dorking, Michelle found herself working under Graham Samuels something she didn't particularly enjoy but accepted, understanding that she had left Clive Francis with little other option. As far as she was concerned, he wasn't the best researcher they had but was assertive and ambitious.

What intellect he lacked he compensated for with cunning and stealth. He was perhaps even devious and Machiavellian. For Michelle, it was difficult to find anything positive to say about Graham Samuels, so she chose to say nothing at all and kept to herself, avoiding communicating with him unless it was absolutely necessary.

'I get the distinct impression that you are holding back research results from me,' he accused her at one of their weekly meetings.

'That's not true. I am not prepared to release any results until I'm sure they have been rigorously tested. If I release results prematurely, I could lead the whole team up a blind alley,' she complained.

'But we need to make faster progress.'

'Well, I would certainly appreciate it if you have something to contribute to that cause,' she said sardonically. Clive Francis intervened as usual while the members of the team looked on with some amusement.

'Look, we'd all like it to progress faster, but we need results that are incontestable otherwise we will create chaos and grind to a halt in confusion,' Clive Francis warned, 'so let's make sure we maintain our discipline.'

A few days later, Graham Samuels came into her office in an unusually buoyant and friendly mood.

'Michelle,' he said, 'there's something I need you to do for me.'

'What's that?' she asked cautiously.

'Well, you know we need to employ another junior researcher, I've just spoken to the University of Birmingham, and they have three candidates for us to interview.'

'Are they coming down to visit us?'

'No, rather than have three people come down here, I've suggested that someone from here go up there.'

'You want me to go?' she pre-empted him.

'Michelle, you are our most experienced researcher. I'd really appreciate it if you could do it.'

It seemed a reasonable request. They did need another researcher, and Michelle would certainly like to meet the candidates face-to-face.

'When do I need to go?'

'I've already arranged it for next Wednesday,' he replied, 'you should be able to get there and back by train in one day. When you get there, just ask for their placement officer. They'll be expecting you.'

At lunchtime, Michelle continued working not wishing to interrupt her train of thought. She was eating a sandwich with a cup of coffee beside her, when Richard Carmichael popped his head through the door.

'Hi Michelle,' he called, 'there's something I need to discuss with you. I don't want to disturb you right now, but can we meet for coffee at Dino's after work.?'

'Sure, but what's it about?'

'Rather not say right now,' he said, becoming a little more serious.

'What time?'

'Five thirty?'

'Alright, see you then.'

At about five-fifteen that afternoon, she packed up her work, storing it in her filing cabinet. She put on her coat, picked up her handbag and locked the door of her office behind her. She passed through security out into the darkness. It was a short walk to the high street and Dino's near the station. When she got there, Richard Carmichael sat drinking a cappuccino. As she sat down, he asked her what she would prefer, rose to fetch it and came back with an espresso.

'What's on your mind?' Michelle asked.

'It's about Graham Samuels,' he said, looking at Michelle for some reaction. It was obvious that the two of them didn't get on.

'I'm not sure it's appropriate that we discuss a colleague,' Michelle said, 'he's our boss right now.'

'There's general dissatisfaction in the team regarding his management style.'

'Why is that? He doesn't interfere with the individual researcher's day-to-day activities.'

'Yes, I know, but it's not that. It's about the Royal Pharmaceutical Society's Annual Conference. In the past, when you were in charge, you invited most of us to attend and we registered as delegates. This time none of us has been invited, only Graham is attending to present a paper.'

'I'm sorry to hear that, but I guess that's his prerogative, although I have to admit it's a little selfish. Have you seen his paper?'

'No, because none of us is registered we haven't received copies of the papers that delegates are presenting.'

'Well that's a bit short-sighted of him, there might be some papers that would interest the team.'

'Also, if anything, he should have asked you to present a paper as well.'

'I haven't been here, so that's understandable.'

'But since you've been back, at least he could have had you registered as a delegate to hear the papers presented including his own.'

'That's true.' Michelle agreed, starting to consider it a bit strange.

'There's something else.'

'And what's that?' she prompted.

'You know that he has asked you to interview those candidates in Birmingham. Well, that's the day he presents his paper.'

Michelle didn't immediately respond but pondered this coincidence.

'What are you suggesting?' she asked cautiously.

'Something's going on. Why would he arrange for you to go to Birmingham on that day?'

'Aren't we a bit paranoid,' she said with a laugh. But Richard Carmichael failed to relax his serious expression.

'No, I believe that something untoward is happening.'

'So, what can we do about it?'

'I'd like to make a suggestion,' Richard Carmichael said. 'Let me go to Birmingham to do the interviews, and you go to the conference centre on the day and make a late registration. It just makes sense that someone from the team attends and comes back with copies of the papers.'

'Well, if you're happy to go to Birmingham for the day I can certainly do that.'

'Thanks, Michelle, that makes me feel a lot happier.'

On her way home in the train, Michelle passed their discussion through her mind. It was almost as if Richard Carmichael knew more than he let on. He was adamant that

Samuels was up to no good. Anyway, there was nothing to lose in her attending, although Graham Samuels would not appreciate her being there without his having sanctioned it. She'd face the consequences of that when the time arose.

When the morning of the day of the conference arrived, she got up at her usual time, took a shower, dressed smartly in a female business suit and ate breakfast. Then she waited past her usual departure time watching the news on the television. Instead of heading for Dorking, she took the tube through to the conference centre, arriving as planned just after proceedings had commenced. She wanted to avoid bumping into Graham Samuels in the reception area. Once registered, she slipped in and found a seat at the back of the auditorium.

The President of the Society was in the middle of his welcoming address and up on the stage was the conference chairman and a panel of distinguished medical research scientists. Studying the programme, she discovered that Graham Samuels would be presenting his paper during the second session after the morning tea break. It followed the usual format with each presenter running through his paper using the overhead projector to display on the screen tables, graphs, and formulae showing the results of his research. At the end of each presentation, there was polite applause and the delegates asked questions or challenged the results.

While this was in progress, Michelle paged through her copy of the papers until she found Graham Samuels's paper. The moment she started reading it she discovered she was reading her own written research contribution that consolidated and augmented the results of project 'Heartburn.' She was shocked that Graham Samuels would stoop so low as to plagiarise her work. But what surprised her even more, was how he had come by her written final report. She had deliberately secured it, making sure Clive Francis's assistant locked it away in the safe in his office pending the patent application. No one would have distributed it amongst the team.

Studying the paper a little closer, she soon discovered that it contained small errors that she had edited out before taking it through to Clive Francis's personal secretary for typing and safekeeping. He had obviously managed to get his hands on her personal file with her research results before she had edited it. If she allowed him to make the presentation without challenging it, he would have used her to enhance his own reputation amongst the research community. He hadn't even had the decency to mention her name as a co-author.

Did she have the confidence to make a challenge in front of all these learned people, especially the members of the panel? How was she to prove that it was her work without any documentary evidence to support her claim? She remembered the incident at the club in Sumbu when Dominic had risked his reputation on her behalf to prevent an injustice. If he were here now at her side, there is no doubt he would insist that she take courage and confront Graham Samuels in front of this whole audience.

Just before the tea break, she slipped out into the reception area, grabbed a cup of coffee and took it outside the conference centre and away from the main entrance. She waited until the delegates had returned to the auditorium after the tea break and re-entered to take her seat. Graham Samuels was the second presenter to take the podium. He introduced himself and went through the paper displaying salient points on the screen. It was a confident and convincing performance, and when he had finished, the chairman thanked him and asked the audience if there were any questions. Graham Samuels waited at the podium not expecting that there would be anything other than encouraging comments.

'Yes, I have a question,' Michelle called out from the back of the auditorium.

'Can we please have your name?' the chairman asked.

'My name is Michelle Simpson.'

The confident expression on Graham Samuels's face changed to one of discomfort and concern as he looked back and forth between the chairman and Michelle.

'Please, go ahead Miss Simpson,' the chairman encouraged making a note in a pad he had in front of him, 'it is Miss is it not?'

'That is correct,' Michelle replied and then continued, 'I would like to ask Mister Samuels to refer to page twenty-three of his paper if he could display that on the screen.'

She was supposed to be in Birmingham, how the hell had she got here. Graham Samuels fumbled through his paper, finding the page she referred to displaying it on the screen. What should he do? Introduce her to the delegates as a co-worker and have to explain, for he knew she recognised her own work. Or should he brazenly try to fight it out? There was still a chance if he contested any of her assertions.

'I'd like you to refer to the formula on line six. It is incorrect,' Michelle said bluntly.

Samuels thought to himself, 'but it's her work and she is claiming it's incorrect, how can I use this against her.'

'Well, I'm sure you know an experienced researcher checked it. You will find it reliable.'

'That may be so, but then the person who checked it is also wrong.'

The chairman whispered to the panel member to his right in a short discussion. If she had studied the paper in that detail before coming to the conference, she might have something to contribute.

'Miss Simpson, I wonder if you could come up to the lectern and show us the correct formula,' he said before Samuels could respond.

Michelle walked to the front of the auditorium and took her place at the podium, forcing Samuels to step aside, looking bemused. He would need to examine the formula she was about to display and after a moment of reflection in front of the crowd acknowledge she was correct. It was, after all, a simple mistake.

Michelle took a transparency, and with a felt tipped pen wrote down three formulae and placed it on the overhead projector. There was a soft mumbling of voices from within the audience as they looked at the three formulae displayed on the screen.

'Here are three formulae that could replace the one I claim is incorrect,' Michelle suggested, 'perhaps Mister Samuels would like to identify the correct one.'

Samuels looked at the three formulae his mind in disarray. If he understood the work in detail, he should be able to choose the right one. But of course, he didn't so she had trapped him. He could still try to crush her with assertive arrogance.

'None of these formulae is correct, they are a product of your deluded mind,' Samuels roared his face contorting in undisguised anger.

Michelle hesitated, and her hand shook a little at this onslaught, but she remained calm and looked at him with contempt. There was now mumbling in the audience who were beginning to enjoy this extraordinary exchange between the two people up at the podium.

'Miss Simpson, please explain by identifying the formula you believe is correct and why.'

'It's this one,' she claimed underlining it with the felt-tipped pen.

'Well, we have no way of knowing if you or Mister Samuels is correct without having the paper adjudicated independently.'

'That won't be necessary,' Michelle replied, 'this is the formula that will appear in the patent that is about to be released.'

'How do you know that?' the chairman asked.

'Because the work Mister Samuels has presented is, in fact, mine. That is why he can't answer the question.'

Further rumbling rippled through the audience, and the chairman summoned the members of the panel to congregate around him in discussion. Michelle stood there her heart beating at an accelerated rated. Samuels stood looking blankly at the wall away from the audience. This was not turning out well for him. There was nothing more for him to say. The panel members resumed their seats.

'Mister Samuels,' the chairman said peering disdainfully over his spectacles, 'would you agree that this paper should be attributed as the original work of Miss Simpson and that you be acknowledged as the presenter.'

'But …' Samuels stammered, but thought better of it and said, 'yes.'

'Then we note that the paper will be amended for publication in the name of Miss Simpson with you acknowledged as presenter.'

During the lunch break, Michelle selected a meal from the buffet and found a table occupied by researchers she had never met. She was now recognisable by all in the conference centre after her confrontation with Graham Samuels, who failed to take a seat at lunch.

'It's happened before,' the middle-aged woman to the left of her remarked.

'But why do people do it?' Michelle asked.

'Well you know it's that "publish or perish" syndrome. Some people will go to any lengths,' a younger man on the other side of the table added.

'It takes some gall to risk such humiliation,' Michelle remarked.

'I suppose you need to be quite desperate,' the older woman concluded.

The next morning, Clive Francis was busy reviewing his operations budget to accommodate the new recruit that Richard Carmichael was recommending they employ when he had a phone call from Hans Bauer of the Royal Society.

'Hello Clive, it's been a while.'

'Yes, but a pleasant surprise, how are things going.'

'Very well, thanks, I think it's time we had a game of golf again.'

'Good idea.'

'But before we arrange that, I believe that you employ a young lady by the name of Michelle Simpson.'

'Yes, I do, is anything wrong.'

'No, quite the contrary, she's a remarkable young lady.'

'Oh, why's that?'

'Well, she attended the Society's annual conference yesterday and put up a remarkable performance. She's having a paper published in her name.'

'But I wasn't aware that she was presenting one. I'd agreed that Graham Samuels present his work.'

'That's the problem, Samuels made a presentation, and it turned out that it was original work done by Michelle Simpson. She convinced the panel of the veracity of her claim. The work is to be attributed to her with Samuels as the presenter.'

'Well, I'm pleased that Michelle is to get recognition. She's an excellent researcher.'

'What about Samuels, you'll need to keep a close eye on him.'

'After what you've told me I'll certainly do that.'

When Hans Bauer rang off with their golf game arranged, Clive Francis returned to his budget with another adjustment in mind. Michelle deserved a bonus for her work and probably a medal for working with Graham Samuels. It was time she resumed her rightful place as leader of the research team. Samuels wouldn't like it, but he would find it difficult to contest after his flawed judgement and poor behaviour.

CHAPTER 20

Despite the rainy season, the fishing business was going as well as expected. Machine drying some of the fish allowed them to keep up with the demand, which had driven up the prices enough to cover any of their extra costs. From time to time, Jimmy concealed the rough diamonds in the small cabinet in the bow of the boat. He carried them ashore when he wouldn't be noticed, transferring them to Omar when he arrived. Transporting the money back to the village and handing it to Moses with the documents recording the transaction was the most fulfilling part of his clandestine side-line. Moses would pay him a small commission depending on the money received. Jeffery noticed that Jimmy was putting on weight, but of course, he was unaware that the man's diet had become far more extravagant with his new wealth.

The shock of the old man's suicide had passed. They buried him next to his wife as requested, the priest turning a blind eye to the circumstances of his death. Although he had stopped attending church after his wife's death, he had continued to contribute. The death notice in the Sunday newspaper resulted in some of his former work colleagues and their wives travelling to Sumbu to attend the funeral. Some of them, particularly those who were retired, chose to stay over for a few days holiday at the visitors' lodge a short way west of Sumbu. George prepared a buffet lunch laid out on the dining room table from which the visitors could place their choice on plates to eat with their fingers. For those who chose to drink, there was whisky and soda or Gin and tonic as well as cold beers. Jeffery mixed with the visitors listening to the tales they related, which revealed things he'd never known about his father. He had always respected his father but now even more so.

When Michelle got the news, she went home early, cried bitterly for half an hour, and then went out for a walk in the rain. She found a pub and spent an hour consuming two glasses of wine. Being alone with nobody close to share her grief was the worst of it. Soon, memories of her father flooded back, and she found herself smiling again at some of their most exciting shared moments. The next day she went back to the office and immersed herself in her work.

When the news of Simpson's death reached Max Freeman, he immediately considered how these changed circumstances might positively affect his plan. Without Simpson around it might be easier to influence the remainder of the family to part with the licence. As far as he could remember, there was a son in Sumbu whom he'd never met and a daughter somewhere in England. He had no desire to travel all the way to Northern Rhodesia again to see the son, so a reasonable course of action seemed to be to try to contact the daughter. He'd heard that she worked for a pharmaceutical company, so he gave his personal secretary the task of tracking her down. Once she had established where Michelle worked, Max Freeman waited a discreet three weeks to allow matters to settle and then asked his secretary to get her on the phone.

'Good morning Miss Simpson,' he said, 'Max Freeman here of Postlewhite International Mining. I just want to say how sorry I was to hear about the death of your father.'

'Thank you, that's very considerate of you, but I'm not sure we've met, and my father never mentioned you.'

'Understandable. We were busy working on a business proposition together and I visited Sumbu to discuss it with him, but we never concluded an agreement.'

'I'm not that familiar with my father's business activities, as you may know, I spend most of my time here in London,' Michelle explained.

'Yes, I thought that might be the case. Let me clarify.'

Max told her about the mining licence and that they wanted to make an offer for it. 'I'm sure you will find it a generous offer, and we would like you to visit us for a meeting.'

'I'll need to discuss that with my brother, but I'm sure he will be interested.'

'Good, if you can do that, we can make the arrangements when you are ready, but please don't leave it too long, we need to move quickly.'

Michelle said goodbye and put down the receiver. Having had her train of thought interrupted by the call, she went back to the beginning of what she had been studying and resumed work putting the call out of her mind.

When she arrived back at her flat in Earls Court that evening, she brought with her fresh cod she had bought from the fishmonger in Earls Court road. For supper, she grilled the fish, boiled some small new potatoes, steamed some asparagus and served it with a hollandaise sauce. Before serving it, she had a small glass of sherry, the habit introduced to her by her father, and retained in his memory.

It was late August, and looking at the time, she calculated that it would be eight-thirty in the evening in Sumbu. If she phoned now, she might catch Jeffery at home.

'What's wrong?' Jeffery exclaimed with some alarm when he recognised her voice. She made a mental note that they should speak to each other more frequently.

'Everything's fine,' she laughed to put him at ease.

'It's so good to hear from you.'

'I should phone you more often, but you know how it is, time just flies. But something has cropped up that may interest you. I've had a call from a man by the name of Max Freeman. He wants me to come to their offices to discuss the sale of the mining licence, but I can't do this alone. I was wondering if you could come through to London to help.'

'I see,' Jeffery said hesitantly. 'I'm not sure I can get away,' he continued, thinking of his political commitments, 'and in any case, I'm not sure I'm the right person.'

'Well, I can't do it alone,' she cautioned.

'It would be better if Dominic came, he'll know what to do.'

Michelle wasn't sure if she was excited or apprehensive. All kinds of mixed feelings raced through her mind.

'Alright, let's do that.' she said, 'He needs to come as soon as possible. They're anxious to conclude some kind of deal urgently.'

'How long do you think he'll be away?'

'Difficult to say, but let's say two weeks and review it after that. Will you be able to manage?'

'The way Dominic has organised everything here, we're both under far less pressure. We have employees running the operations so one of us can manage. Anyway, it's the rainy season, so we're just ticking over.'

'If Dominic agrees, just let me have his flight details as soon as you know, and I'll pick him up at the airport. I'll also arrange hotel accommodation.'

When she hung up, she wondered how she would manage meeting Dominic again. Suddenly she felt excited. It would be good to have a man in her life again. What kind of relationship did she expect? Would he still feel the way he did about her, but what was it he actually felt? Unlike Misheck, he had never discussed his feelings. The intimacy she had encouraged had aroused her to a never before experienced level of passion. She wouldn't do that again. If it happened, it would need to be at his urging.

Jeffery returned to the dining room table, where Dominic was sitting having coffee. The storm outside was driving the rain right across the veranda, and somewhere a window shutter was banging in the wind.

'That was Michelle,' he said.

'How is she?' Dominic asked, swivelling his chair around to face the head of the table where Jeffery now sat since his father died.

'Sounded happy enough, but there is something that needs to be done, and I hope that you will do it for us,' Jeffery prompted.

'I will if I can, what is it?'

Jeffery explained what Michelle had told him. Dominic tried not to show the excitement that gripped him. This was precisely what the old man had prepared him for and he was to meet Michelle again. His hesitation was a result of this unexpected development rather than reluctance.

'But of course, I'll go. We can't turn down such an opportunity even if it turns out to be a red herring. Your father certainly didn't trust that man.'

'I'm sure you can manage him,' Jeffery said optimistically.

'I'll give it my best shot. It's a great challenge.'

The next day Dominic started to make the arrangements. Checking the flights, he chose a connecting flight from Ndola to Lusaka and then on to London. Once he'd made the booking, he phoned Omar and arranged for him to pick up the fish three days before his flight so he could travel back to Ndola in the truck. That would give him a day in Lusaka to visit the Department of Mining and Geology to pay the fees for the renewal of the licence.

Under the old man's bed, he found a suitcase. Looking at the old man's formal clothes in his wardrobe, he decided that if he was to do business in London, they were unsuitable. However, while for daily wear, T-shirts, jeans, tennis shoes and commando boots might be acceptable in Sumbu they wouldn't be much good for a London winter. His first task when he got to London would be to go shopping for a new clothes. But he did decide to take one of the old man's sports jackets to fend off the cold until he could find something better.

At Heathrow airport the Vickers Viscount came into land. He looked down through gaps in the clouds on the unfamiliar scene of terraced houses and green spaces. He passed through immigration and customs without trouble and found Michelle waiting in arrivals. She gave him a big smile and a hug and seemed genuinely happy to see him. As they left the airport building to join the waiting taxi, a cold breeze reminded him that he was far from home. In the taxi with his luggage stowed, after she had given the destination hotel to the driver, they both started talking together; laughing at their eagerness. He removed a small gift-wrapped packet from his jacket pocket, presenting it to Michelle, who expressed genuine surprise. When she opened it, there was a bottle of Helena Rubenstein apple blossom perfume. She leaned over and kissed him on the cheek, smiling with delight.

'You remembered, it's my favourite,' she exclaimed.

'How could I ever forget,' he replied, squeezing her hand.

For the remainder of the journey, which took about forty minutes, they talked about Sumbu and the time she spent there. Inevitably, it got round to the attempt on his life and her father's action that prevented it succeeding.

'Your family seem to spend their time saving me,' Dominic commented gravely. 'I hope I can repay the debt.'

'You owe us nothing,' she replied. 'You've already changed Jeffery's life for the better.'

'What about yours?' he prompted.

'You gave me confidence, and that's a wonderful gift,' she replied. 'I ask no more.'

The small hotel turned out to be a short walk from where she lived, and they agreed to meet at a restaurant for dinner that evening giving him time to clean up and try to catch up on his sleep.

'When is the meeting?' Dominic asked.

'It's in three day's time, nine-thirty in the morning on Friday. I've taken a week off in case we need to make preparations or discuss their proposal. What's the first step?'

'I need to go shopping to get some clothes.'

'You came all this way to go shopping in London?' she teased.

'Well, look at me,' he exclaimed.

'Now you mention it, you look disgusting. I'll take you shopping tomorrow.'

They got out of the taxi, and she paid off the driver, then she went in the direction of her flat, and he entered the hotel. That evening over dinner, he repeated the discussion he had had with her father and what the old man had asked him to do.

The next day, Michelle took Dominic to Burton's to choose a suit. He had no idea where they were because Michelle and the busy crowd of commuters rushed up-and-down stairs and escalators pushing on-and-off the red tube trains. Underground he lost all sense of direction. The names of the stations didn't mean a thing. When they arrived at the shop, he had expected to be able to choose a suit off the peg, but Michelle insisted on a bespoke one. He chose charcoal coloured wool as the fabric and Michelle insisted on single-breasted narrow lapels and slim look trousers. While the tailor took his measurements, she argued about when they could deliver the suit. In the end, after being told that the best delivery they could manage was five days, Michelle took a stand. She would take a wool overcoat, six shirts, six pairs of socks, three ties, a scarf, a cravat, two sets of slacks, two sports jackets, two belts and a pair of brogues, if they could make delivery in two days-time, in the afternoon. When they left, he paid using some of his traveller's cheques. They departed with numerous carrier bags, Dominic in shock and Michelle walking happily along. One thing he learned that morning was that when it came to shopping, women had no equal.

During the following days, Dominic found time to study the map of London. He memorised as best he could the major street layout and location of recognisable landmarks, not forgetting the major tube and British rail connections. He and Michelle opened a bank account for the Simpson Family Trust with both of them as joint signatories. Dominic was gradually adjusting to the hustle and bustle of London and to give him a feel for the city, Michelle took him to Oxford Street. Sturdy facades of the mainly Victorian-era buildings rose majestically above them. The shop windows were filled with luxury goods. The street was alive with fashionably attired office workers. Casually dressed tourists of various nationalities sauntered along less urgently, oblivious of the chill autumn air. Black taxis darted in and out of the traffic, occasionally stopping to drop off or pick up passengers. Nothing could have been further from the vast quiet spaciousness of Sumbu.

One item that Dominic still needed was a briefcase to complete his new business identity and to carry the documents relating to the potential mining business. So, as it turned out, their visit to Oxford Street had a practicable purpose. They found a crowded coffee shop and had coffee with Roy Orbison singing "Only the Lonely" in the background and then made their way back to Earls Court.

The morning of the meeting with Max Freeman, they met outside Dominic's hotel and caught a cab to Postlewhite International Mining's offices in Lombard Street.

'You look great in that suit. It's a transformation. I really could fall for you,' she commented cheerfully.

'Well, I might look the part, but let's see if I can play the part,' he replied a little more seriously.

The lift took them to the third floor, where they found Max Freeman's secretary waiting for them. She ushered them to a mahogany panelled boardroom and asked them whether they would prefer tea or coffee, leaving with the promise that Mister Freeman would not be long.

'Ah, Miss Simpson, so good of you to come,' he said with outstretched hand, 'and this is…'

'Dominic Harrison.' Dominic reminded him.

'Ah yes, I remember we met in Sumbu. I wouldn't have recognised you,' he said. That was understandable, but Max Freeman was exactly as Dominic remembered him, excepting he had put on even more weight. The secretary came back into the room, set down the coffee tray on a side table, and served them where they sat at the boardroom table.

'First,' Max said, looking at Dominic, 'thanks for coming to London. It's much easier here because I have a support team to assist in concluding the agreement.'

'What do you propose?' Dominic asked.

'Well, as you know we are interested in acquiring the Simpson mining licence providing we can arrive at suitable terms and price. This is our offer, which I'm sure you will find to be quite generous,' he said, passing a copy each to Dominic and Michelle. Dominic took a few minutes to read the document while Max addressed Michelle.

'Miss Simpson, I'm sure you're not interested in becoming involved in mining. You would be much better off with the money.'

Michelle smiled sweetly, and countered caustically, 'It will take quite a lot of money to render me disinterested.' Dominic heard her response while still reading the document and smiled to himself at her incisiveness.

'But this is no better than the offer you made to Mister Simpson when you visited Sumbu,' Dominic remarked feigning surprise.

'Well, nothing's changed on the ground since then.' Freeman said petulantly.

'So, you've brought me all this way to make the same offer?' Dominic exclaimed. Max Freeman's mind started to race. Things weren't going as he expected.

'Circumstances have changed,' he said. 'I believe that the licence is worth even less than we have offered. If you don't take our offer, I believe you are in danger of getting nothing for it.'

'I disagree,' Dominic countered, 'in fact I believe it's worth a great deal more.'

'Nonsense,' Max asserted.

Dominic didn't immediately respond to Max's interpretation of the situation. He'd come all this way, and if he was going to be faithful to the old man's belief, it was his duty to find a way to improve on the offer. They now had a recently dated offer, so they needed to find another party who might see the logic behind the old man's reasoning. But there was no reason to reject the offer out of hand. Rather delay, to give them time. Let Max Freeman stew for the moment.

'All right,' Dominic conceded, 'you may be right. I need to discuss it with one of the other trustees before we make a decision. We'll get back to you after we've had time to consider.'

They shook hands politely and left. Going down in the lift, Michelle turned to him and said, 'Why on earth did you say we would consider it?'

'Don't worry,' I do not intend to accept his offer. I'll start immediately looking for an alternative strategy in the morning. If he has competition for it, he'll change his tune. I believe your father. It's worth more than he's offering.'

That weekend, Dominic spent time at the desk in his hotel room, making notes and trying to work out the best plan of action. Since he arrived, he had bought a copy of the newspaper each day, accumulating them on a shelf in the built-in cupboard, with pencilled circles around articles of interest. Browsing through the business section, he was gradually getting a feel for the issues of general concern in the British economy, as expressed by journalists, and the opinion of respected economists.

Company news and the quarterly results of leading companies quoted on the London Stock Exchange attracted his attention, particularly those in the mining sector. Unlike other commodities, which tended to vary according to the principle of supply and demand, gold had a fixed price. This meant that the cost of mining, played a critical role in the value of a company; a matter of concern for potential shareholders seeking dividends.

Eventually, he concluded that they needed to form a company; cede the licence rights to it by agreement and then find investors to take up shares to fund further exploration. This was understandable in principle, but how would they establish the value of the licence? What they needed was to find a potential investor interested in mining, who would also have a team capable of analysing the geology, mining economics and financial implications necessary to form an opinion on the value of the deposit. That could only produce an estimate because no drilling had taken place in the concession area. But they did have the lab reports based on the samples taken from the outcrop of which Max Freeman was unaware. Someone could surely establish something from the report?

On Sunday evening, Michelle joined him for dinner at the restaurant in the hotel, and he explained what he believed they should do. She listened attentively determined to understand as much as she could.

'We can't start looking for an investor until we have formed a company. In the morning, I'll arrange a meeting with a firm of solicitors I picked up in the Yellow pages. They're not far from here in South Kensington. They will set up the company and handle any other legal matters that are required. Setting up the company will take a little while, and I need to make a start finding a potential investor before we form it to avoid wasting time. If we are to talk to a potential investor, we need to provide all the information we have about the concession. You know, its location, the geological report and so forth…'

'But isn't that a bit dangerous? They can just run off with what we have,' Michelle interjected.

'You're right of course, and that's why we need the solicitor to draw up a non-disclosure agreement in a form where we can merely enter the name and details of the potential investor and get it signed before we release any information.'

'That seems reasonable. Is there anything I can do to help?'

'Yes, there is. Many things that we will have to do will require Jeffery's signature. We can't wait for documents to travel between here and Sumbu. The best would be if you could obtain from him power-of-attorney to sign all documents on his behalf. The solicitor can draw up that document for you to send to Jeffery. From there on if you can work with the solicitor, I will start to track down an investor.'

'You have thought it through,' she commented, 'it sounds ambitious.'

'I just keep following what I think your father would have done. I'm sure he would have taken an aggressive approach as well. I don't want to let him down, or you and Jeffery either.'

'He made an impression on you, my father,' she said with a grin.

'You should have seen him standing there with that rifle,' Dominic responded with a laugh, 'an unforgettable sight.'

CHAPTER 21

By the time the Bentley arrived outside Dominic's hotel the following Friday, he had been waiting in reception with his suitcase for about ten minutes. A smartly uniformed chauffeur came through the hotel entrance looked around, saw Dominic standing there with a suitcase, approached him, and said, 'You're Mister Harrison?' When Dominic acknowledged that he was, the chauffeur grasped his suitcase with the words, 'Please follow me, Sir Peter is waiting.'

Finding a potential investor had turned out to be a frustrating exercise. He'd perused the current and back copies of The Times business section for leads, contacted several companies, only to find he couldn't get past the receptionist and secretaries to anyone who would even listen to his business proposition. That was until he contacted Faulkner Investments. An eighth of a column in The Times reported that they were sitting on a large cash reserve and in negotiations with a few mining companies that were seeking venture capital for start-ups, or expansion of existing operations. Fatigued, Dominic was about to pass it over but was running out of candidates. 'One more and I'll call it a day,' he thought.

When he phoned, the operator put him through to a secretary at Faulkner Investments. He explained the reason for his call and to his surprise; she put him through to Sir Peter Faulkner, the Chairman. The voice that answered had the accent that

Dominic associated with aristocratic privilege that he had heard on the radio and in films. It had that calm warmth that belied his status and prominent position of power. After listening to what Dominic had to say, he suggested that he come through to their offices for a meeting.

The next day, Dominic took the District Line tube from Earls Court to Monument station and walked the short distance to the offices of Faulkner Investments in Mincing Lane. Before leaving, he bought an umbrella from a shop in Earls Court Road as it looked like rain. A middle-aged woman, bristling with efficiency, led him from the reception to Sir Peter's office.

Sir Peter was much as Dominic had imagined, tall with a shock of grey hair, piercing blue eyes and a leathery skin that was out of keeping with someone who spent much time in an office. He stood up, removed the reading glasses, and placed them on the antique desk, then shook Dominic's hand.

'Ah, Mister Harrison, please sit down,' he said. Dominic sat down, and Sir Peter leaned back in his chair, studying him closely.

'Sir, thank you for seeing me at such short notice,' Dominic said.

'It's no trouble, young man. I want you to tell me all about yourself.'

Dominic was somewhat taken aback, but gave his background; accountant, studied at Rhodes University in South Africa, practised in Salisbury, had an interest in a fishing business in Sumbu in Northern Rhodesia and had been tasked with promoting a mining opportunity there. He skipped the part about being in the Congo. Sir Peter asked him a few more questions of a personal nature, smiled warmly, and said, 'Give me some time to consider, my secretary will give you a call.'

It had been a rather short and disappointing meeting, no business discussion, and it ended with the 'don't call us, we'll call you' type of message. But Dominic was wrong about that. Two days later, when he returned to the hotel from a meeting with Michelle and the solicitor, a message to call Sir Peter's office was waiting for him in reception. From his room he immediately phoned, and the operator put him through to Sir Peter's secretary who informed him that he was to spend the weekend at Sir Peter's country estate in Surrey for business discussions.

The Chauffeur opened the back door of the Bentley, and Dominic found himself seated next to Sir Peter in the rear of the car.

'Ah Dominic,' he said, 'pleased you could make it.'

'Well,' Dominic responded, 'thank you for the invitation.'

After stowing Dominic's luggage in the boot of the car, the chauffeur pulled out into the Friday afternoon traffic.

'Please excuse me, I have some documents I need to study, you might want to read this in the meantime,' Sir Peter said, handing him the newspaper.

By the time Dominic reached the sports section, they were leaving the built-up area and heading into the country. Fields of wheat and hedge rowed meadows gradually became more frequent as did the thickets of forest trees. From time to time, the car would slow to pass through a small village and between them, one or two farms with barns and farm equipment appeared a short way off the main road. Eventually, Sir Peter slipped the documents he had been reading into his briefcase.

'I've just been reading the latest annual Colonial Office report on Northern Rhodesia,' he said, 'trying to weigh up the business risk, taking into consideration the political uncertainty.'

'Have you arrived at a conclusion?' Dominic asked.

'Not yet, but perhaps I'll be persuaded later when we discuss your proposal.'

'I'm looking forward to that, I'm sure you'll find it interesting,' Dominic said.

'I understand that you've been fighting recently with the mercenaries in the Congo,' Sir Peter remarked. Dominic cursed himself under his breath. Why had he not been open about that from the outset?

'Yes, but how do you know that?'

'I had the Colonial Office run a check on you with the District Commissioner's office in Sumbu. They sent me a telex report. I always check up on the people I do business with, you can't be too careful,' Sir Peter said soberly.

'I'm not a professional mercenary, it was circumstantial, and I'm trying to put it behind me.'

'I believe you, so let's say no more about it.' The warm smile had returned, and Dominic felt embarrassed but relieved. To change the subject, he commented, 'I'm looking forward to seeing your country house.'

'I'm sure you'll like it, it's a grand old place, been in the family since the middle of the last century. My great, great grandfather John Faulkner was a tea trader in the days of the clipper ships. When he bought Westlake Hall in 1868, it was a time when tea enjoyed considerable growth in demand as the taste for it became popular in England, and he accumulated great wealth. At the same time, the stately homes of England were in decline, the cost of the staff needed to run them and of increasing taxes was becoming too high for the owners to bear. Aristocrats were selling some of them off for only the value of the construction materials, so John Faulkner got a bargain. Of course, he and his heirs have had to maintain the estate since then, no mean task.

'My grandfather founded the Faulkner Bank with the assistance of a New York bank during World War I while my father was fighting in France and Belgium. The war had destroyed the tea business with blockades at sea and rationing at home. My father took over the running of the bank during the Great Depression by which time my grandfather had retired. During World War II, the war office gave me a commission, and I fought in the desert war in North Africa. When the Americans entered the war, they used Westlake Hall as an intelligence command centre. After the war, the Americans bought out our interest in Faulkner Bank and renamed the company. My father and I formed and carried on as Faulkner Investments. I took over the running of the business in 1949 when my father retired, and all going well, my eldest son George will take over from me one day. He's presently working for a New York bank to maintain the connections we've established over the years.

'When we get there, you will notice that we only occupy part of the building. A joint American and British group is using the rest as a research and development centre. Not quite sure what they're up to, something to do with computers I believe.'

Ten minutes later, they turned through the gate which was flanked by a disused gatehouse and up the long driveway towards Westlake Hall. A high portico with columns either side formed the entrance to the two-storied building. They stepped out of the car and climbed the steps leading to the front door. The chauffeur reached it before them, ringing the bell and instructing two servants that appeared to fetch their luggage. Once in the hall, in front of them rose a heavily wooden staircase leading up to the second-floor landing. The doors to the left were sealed off, but to the right, there was a gallery leading to a ground-floor living area. Dominic was relieved of his overcoat by an attentive middle-aged woman servant who hung it in a cloakroom off the entrance. He was ushered up the staircase with his suitcase to his quarters by a young servant in a black and white uniform matching that of the other staff.

'We've been expecting you, Sir. I hope you will be comfortable here,' he said setting down Dominic's luggage. 'My name's Horace. If you need anything during your stay please ring the bell, and I'll attend to it. When you're ready, go down and turn left at the bottom of the stairs. The parlour is a short way along the gallery.'

Dominic thanked him and he left. The room was large with heavy drapes hanging from the high window, which faced out onto the grounds at the front of the house where he could see a path leading through the lawns to a large ornate fountain. Looking to the right, there was a lake partly surrounded by trees. He noticed from the shape of the room that the owners had added a modern bathroom at some time in its history. A heavy highly polished mahogany double bed with an ornately carved headrest with large pillows occupied an insignificant part of the space in the room. He placed his briefcase next to the desk situated near the window. With his suitcase on the bed, he unpacked his clothes, hanging the coats and jackets in the wardrobe, and other items he placed on the shelves and in the bathroom.

When he arrived in the drawing-room, he found a well-groomed slightly greying woman seated at a bureau writing letters with a black fountain pen. She rose, smoothing her grey woollen skirt with her hands as she did. Peering at him imperiously over her reading glasses, 'I'm Lady Faulkner,' she said, extending her hand.

'Dominic Harrison,' he replied.

'Welcome to Westlake Hall. I trust Horace has made you comfortable.'

'Yes, thank you. I hope that I'm not intruding.'

'Not at all, my husband regularly brings his business associates here.'

Sir Peter entered the room greeted his wife warmly with a kiss on the cheek and went to a tray on a side table on which there were glasses and a couple of cut-glass decanters.

'A drink?' he asked his wife.

'No thanks darling, I'll leave you two to your business. Don't forget that you are expected to attend the dinner at the church hall this evening. Have you prepared your speech?'

'Oh, yes, of course, I had forgotten, but I'll be ready.'

Lady Faulkner left, and the two men each took a whisky and sat either side of the fireplace where wood burned, occasionally crackling and spitting causing ash to fall through the grate.

'I'll have to excuse myself from dinner this evening, but I'm sure you won't mind dining with my son and daughter. Now, let's get down to business for a few minutes. We have the rest of the weekend, but we may as well make a start.'

'If you don't mind, Sir, can I ask you to sign this non-disclosure agreement between our new company and Faulkner Investments before we start?' Dominic asked cautiously.

'But of course, my boy,' Sir Peter said with a laugh, 'good thinking, as I said, one can never be too careful.'

Dominic went upstairs, fetched his briefcase and after Sir Peter had signed the agreement, he brought out the geological report and the map, spreading the latter out on the carpet between them.

'This is the Postlewhite Mining concession here in the south, and this is the Simpson Mining concession in the north, Dominic explained. 'This is the location of the outcrop to which the geological report refers. The late Mr Simpson believed that the northern concession would be more economical to mine and consequently of greater value. Here is the most recent offer from Postlewhite Mining that I have rejected.'

'I'm no expert when it comes to mining geology, but I have members of my team that are, and they can give us an opinion next week. If it turns out to be of interest to us, we could then propose a financial plan to raise enough capital for the next step.'

'Alright, I'll leave the map and the geological report with you to hand to your experts and we can review it as soon as you have their opinion.'

'Agreed, now if you'll excuse me, I must go and get ready to leave. Dinner is at eight, so please introduce yourself to my daughter Cynthia and youngest son James. They're both out at the moment but will be back soon.'

Dominic repacked his briefcase and went up to his room, took a hot shower, dried himself and came out of the bathroom, appreciating the central heating. He dressed in a shirt with cravat, slacks and a sports jacket, browsed through the books in the bookshelf on the right side of the bed, chose a book, and commenced reading while waiting for dinner time.

When he came down to dinner, both of Sir Peter's children were sitting politely waiting for him to take his seat before the servants served the meal. He introduced himself, and they both examined him with interest.

'Mr Harrison, I understand that you are from Africa?' the boy asked. Dominic estimated he was about fifteen.

'I am indeed, from Salisbury in Rhodesia but more recently from a town in the south of Lake Tanganyika.'

'Do you have lions wandering around outside your house?' James asked.

'Don't be silly, James, of course they don't. Otherwise, the lions would eat them.,' Cynthia exclaimed earnestly but with a mocking tone. James didn't respond but just glared at her across the table. 'Do you mind if I call you Dominic?' Cynthia asked.

'Not at all,' Dominic replied. She seemed to be in her early to mid-twenties, pretty with blue eyes and a broad mouthed smile.

'It's so exciting, James,' she exclaimed, 'he's a real live mercenary fighter from Africa.'

'How on earth do you know that?' Dominic asked sharply.

'I know I'm naughty, but I read it in the report on daddy's desk in his room. He was in such a rush to leave that he forgot to put it away. You're not angry with me, are you?'

'Well, I should be. It's very personal and not at all romantic.'

'Oh, but it is. There's so little opportunity for adventure around her.; It's so boring.'

'Wow, the chaps at school will be impressed,' James exclaimed. 'I say, we have an important cricket match tomorrow afternoon, do you think you could come?'

'I dare say I could unless your father has something else planned for me.'

'Oh, but he won't, he's coming to watch too.'

'I'll come on one condition, that you don't mention the word mercenary to any of your friends.'

'It's a deal,' James cried, 'extending his hand across the table.'

'Well, I can't wait to tell Judith and Mary,' Cynthia giggled smiling at him defiantly, 'you're such an attractive man too.'

Dominic concentrated on his meal, not quite knowing how to handle this self-confident extroverted girl.

'If you're going to the cricket then I insist that we go riding together in the morning. You do ride, don't you?'

'A little,' he said remembering the ponies he and his mates at university had ridden in the Drakensberg Mountains, 'but I've not come prepared,' he added, hoping she would pass it over.

'All you need are some riding boots, and we have plenty of spares down at the stables. I'm sure we'll find your size.'

At this point, Dominic simply nodded realising that this headstrong girl would never take no for an answer. When they finished their dinner, James excused himself saying he had school homework to complete, leaving Dominic and Cynthia to retire to the drawing-room.

'My father instructed me to look after you this evening. It's all arranged. We're meeting some of my friends at the pub. After all, it is Friday night, and you can't just sit around here doing nothing.'

They walked together around the side of the mansion to some garages where Cynthia reversed the hardtop MGA out, turning it sharply, so it faced the exit. Once in her seat, she put her foot heavily on the accelerator, so the back wheels spun on the gravel. After a while, she slowed to a safe speed the lights illuminating the narrow road ahead.

'It was a lie,' he accused grinning.

'What was?'

'Your father never asked you to look after me.'

'Only a little one,' she laughed, 'you might not have agreed to come with me if I hadn't.'

'What do you do?' he asked.

'Well, at the moment I'm writing a screenplay. I studied English, History and Drama at University.'

'What's it about?'

'It sets out to define the changing role of women in today's society. Take my mother, for example. I love her dearly, but she has merely spent her life as an adjunct to my father. She was on the periphery of our upbringing. Nursemaids and governesses attended to that. She was busy with the woman's league, or the church, or fundraising for this and that. But the real change is coming with middle-class women seeking more than being housewives and servants to their husbands. What do you think?'

'I've never been married or had children so I suppose if one starts out life with the woman's role defined differently to what it is now, one wouldn't feel it unusual.'

'Ah, you see, I think I'll write what you've just said into my work.'

'As long as you don't use my name,' he laughed.

Smoke permeated the air inside the pub and voices, laughter and the clinking of glasses enveloped them as they entered. She led him by the hand to a side room, exclusively reserved for Cynthia and her friends for the evening. It was an extravagance because as she explained, there were only two other couples. Judith and Mary and their boyfriends were already drinking. The girls were sipping Babychams from champagne glasses and the men rum and coke from tumblers.

'Look who I've found darlings,' Cynthia offered as an introduction, 'Dominic Harrison a real live mercenary. Isn't it exciting?'

The girls beamed and made suitably impressed comments whilst the men looked more doubtful but shook his hand politely.

'I say are you truly what she says?' one of the men ventured.

'Well yes, but not any more,' Dominic replied. 'I was a reluctant one, put it that way.'

'An African adventurer,' Cynthia exclaimed, her tendency to drama getting the better of her.

'What's the celebration?' Dominic asked, trying to steer the conversation to a different subject.

'Oh darling, this is what we do for entertainment,' Cynthia enthused, 'what else is there to do on a Friday evening?'

'I could make a suggestion,' Judith's partner said lecherously.

'It's too early for that and in any case, when push comes to shove, you'll fall down drunk,' Judith countered mockingly. Mary sniggered in a way that left Dominic wondering whether it was embarrassment or anticipation.

The evening passed and as the alcohol took over, they all became happily mellow and affectionate. Dominic and the men had become good friends.

On the way back to Westlake Hall, Cynthia rested her hand on Dominic's thigh steering erratically with the other one.

'I enjoyed myself this evening. The men around here are such bores. Let's meet up in London. I live in our townhouse in Knightsbridge with Daddy during the week, but when he comes home over the weekend, I have the place to myself.'

'I'm sure we can manage that,' Dominic replied, not sure that it was a good idea but not knowing what else to say. When they arrived at Westlake Hall, there were still lights on in the office section, and people were moving about working. The rest of the building was in darkness other than the entrance hall. They stood at the bottom of the stairs, and Cynthia leaned up and kissed him lightly on the cheek but then put her hands behind his head and kissed him passionately on the lips pressing her body close into his.

'Let's have a nightcap in my room,' she murmured.

'Let's keep a clear head for that riding in the morning,' he said, pulling away, 'if I don't sleep now, I'll fall off the horse.'

The rest of the weekend went off well. When they went out in the morning, Cynthia tested his riding skills by trying to promote a gallop, laughing happily at his ineptitude. James turned out to be captain of the cricket team and scored thirty-two runs, but his team-mates failed to live up to his example, and they lost by fifteen. There were further discussions with Sir Peter on Saturday evening. On Sunday morning, they all went to church, something Dominic had not done for years excepting for weddings or funerals.

Late Sunday afternoon the chauffeur dropped Dominic off at his hotel in Earls Court before driving Sir Peter to his townhouse in Knightsbridge. Cynthia was out when they left Westlake Hall, so he assumed she had driven herself back to London in her car.

CHAPTER 22

A few days later, Sir Peter Faulkner sat with his financial director Jeremy Fielding and two members of his support team in an informal meeting in his office. Francis Taylor was a geologist, and Quinton Braun, a mining engineer. The map was spread out on his desk and a report compiled by the two men in his hand.

'Before I read the details, perhaps you can give me a summary,' Sir Peter suggested.

'Well the lab report from the ore outcropping on the Simpson concession is consistent with the findings from the drilling on the Postlewhite area to the south,' Taylor remarked. 'At this stage, one could expect the gold yield to be similar on each concession.'

'And the mining economics?' Sir Peter asked, looking at Quinton Braun.

'The strike and dip angles of the ore body established from the drilling confirms that one would expect it to outcrop approximately where it occurs on the Simpson concession. What it means is that whereas on the Postlewhite area underground mining would be a requirement, on the Simpson area the ore body is much closer to the surface. Open-pit mining offers a more economical solution.'

'We can conclude that the Simpson concession is more valuable?' Sir Peter mused.

'Yes, I've come to that conclusion, but a magnetic survey followed by drilling would be necessary to confirm it,' Taylor added.

'So, if we were to encourage investors to go with the Postlewhite deal and Harrison makes his report public we could be seriously embarrassed,' Sir Peter exclaimed.

'Yes, there is no doubt about that.'

'Has Harrison spoken to anybody else about this?' asked Jeremy Fielding.

'No, not as far as I know, only Postlewhite who he has turned down' Sir Peter said thoughtfully, 'I think we need to get an exclusive agreement on this. What do you think?'

'I agree. Should we offer him a loan secured against equity? He'll need the funding for the drilling.'

'I tried that. He's not interested in debt at this stage. We need to tie it up with an option to secure some shares for ourselves. Get the lawyers onto it, and make sure we have a director on the board.'

'How much do we pay him for the option?' Fielding asked.

'Find out how much the drilling is going to cost, add some working capital, and we'll ask for an option to purchase forty per cent of the shares. I'm sure he'll drive us down, but if we come out with twenty it should be fine,' Sir Peter said, 'and Jeremy I'd like you to be appointed to their board so you can advise on the drilling program and Jeremy, make sure we have an exclusive on raising the finance.'

Michelle was back at work. The Simpson Mining and Exploration company was now registered and the details had been passed on to Faulkner Investments. Apart from the lectures she was giving at the University, she was busy in the evenings assisting in strengthening the Anti-Apartheid Movement. Their main objective was to persuade the government to introduce a boycott of sports, cultural and academic contacts with South Africa. More ambitiously, they were working towards the introduction of international sanctions against that country.

Other than meeting for coffee for Dominic to give her feedback on the progress with Faulkner Investments, she saw little of him. Then one evening, when she was home, she got a call.

'Are you free on Thursday evening?' Dominic asked.

'Well, hello stranger, yes I am.' Michelle responded happily.

'I've booked a table at the Marquee Club.'

'What's the occasion?'

'I'd just like to take you to hear some outstanding jazz.'

'That sounds wonderful.'

'I'll get a taxi and pick you up at seven.'

'See you then.'

Michelle put the receiver down, feeling rejuvenated after devoting so much time to working with hardly a break. She had missed not seeing Dominic but knew he had been equally as busy and was not avoiding her. Or at least she hoped that was the case.

Dominic arrived in the taxi on time dressed in his suit, clean-shaven and smelling of aftershave. Quite a transformation from how he appeared in Sumbu. The taxi dropped them off outside the Marquee Club in Oxford Street and as they climbed down the stairs into the basement, a big band sound rose to meet them. It was still quite early, but the place was already almost full.

A waitress showed them to their table, and they ordered drinks, which took a little while to appear. While they were waiting, Dominic took a document from his jacket pocket and placed it on the table in front of Michelle.

'What is it?' she asked.

'It's an offer from Faulkner Investments. They're prepared to back our new company with a quite considerable amount of money.'

'So that's the celebration,' she said accusingly.

'Not really, I wanted to be with you. It only came this morning.'

'What do you think of the offer?'

'It's quite fair, much of the funds are to be used for drilling to add value to the company, but there's enough for us to be able to work on the project full time covering our living expenses for about eighteen months. By that time, if all goes well, Faulkner Investments will raise more finance to continue with the exploration.'

'That's fantastic news,' she exclaimed, leaning over and kissing him on the cheek, 'I knew you would do it.'

'Well, it's not signed yet, you need to read it carefully and discuss it with Jeffery. When you're both happy with it, we can then sign.'

'I'll phone him tomorrow. I'm sure he'll be pleased,' she said, smiling.

A black jazz singer appeared to applause and was soon singing, causing a lull in the bubbling voices of the crowd. Michelle listened to this beautiful woman, entranced. Had Dominic subtly or subconsciously engineered this to boost her self esteem? She didn't need it. But it was good to see someone similar to herself so appreciated by the crowd.

After singing a few songs, the band took a break and the voices in the crowd resumed at an increased pitch. A pretty blonde was making her way towards their table. Michelle noticed her first., but Dominic was studying the menu.

'Darling, how good to see you,' Cynthia cried, placing an arm around Dominic's shoulders and kissing him on the cheek. Dominic caught entirely by surprise, stood up, smiling weakly.

'Michelle, this is Cynthia Faulkner,' Dominic said as Cynthia looked critically at Michelle with undisguised disapproval.

'Such a pleasant surprise, do you come here often? I come with friends every Thursday evening. It's so entertaining and the "in" place. Surprising who you meet here.'

'No,' Dominic managed to blurt, 'It's our first time.'

'Oh, you must drop by on a Thursday, and I'll introduce you to some of my friends,' Cynthia promised without looking at Michelle. 'And do give me a call sometime so we can meet. Well, I must get back. I'll be missed.'

Dominic sat down feeling deflated. Michelle sat there silently looking down at nothing in particular on the table, not daring to look Dominic in the eyes.

'I want to go home,' Michelle said softly.

'Please don't let her get to you, let's stay, and enjoy ourselves.'

'No, if you want to stay then do so, I'll go out and get a taxi.'

'I can't let you go home by yourself. I'll come with you,' Dominic exclaimed.

They travelled silently back in the taxi each consumed in their own thoughts. She's had a relapse into excessive sensitivity, why can't she just treat such behaviour with the contempt it deserves. Michelle, on the other hand, was furious that this woman had shown obvious affection for Dominic, how had that familiarity developed if not with Dominic's connivance?

When the taxi arrived outside Michelle's flat, they both got out, and while Dominic was paying the driver, she walked up the steps to the door fumbling with the keys.

'Wait, aren't you going to invite me in?' Dominic called.

'Go home,' she insisted the tears running down her cheeks.

As he walked, he tried to understand how an intended fun night out had turned into such a disaster.

Back in her flat, Michelle made herself a sandwich and a cup of tea and allowed herself to calm down. What really upset her? Was it the woman's look of disdain in her direction or her affection for Dominic? When she heard that Misheck had married, she felt happy for him not jealous. Was she in love with Dominic, or was he becoming like one of the family? Another brother? Other men found her attractive; he was not the only man in the world. But did she have the courage to go out of her way to find one? The one advantage of London was its cosmopolitan nature. She didn't feel that different because there were people from all over the world, particularly the holidaymakers, only it was autumn and quite chilly, so there were not so many around, mainly residents.

She put on her coat again, left the flat walking down Earls Court Road and caught a tube to Kensington High Street. She could have chosen a pub in Earls Court, but that felt too close to home. If she was a little further away, she could feel liberated and anonymous. When she arrived, she found a pub a short walk from the station went in, bought a gin and tonic at the bar and found a table with two stools in the corner. Now, rather than feeling upset, she felt rebellious anger towards Dominic, a desire to punish him for humiliating her. Reckless energy assailed her and she looked around the pub, which was only half-full for a suitable companion, a man who might be alone and looking for company. At a distance, how would she know if he was married or not, could she see a ring from this distance?

'Do you mind if I join you?' A half-whispered voice said, coming from the opposite direction to which she was looking. Turning, she found herself looking at a young white man with long dark hair and dark, sad eyes with a beer in his hand.

'Please do,' she said swivelling on the stool to face him on the other side of the small table.

'My name's Sergio Ortega,' he said, extending his hand.

'Michelle Simpson,' she replied with a smile.

'Are you waiting for someone?' he asked, looking around rather nervously.

'No, I'm here alone,' Michelle mused.

'You're very beautiful. I'm surprised to hear that.'

'I had a fight with my …,' She was going to say boyfriend but hesitated.

'…boyfriend,' he asked, finishing the sentence for her.

'Something like that,' she admitted.

'Girlfriend?' he asked with raised eyebrows.

'No, I'm not like that,' she said with half a smile.

'It wouldn't matter if you were.'

'How do you mean?'

'Well, I'm a homosexual,' he said quietly looking around, 'would you rather I left?'

'No, please stay.'

They sat in silence for a while, sipping their drinks.

'What do you do?' Michelle asked him.

'I play the cello and write poetry. Not attractively exciting, I'm afraid.'

His vulnerability brought out some dormant instincts in her. She leaned over and took his hand in both of hers.

'But that is exciting you create or express beauty from nothing but your mind.'

'I'd never thought of it like that. I just allow my emotions to guide me.'

'You're very sensitive,' she remarked.

'But aren't you?'

Michelle didn't respond for some time trying to find the answer. Yes, she was, but no, she wasn't.

'I'm a medical researcher. It's scientific and analytical work. Perhaps I spend too much time trying to analyse my feelings instead of allowing my emotions to guide me as you put it. Or perhaps I don't react spontaneously to my emotions.'

'Is that stressful?' he asked.

'I suppose it is now that you mention it.'

'Do you love someone?' he asked, looking directly into her eyes demanding the truth. Michelle hesitated her mind racing. 'You're not sure,' he stated before she could answer. They sat in silence for some time drinking.

'Will I always be like this?' she asked, appealing to him.

'I don't know. But isn't it because science always leaves a theory open to question? Are we ever really sure about anything?'

Michelle finished her drink and smiled at him, warmly squeezing his hand.

'I must go now.' She said, standing up. 'Thank you. You just stopped me from doing something I was sure to regret.'

Back home, Michelle took out the Faulkner Investments agreement and spent an hour and a half reading it. By then it was past midnight, so she went to bed, setting her alarm clock for five in the morning. If she called Jeffery then, it would be six in Sumbu so she would catch him before he left the house.

CHAPTER 23

When Dominic found the two copies of the agreement signed by Michelle waiting for him in the hotel reception the next morning, he opened the envelope they were sealed in, and out dropped a note. It was curt and to the point, to the effect that Jeffery had agreed that they proceed. Between the few lines, the tone delivered another message that Dominic interpreted as a significant setback to their relationship. For the moment, he put that matter aside and added his signature to the agreement as a witness.

It was after nine in the morning when he phoned Faulkner Investments to arrange to take the agreement to their offices for Sir Peter to sign.

'Jeremy Fielding,' the voice said over the line when the switchboard operator put him through.

'It's Dominic Harrison. I was hoping to speak to Sir Peter.'

'He won't be in the office for the next few days, can I help you?'

'I have the signed agreement for his signature,' Dominic said.

'Yes, he was expecting it. It would be better if you delivered it to his townhouse in Knightsbridge. He'll be home each evening,' Fielding advised him.

'Alright, just give me the address, and I'll get it to him today,' Dominic replied.

The previous days had been quite hectic, so Dominic welcomed the rest of the time he had that day to devote to something a bit different. He took a tube to Leicester Square and walked to the Westminster Reference Library. If he were to become involved in mining, he might as well familiarise himself with mining economics and investment banking. There was a wealth of books on the subject, so he spent the rest of the morning sitting there reading. At lunchtime, he went in search of a pub, had half a pint of beer and sausage and mash. Back at the library, he spent the rest of the afternoon studying the subjects he had chosen until the library closed.

Having spent most of his time during the past two weeks, sitting at his desk, or in meetings, he needed exercise. He made his way to Piccadilly and walked west until he reached Hyde Park Corner, then bought a newspaper and crossed the road to enter the park. It was a diversion but, as it was a cloudless day with the low sun still giving some warmth, he walked along the Serpentine until he found a bench. When he sat down, some ducks paddled expectantly towards him those further away flapping their wings as their legs propelled them to catch up with the others. When no food appeared, they gradually dispersed, leaving a few foraging near the water's edge.

He sat, reading the newspaper from front to back using up time so he wouldn't arrive at Sir Peter's residence too early. When he left the park, he disposed of the newspaper in a refuse bin.

Using his map of London on his walk from Hyde Park, he soon found a row of Georgian terraced houses. The white façade of the buildings rose five floors, and he admired the architecture with its inset sash windows and doors crowned with classical pediments and decorative mouldings. A balcony at the first-floor level formed the roof of a small portico at each entrance. He found the correct number, climbed the steps to the door, and announced his presence using the brass knocker. A housekeeper, in a black tunic with a frilly white apron and cap, answered the door. She took his name, and the purpose of his visit closed the door and left him waiting on the doorstep. When the door opened again, she welcomed him in with a wave of her hand and indicated he should follow her, leading him into the living room.

'Darling, what a pleasant surprise,' Cynthia cried rising from an easy-chair and offering him her cheek to kiss in greeting.

'Hello Cynthia,' he said guardedly, 'I've come to see your father.'

'Oh, Daddy won't be back for a couple of hours,' she said, then, 'Doris, bring another cup so Mister Harrison can join me for tea.'

'Well, it's not Westlake Hall, but it's certainly comfortable and ideally located close to your father's office,' Dominic remarked, looking around and trying to make conversation.

'Not only that,' she explained, 'when my brother George comes through from New York on business he has his own suite here on the fifth floor, and of course, other members of the family regularly pass by London and use the visitors' accommodation. Only my father and I are permanent residents. My mother and James live permanently at Westlake.'

'Where will James live when he goes to university?'

'Depends on how hard he works. If he gets into Cambridge, he'll live in digs up there. Otherwise, he might go to University here in London, in which case he can live with us here. There's plenty of room, Daddy has a suite on the first floor, and I'm on the second. Doris and our cook live below here. Let me show you around,'

Dominic followed her to a second reception room, dining room, and kitchen on the ground floor and up the stairs to her father's suite. In addition to his suite, there was another bedroom and bathroom. Everything was tastefully furnished, and the bathrooms had been modernised. The second floor where Cynthia lived followed the same layout as the one below. She opened the door of her suite, and he followed her in. It was a large room with two easy-chairs and a coffee table, a double bed with side tables and lamps, dressing table, two overflowing bookcases, and two desks. One of the desks showed evidence that she had been working here recently, a few piles of papers, an open book, and other writer's paraphernalia. On the second, there was a typewriter and a neat pile of unused foolscap paper.

'So, this is where you do your creative work,' Dominic said.

'Yes, this is where I allow my imagination to run wild. This is where characters emerge and become real, evil characters, courageous characters, virtuous characters and passionate characters. I work alone most of the time, and that's why I like to go out at night and let my hair down, seeking interesting people to absorb into my fictitious world. I can't write if the characters don't come to life.'

'You fantasise?' he asked, smiling.

'No, you're not a fantasy, you're real, a real-life heroic and passionate character,' she breathed, moving up close and looking into his eyes. She took his hands and said, 'You're real, I can feel you, I can hear your heart beating.' Her ear was against his chest. Darling, undress me,' she commanded.

'Your father will be home soon,' Dominic warned.

'No, he won't, and even if he does, he won't come up here, and Doris is down on the lower level, she won't come either.'

He tried to pull away, but she slipped her hand down the front of his shirt. She paused when she felt the scar on his right side, which had left a deep indentation.

'What is this?' she gasped.

'It's a scar from a bullet wound.'

Then she whispered, 'Che Guevara, Che Guevara,' continuously. It was possible. He had taken on the persona of the revolutionary guerrilla fighter as far as she was concerned. She was playing out some scene for inclusion in her writing, trying to use him as a physical manifestation of her imagination, to convert this contrived experience into words representing a convincing scenario.

'You believe that I compare to Che Guevara?' Dominic asked.

'Yes, I do, it's wonderful.'

Dominic laughed and walked to the door, looking back to find her not the least offended by his contempt. Her self-confidence was unsettling and he almost admired it.

A little while later, Sir Peter arrived and signed the agreement. Dominic caught the tube back to Earls Court station and walked to the hotel. It should have been a moment for celebration, but he felt no excitement just a numb feeling. How was he to tell Michelle that Sir Peter had signed the document? Why did he feel guilty about his time with Cynthia in her bedroom? After all, he was not Michelle's favourite person right now.

Within three days, Faulkner Investments paid the funds into the Simpson Mining and Exploration's bank account, by which time he had gathered the courage to phone Michelle.

'Dominic, I thought you had given up on me,' she said brightly. Her warm bubbly voice was as appealing as ever. His heart gave a little leap, and suddenly a weight fell from his shoulders. Was she capable of influencing his mood to that extent?

'Good news,' he said cheerfully, 'the money's in the bank.'

'Excellent, what do we do next?'

'Well, some fees are now due to the trust for the use of the licence. I can make out a cheque to transfer the funds but need your signature as well as my own. You should phone Jeffery and tell him that when the funds are in the account, we can pay back the loan we took out from the bank in Sumbu.'

'He will be delighted,' she said, 'you're a star.'

They met briefly at a nearby coffee shop the next morning before Michelle was due to give a lecture at the University. For the few minutes they were together having coffee she seemed happy and his humour had also returned. They left together, she on her way to her lecture and he in the direction of the bank.

When he had finished at the bank, he returned to the hotel and put a call through to Michael Nicholls, the bank manager in Sumbu.

'Where on earth are you?' Nicholls asked as the line crackled and Dominic's voice seemed distantly faint.

'In London,' he shouted down the mouthpiece, 'I need you to follow the written instructions I left regarding the savings account. The loan is to be settled within days so you can drop the surety attached to the savings account and do what's necessary.'

'I remember, don't worry, I'll do it.'

'Thanks, the line is bad, so I'll say no more. Goodbye,' Dominic said as he hung up.

A few days later in the mercenary recruitment centre in Salisbury, the adjutant entered the Colonel's office with a telex in his hand.

'You're going to find this hard to believe,' he announced laying the telex in front of the Colonel.

'What's this?' he asked.

The Colonel read it through and said, 'Well I'm damned, it means that Dominic Harrison opened a bank account in Sumbu in the name of the Commando Unit and deposited the missing money there. It's even been earning interest. What's more, the bank has posted us the cash book that Major van der Walt kept with the money.'

'We've already written it off in the books,' the adjutant reminded him.

'Well, make the necessary adjustments and reply to the telex. Give the bank our account details and ask them to transfer the money.'

When the Adjutant left the office, the Colonel sat there wondering. This Dominic Harrison had turned out to be unusually honest.

CHAPTER 24

One late autumn afternoon, Max Freeman received a phone call from Jacob Gomani in Lusaka.

'Mister Freeman, I have some news for you. We are sending someone to set things up as we discussed when I was last in London. He will bring with him the documents. Deliver it to Dominic Harrison at the address given to us on his licence renewal application. It will show that we have revoked the licence. He will also bring with him other forms for your signature to secure the concession.'

'That's excellent news,' Max Freeman exclaimed, 'this will be to our mutual benefit.' Jacob Gomani gave him the name of the UNIP representative that was to be arriving in London in the next three days and hung up.

Max was ecstatic, he got up from his desk bouncing around the office yelling, 'Yes … yes…yes…'

Hearing the commotion, the Chairman walked down the passage to Max's office.

'What's going on?' he asked, putting his head through the door.

'They've revoked the Simpson licence,' Max exclaimed in excitement.

'They have? Well, that's wonderful news. It's effective from when?'

'With immediate effect, they're sending someone from Lusaka. He should be here within the next three days with the documents.'

'Has the licence been transferred?'

'No, but he will bring the application forms to take it over with him, ready to take back. All we need to do is fill it in and sign it. It's a formality,' Max assured him.

'Good work Max, I'll notify the other board members,' the Chairman said and left the office.

Max leaned back in his chair and lit a cigar, puffing too quickly he was so excited. The room gradually filled up with smoke creating a blue haze. This would put that upstart pessimist Frank Osborne in his place. Then he considered how to break the news to Dominic Harrison. He knew that Faulkner Investments were looking for investors for the Simpson concession and they seemed to be succeeding. It couldn't be better they were out there creating interest and finding investors for the concession that would soon be in the hands of Postlewhite. So why notify anyone. The longer he waited, the more interest Faulkner Investments would generate. Once he had the document, Faulkner Investment would join up with Postlewhite to share the fund-raising fees. The Simpsons would be totally out of the picture.

A plan germinated in Max Freeman's mind. It would be dramatic. He would invite the Chairman and Frank Osborne if only to rub the latter's nose in it and the Faulkner team to a meeting at Postlewhite's board room to receive the news when the UNIP representative arrived with the document. His success would filter out to the financial pages and Max Freeman would enjoy a moment of fame. He picked up the phone and asked his secretary to put him through to the financial director.

'Have you heard the news?' he asked the moment the man picked up the phone.

'Yes, sounds like it's all go,' he said.

'Just remember to have the funds ready for transfer to the bank account our visitor nominates. We need to show good faith.'

'Don't worry. I can do it whenever you require,' the financial director assured him.

Visiting the Westminster Library turned out to be a great help in advancing Dominic in his presentations to potential investors. At first, he went with an experienced member of Sir Peter's team to learn how to make the presentation attractive and convincing. Now, after a few days, he was confident enough to operate alone. He made the contacts from a list supplied by Faulkner Investments, set up appointments for the presentations, and travelled to offices mainly in The City. He didn't immediately appreciate his measure of success because potential clients referred back to Jeremy Fielding their financial director.

It was such a busy time that he had little contact with Michelle although they spoke to each other from time to time on the phone. On certain occasions when the potential clients were, from Faulkner's experience, considered high probability, if the presentation were in the morning, he would entertain the executives to lunch in one of the many upmarket restaurants in or near to The City. At first, he found the amount of money flowing into the restaurants quite disturbing, but he soon got over that and became generous in entertaining these men of extravagant tastes. Very soon, the restaurants knew him by name and they were treating him with much respect. He consumed too much alcohol keeping up with his potential clients, but fortunately was not required to drive, being able to take a tube back to the hotel. On these occasions, he skipped dinner and turned down Michelle's suggestions that they should dine out.

Eventually, he bought some running shoes and a tracksuit and would rise early and go for a run through the streets and around Hyde Park before setting off for work.

Cynthia contacted him a few times complaining that he worked too hard and should join her at the Marquee Club. He turned her down as diplomatically as he could, but the truth of it was that he was so busy he wasn't in the mood. Just when he was beginning to tire of the whole process, it ended.

'It's oversubscribed,' Sir Peter told him. 'We've raised more funds than we can offer shares. Take a break.'

'And after that, what's the next step?'

'We need to do a magnetic survey and then plan the drilling programme. We'll need you for the project management.'

Dominic was pleased. At first, entertaining people in restaurants was fun, but after a while, it just became work and he was sure it wasn't doing his health any good. How was he going to take a break during the week? Michelle was working and had run out of leave, so he'd be at a loose end. Touring around England was one possibility, but he hadn't bought a car and in any case, where would he park it. At some point, he would need to become better organised. Staying at the hotel was becoming tiresome, a place of his own with parking would allow him more freedom.

When he phoned the Faulkner's townhouse, the housekeeper answered the phone and he asked for Cynthia.

'Dominic darling, how good of you to call,' she said enthusiastically.

'Well, I was beginning to feel bad about not going to the Marquee Club when you asked. I was just so busy.'

'Do you want to go on Thursday evening?'

'No … I mean I could, but I have another idea. I'm taking a few days break and want to know if you would like to go to Paris. We could drive down to Dover in your car and catch the ferry across. That's if you're free, of course.'

'What a wonderful idea, you are a darling. When do you want to go?'

'How about tomorrow?'

'Well, we'll need to get visas, if we use Faulkner Investments travel agent, they can get them quickly. I'll phone you back with the address. Take your passport there this morning, they'll be expecting you, and we should be able to pick them up tomorrow.'

'Can they make a hotel reservation?'

'One bedroom or two?' she giggled.

'Two,' he said with feigned shock.

'You are a spoilsport darling,' she said still giggling, 'leave it to me.'

Two days later, she picked up Dominic from his hotel and they set off for Dover in her MGA, two small bags in the boot. It wasn't the best weather, and the windscreen wipers kept busy. They drove onto the ferry at Dover and went into the restaurant for coffee. Two hours later, they were driving out of Calais on their way to Paris.

It was a small comfortable hotel near the Opera House, and their rooms turned out to be on different floors. Both had en suite bathrooms but were small, not that it mattered, as they would be out most of the time. Cynthia spoke acceptable French, and he found himself reliant on her, which inflated her ego even further. She turned out to be a revelation; if he had needed a personal tour guide, he couldn't have done better, although she chose to visit what interested her most.

The day after they arrived, they visited the Louvre and went on to The Orsay Impressionist Museum, where he discovered that Cynthia knew the history of the artists and their work in great detail. After that, they visited Notre Dame Cathedral with its spectacular rose window and towering interior vaulting. Outside in a yard at the back of the church, they stopped for a moment, to watch the stonemasons dressing stone to produce replacement parts for the structure. They crossed the bridge to the Ile Saint Louis wandering through the streets until they found a little shop selling pastries. Sitting, dangling their legs over the wall along the Seine, eating their pastries and watching the boats go by, Dominic felt comfortable. He glanced at Cynthia, smiling with a far-away look on her face, wondering what fantasy she was enjoying at that moment in the weak late autumn sun. Which period of the history of this romantic city consumed her at that moment?

'Tomorrow,' she said, 'I want to take you to Giverny to see a beautiful garden and the house of Monet, one of the great impressionist painters. You saw some of his painting today, in fact of that very garden. From there we can carry on to Auvers and see the church that Vincent van Gogh's painted. A short walk from the church are the graves of Vincent and Theo, his brother. It's so beautiful there, and you can feel their spirits.'

'You like it here, don't you?'

'Yes, darling I do, it's so romantic,' she enthused, squeezing his hand.

'Where shall we dine this evening,' Dominic asked, having learnt to allow her to lead him wherever she pleased.

'It's a surprise, but we'll take the Metro.'

That evening by the time they left the hotel for the Metro, it was already dark. They got off at the Champ de Mars Metro station, and then Dominic realised where they were going. They took the elevator up the Eiffel Tower to the restaurant where the Maître d' showed them to their table. Sitting right next to the window, they could see the lights of Paris spread out below them and the lights of the boats snaking along the Seine.

'Isn't that romantic?' Cynthia marvelled.

'I have to admit it's quite breath-taking.'

'You're a most attractive man,' she mused.

'And you're a very pretty girl.'

'Does that mean we can spend more time together? Get to know each other more intimately.'

'You know I'm attracted to you, but I just feel that we come from such different backgrounds. I don't fit into the society you move in down at Westlake Hall.'

'But that is why I'm so attracted to you,' she exclaimed.

'For now, yes, but later on, that fantasy will evaporate, and you'll find out that I'm just quite ordinary. You'll gravitate towards someone more fitting to your parent's expectations.'

'I'm not going to let my parents influence who I want to marry.'

'Perhaps not, but what if the man that you fall in love with is not prepared to live forever at a social disadvantage? Who will ultimately influence the children? No, I don't believe you can so easily escape your upbringing. Live and enjoy your fantasies, but when it comes to choosing a partner, follow your head, not your heart.'

'Then perhaps I'd rather just live with my fantasies, and not get married at all. I just want to be happy,' she countered with disarming honesty. He could tell she was quite serious.

'If you do that, you will probably become a fascinating Aunt to some nephews and nieces,' Dominic laughed.

The next day they travelled to Giverny and Auvers to complete Cynthia's magical tour. By the time they had finished and got back to the hotel, Dominic was in culture shock. Compared to Paris, places in Africa could be on another planet, beyond his imagination.

When they arrived back in London the day following, Dominic thanked her outside his hotel before she drove away.

'Thanks for a wonderful tour of the romantic city,' he said.

'It could have been more romantic if you'd shared my bedroom,' she stated with a wicked laugh.

'That might have been dangerous,' he replied.

'Not true, I'm now on that new pill that's just been released. What a waste!'

She drove away, leaving him to ponder. There was something almost mesmerising about this intelligent and eccentric girl.

CHAPTER 25

At Faulkner Investments' offices in Mincing Lane, planning for the further exploration of the Simpson concession was progressing well. Dominic was concentrating on refining the preliminary expenditure budgets he had assembled at the beginning when they worked out their capital requirements. They were to bring in a consulting geophysicist to plan and interpret the results of the magnetic survey, and Francis Taylor was busy with this task. Once they had the analysed the results of the magnetic survey and the drilling pattern with ore body depth estimates, Dominic would be able to refine the expenditure budget. This would lead to the appointment of a contractor who would establish themselves on-site with their staff and equipment.

One early winter's morning when an arctic wind brought a chill to the air, Sir Peter received a call from Max Freeman.

'How are things going with your Simpson concession project,' Max asked. 'What's that got to do with him,' Sir Peter thought, and said evasively, 'As well as can be expected.'

But he knew that finding investors for the Simpson concession had been made a lot easier by the drilling results from the Postlewhite's concession that were by now common knowledge. Knowing the existence of the outcrop on the Simpson concession to the north made it possible to offer investors the prospect of better returns from opencast mining.

More lucrative than the Postlewhite concession which would require underground methods.

'We're about to make an important announcement that will be in the interest of your investors and ours. The outcome might well mean that we can join forces to our mutual benefit,' Max said somewhat enigmatically.

'Tell me more,' Sir Peter encouraged him.

'I will elaborate at a meeting at our offices on Thursday morning at ten o'clock. I'd like you to attend and bring with you Harrison and the Simpson girl.'

'Alright but, let me check that everyone is available, and I'll get back to you to confirm.'

Sir Peter put down the phone and sat there, contemplating what Max Freeman had just suggested. The man had a reputation for being unscrupulous and devious. He was not to be underestimated. The two of them had clashed a few times in the past, but this time Faulkner Investments seemed to be in a stronger position. They had already raised the capital they needed, whereas he knew that Postlewhite was still struggling in that regard. He had given himself time to consider before confirming that they would be prepared to attend the meeting.

'There's an interesting development,' Sir Peter said to Dominic when he arrived at his desk, 'Max Freeman wants us to attend a meeting at his offices on Thursday. I don't trust that man.'

'I feel the same way. He tried to take over the Simpson licence for a song. I can't blame him for trying, but we have proven that instead of being greedy, he should have upped his offer. I'm pleased he didn't otherwise you and I wouldn't be working together and I would probably have not been in business at all.'

'Do you think we should attend?' Sir Peter asked.

'Well, there's no harm in listening,' Dominic observed.

'I'll get back to him and confirm. He specifically asked for Miss Simpson to attend.'

'I'll make sure she does,' Dominic assured him.

On the Thursday Sir Peter, Dominic and Michelle assembled at the Postlewhite offices just before ten o'clock. Jeremy Fielding, Faulkner's financial director, joined them at Sir Peter's request. When the receptionist showed them into the boardroom, they found Postlewhite's chairman at the head of the table supported by Max Freeman and Frank Osborne. The chairman made the introductions which included Bernard Argent, who was heading up Postlewhite's fundraising activities. He opened the meeting when they were settled.

'Thank you for coming we've called this meeting to give Max Freeman the opportunity to make an announcement that will affect the future of our two companies. Max if you can take over and explain.'

'To get straight to the point, I have to tell you that the Mining Ministry in Northern Rhodesia has rejected the renewal of the Simpson licence and revoked it.'

The Simpson team sat there for a moment speechless, trying to absorb what Freeman had said. Dominic's mind raced as he tried to figure out what had gone wrong. They had met all the conditions in the renewal application. How was this possible? Sir Peter immediately ran over in his mind the negative impact this would have, if it were true, on his investors and to the credibility of Faulkner Investments. It would be a disaster.

'How do you know this? We haven't been notified,' Dominic exclaimed.

'That's because a representative of the Department in Northern Rhodesia, is to deliver the notification document to this meeting in a matter of minutes,' Max announced rather pompously. Frank Osborne gritted his teeth at this showboating.

'I suppose you know the reason why they have revoked the licence,' Dominic exclaimed accusingly.

'My understanding is that it's because there has been no exploration work undertaken or reported since the concession was awarded.'

'But there is no legal limit on the term of the licence,' Dominic claimed.

'I believe that is at the discretion of the Department of Mining and Geology,' Max suggested smiling with satisfaction. He had prepared his answers carefully. 'It is also at their discretion to which company they award or transfer the licence.'

'I suppose I needn't bother to guess who that might be,' Dominic growled.

'I think this presents a good opportunity for Postlewhite and Faulkner Investments to combine forces,' he proposed ignoring Dominic and addressing his suggestion to Sir Peter.

'Don't think you will get away with this that easily,' Michelle said aggressively, 'we'll fight you every inch of the way.'

'I think doing that will be extremely costly and a futile exercise. You will be fighting both the present and future governments of Northern Rhodesia.'

Sir Peter looked at Max Freeman with a measure of scepticism.

'Well, where is this, so-called representative, from Northern Rhodesia,' he demanded. Max Freeman got up, went out of the boardroom, and returned a few moments later, followed by a black man.

'I'd like to introduce you to Mister Mazabuka,' he said, presenting the man with an up-facing open palm.

For a moment, Michelle and Dominic sat frozen where they sat in surprise, for there stood Jeffery with a broad smile on his face. Michelle leapt up and ran around the table and embraced him.

'Jeffery, what on earth are you doing here?' Michelle exclaimed.

'Looking after our interests, I hope,' he replied.

Around the boardroom table, there were contrasting reactions. Sir Peter was not sure what was going on, but from the smile on Dominic's face, he gathered that it was a positive development. The chairman sat there totally confused as did

Bernard Argent who detected that something unexpected and significant had just occurred. Frank Osborne sensed that this was not going to turn out well for Postlewhite. Max Freeman sat there stunned, but not sure, how the Simpson girl knew his new UNIP contact man.

'Just to repeat the introduction, I'd like to present my brother Jeffery Simpson,' Michelle announced.

'An imposter,' Max muttered half under his breath.

'No Mister Freeman, an alias. It's our mother's maiden name. Jeffery prefers to use it in Northern Rhodesia otherwise, people might expect him to be white.'

By now Max Freeman was recovering slightly, he needed to fight back, or he was doomed.

'This is a conspiracy,' he spat, looking at Jeffery. 'You've misrepresented yourself, there will be legal consequences.' His contact in the Ministry of Mines had been so confident that all was going well, even how he was looking forward to working with them in London.

'Oh, quite the contrary,' Jeffery announced. 'I've got all the documents exactly as promised.'

'What the hell is going on?' the chairman intervened banging his gavel. There was a pause while they waited for him to resume control of the meeting. 'Mister Mazabuka, please explain.' Jeffery sat down and drew some documents out of his briefcase, setting them down on the table in front of him.

'Yes, it's true, the Simpson licence has been revoked,' Jeffery stated. Max Freeman was at a loss. 'But so has the Postlewhite licence,' Jeffery continued.

'But that's outrageous,' Max exclaimed, 'we've already drilled on the site.'

'If that's the case, why did you need the Simpson concession?'

Dominic smiled to himself. He could see Bernard Argent's questioning frown. It was time to bring them down to earth.

'Because the Simpson concession is more valuable and offers a better prospect for mining. It's more attractive to investors,' Dominic stated.

'How can you say that?' Max responded, looking for an exit hole.

'Because our initial share offer is oversubscribed,' Dominic explained.

Bernard Argent was looking sternly and expectantly at the Chairman. Frank Osborne looked like thunder and Max Freeman stared gloomily at the table in front of him. Jeffery opened the folder, took out the documents, handed one set to Max Freeman and the other to Dominic.

'The situation is as follows,' he explained, 'each set of documents has the letter revoking the licences. The other document is an application to re-instate them.'

Max Freeman felt a glimmer of hope. All was not lost.

Jeffery continued, 'I've been instructed to draw your attention to the conditions of the application for reinstatement. Suppose you look at the clauses dealing with a company's suitability to hold a licence. One deals with the matter of the applicant ever, now or in the past, being involved in offering inducements, or other corrupt activities to secure it.'

Max Freeman's life had just collapsed. Frank Osborne stood up and made for the boardroom door. When he got there he turned to Max and growled, 'You bloody fool.' He slammed the door as he went out.

Sir Peter stood up and addressed the chairman.

'If you'll excuse us, I think it's time we departed.'

'I believe we have something to discuss,' Bernard Argent said, looking at Sir Peter. 'Do you mind if I leave with you?'

'Not at all,' Sir Peter responded.

As Dominic, Michelle and Jeffery exited the boardroom, Sir Peter and Bernard Argent followed already in earnest discussion.

It was quiet in the boardroom with the two remaining men both grappling with what had transpired. Max spoke first.

'Well, you can't win them all.'

'You know what you have to do,' the chairman said.

Max's mind was working overtime. A scheme to rescue the situation was emerging. He smiled with anticipation.

'Yes, I'll have a rescue plan on your desk before lunch tomorrow. I'm sure you'll find it ingenious. If not, you can have my resignation.'

Later that evening when Dominic, Michelle, and Jeffery were having dinner at a small bistro in High Street Kensington, Jeffery described how he came to make his dramatic entrance to the meeting.

'Why didn't you tell us what was happening?' Michelle asked him.

'If I'd told you that the licence was going to be revoked, even although the Department would reinstate it, the investors would have been discouraged unless you withheld the information. It saved you from failing to make full disclosure.'

'How did you find out what Max Freeman was up to?' Dominic asked.

'He tried to bribe Jacob Gomani subtly inferring that it was contributions to UNIP. I was supposed to come here to set up the bank accounts and distribute the funds to individuals with influence in the party. But that astute old character Gomani soon discovered that the party's representative in Sumbu was part owner of the licence. He also found out who Postlewhite were using in the Department of Mining and Geology to help them promote the revoking of the Simpson licence. We turned him, with the promise that the Department would take no action if he cooperated with the authorities. After that, he worked under Gomani's direction implementing the plan that we carried out today.'

'Jeffery,' Dominic said, 'that's the second time you have arrived at the critical moment to save me.'

'Not quite, I was trying to save us all, and my father's legacy. We're a family.'

'Are they certain to reject Postlewhite's application for reinstatement.' Dominic asked.

'It's an interesting dilemma. If ever there was an opportunity for a further bribe this is it.

Postlewhite will feel now that it's the only way to rescue themselves, so they'll start searching for another person with influence.'

'There is one factor that may cause them to abandon their quest,' Dominic answered. 'Even if they have the licence, I think the investors will be well aware now that it's not an attractive proposition.'

Jeffery stayed with Michelle for a week, she took unpaid leave to show him around London and some historical sites a little further afield, which they travelled to in a hired car. Dominic continued working at the Faulkner offices, but his confidence was growing and he started thinking about renting their own offices. He couldn't go on taking advantage of Sir Peter's generous hospitality. Bernard Argent was now a regular visitor to the offices engaging in discussions with Dominic and Sir Peter looking a year to eighteen months ahead for the financing necessary to start the mining.

In the middle of the week, Dominic received a call from Cynthia.

'Darling, I'm really missing you,' she complained.

'Sorry, I've been busy. I should have given you a call.'

'It's nearly Christmas, and I'd like to invite you to spend it with me at Westlake Hall. It would be such fun, and you can meet the rest of the family.'

'Oh, that would be wonderful, but I've already made arrangements to spend Christmas here in London with friends,' he lied.

'Well alright but then I insist that you spend New-year's eve with us at Westlake, just a crowd of young people. My parents will be busy entertaining, but we can go somewhere and have a roaring party.'

Dominic hesitated but knew he couldn't turn her down twice with the same excuse.

'All right, that sounds like a great idea.'

'Wonderful darling and bring a suitcase so you can stay over for a few days.'

'I'll try,' he replied doubtfully.

Jeffery flew out on a Saturday anxious now to get back to the fishing business but satisfied that he had contributed to their venture in London. Michelle shed a tear at the airport as he went through into departures, not knowing when next they would see each other. Overall, his visit had been an outstanding success.

CHAPTER 26

A week before Christmas, Simpson Mining and Exploration opened their offices in the same building as Faulkner Investments. Dominic hired a small number of staff to help him run it. All this was possible from the sale of twenty-nine per cent of the shares to the investors. Faulkner Investments exercised their option to purchase twenty per cent of the shares at par, leaving the Simpson Trust retaining control with fifty-one per cent. At the first shareholder's meeting held in the boardroom of Faulkner Investments in the late afternoon, Sir Peter was appointed chairman, Dominic as Managing Director, Jeremy Fielding as financial director, and Michelle as the third director.

After the meeting, Dominic and Michelle decided it was time to do some Christmas shopping, so they took a tube to Oxford Circus.

'Cynthia invited me to spend Christmas at Westlake Hall,' he said as they sat next to each other on the train.

'Well, that should be grand,' she replied, trying not to show her disappointment. She would probably be alone for Christmas.

'I turned it down. I want to spend Christmas with you if you'll have me.'

She reached into her handbag and took out her diary.

'Now let me see… Oh, I just happen to be free,' she smiled.

'You little devil,' he exclaimed, putting his arms around her and kissing her.

Out on the street, it was bitterly cold, and as they exhaled, they made their own little puffs of mist. To counter the cold, the decorative lights along Oxford Street and crowds of shoppers made for a warm atmosphere. Children ran ahead of their parents putting their noses on the windows of shops displaying toys or excitedly admiring the shop window models of Santa with his sleigh and reindeers. Coming from somewhere, they could hear Brenda Lee singing 'Rockin' Around the Christmas Tree.'

They encircled their arms around each other's waists as they walked to prevent themselves from being separated by the crowd on the street. Michelle was in high spirits.

'Let's split up and do our shopping, I don't want you to see what I'm going to buy,' she said with a smile.

'Alright, but let's meet back here in an hour, and we can find a restaurant.'

'No, rather meet me at Bond Street station, and we'll take the train back to my flat. I'll rustle up something for us to eat there.'

When they met up an hour later outside Bond Street Station, they each had a carrier bag concealing their purchases.

'What did you buy?' Michelle asked, sidling up to him feigning to peek in his carrier bag.

'None of your business, you'll have to wait till Christmas.'

Back at her flat, they hung up their overcoats pleased to get in from the cold. It was the first time Dominic had been there in all the time he had been in London. It was comfortable and tastefully furnished with fresh flowers on the mantelpiece over the fireplace. There were a couple of African woodcarvings in one corner, and he wondered if these had been a gift from Misheck. Michelle went into the kitchen and Dominic sat down on the couch.

'Put on some music,' Michelle called from the kitchen, 'I won't be long, I just need to put something in the oven.'

He looked through her collection of records and chose Ella Fitzgerald's album 'Ella Fitzgerald Sings the George and Ira Gershwin Songbook' took out the record and put it on the turntable of the record player. The warm caramel of her voice soon occupied the room.

After a while, Michelle came through from the kitchen with an open bottle of wine and two glasses.

'Couldn't find any Lagosta,' she lamented with a smile, 'you know what happened the last time we drank that.'

'Yes, the most romantic day of my life,' Dominic said, squeezing her hand as she put down the glasses. They sat there quietly listening to Ella Fitzgerald and drinking the wine until she started singing '*But Not for Me.*'

'Dance with me,' Dominic said.

As they shuffle-danced, swaying to the song, Dominic picked up the fragrance of apple blossom.

'I've been thinking,' he said, 'I need to move out of the hotel into a place of my own. To a bigger place than this, with more bedrooms, enough for the children. Will you move in with me?'

'Is that a marriage proposal?' she asked with a hint of indignation.

'Yes.'

'He loves me,' she thought, putting her arms around his neck, drawing him close, kissing him on the lips.

As they danced, his right hand found her left, and she felt something pressed against her palm, a small box. He gently curled her fingers around it and then enclosed her hand in his, so they danced with their hands clasped together held close to her heart. She opened her eyes and drew their hands to her lips, kissing the smooth skin on the back of his hand.

'What is this?' she asked

'Open it,' he whispered in her ear.

She released her hand and held the little box upward in her palm. Opened, she gazed upon a diamond with two sapphires mounted either side in a gold ring.

It's beautiful.' She breathed, 'but you didn't pick this up in London today. There wasn't time to do the setting.'

'I was thinking of you in Paris, and a jeweller made it for me whilst I was there.'

He slipped the ring on her finger and said, 'I love you, am I going to be able to make you happy?'

'Yes, this time, I'm sure. I couldn't be happier. I had my doubts you would ever ask me.'

'I knew I would at the right moment. In the beginning, I didn't have much to offer. Now we can start a new life with great promise.'

She looked at him with a broad smile, but it quickly faded, and she sniffed a couple of times. Was she going to cry, he wondered?

'What's wrong?' he exclaimed, 'I thought I made you happy.'

'Oh my God, it's burning,' she cried, breaking away and running to the kitchen.

He could hear her rummaging in the kitchen, water spluttering from the tap in the sink accompanied by a hissing sound. Better not to go and have a look he concluded. Her sense of humour had evaporated with the steam.

'It's ruined,' she called from the kitchen.

'Forget about it. It's time to celebrate,' he called back, 'let's go out and find a good restaurant.'

Michelle emerged from the kitchen with a newspaper.

'Excellent idea,' she agreed, 'but before we go, I'd like to read you something I found in the newspaper.' She spread the newspaper out on the table, sat down and read:

'Postlewhite shares fell sharply on opening in London yesterday morning and continued to trend lower, closing at a two year low; this on news that there are problems with their Northern Rhodesian mining investment. Details are still sketchy, but the resignation of Managing Director Max Freeman signals the seriousness of the situation. Postlewhite's chairman announced that Frank Osborne had been appointed Managing

Director with immediate effect. The Ministry of Mines in Lusaka declined to comment.' Michelle folded the paper with a smile of satisfaction.

'We shouldn't gloat,' Dominic said, 'but now we have even more reason to celebrate. Let's go.'

Old year's night at Westlake Hall had initially been a Faulkner family tradition confined to members of the extended family. Over time, the cost of running Westlake Hall forced Sir Peter's father to use the occasion to entertain business associates and supporters with the result that the costs were borne by Faulkner Investments, which then enjoyed the tax relief that this presented. When Sir Peter rented out half the Hall to the American computer company, visitors' accommodation reduced, limiting the number of invitations issued. Carefully composed, the guest list included those who were closest to and most important to their business interests. They always invited a Cabinet Minister (most often declined), and one respected business journalist from a major newspaper with his or her partner.

When the written invitation arrived at the flat, Dominic and Michelle were delighted if unaware of its significance. They had joined a select few of Sir Peter's associates. Dominic had been trying to build up the courage to phone Cynthia and use his engagement to Michelle as an excuse to decline her invitation for him to join them for the occasion. Knowing Cynthia, he did not doubt that she was quite aware that he and Michelle were invited.

While Michelle was out shopping, he rang the number for their townhouse in Knightsbridge and waited while the housekeeper called her to the phone.

'Dominic darling, how good of you to call,' she said happily.

'I should have called sooner; it's about your invitation to …'

'Oh, I'm so sorry; I'm not going to be there this year. I'm in love, isn't it wonderful.'

'That was sudden,' Dominic chuckled with nervous relief.

'He's so romantic, an officer in The Guards.'

'Are you happy?'

'Very, surely you can tell. Pity we'll not be at Westlake for the celebration. I'd love you to meet him.'

'I'm sure Michelle and I will bump into you both some time,' Dominic said.

Why had he been concerned about hurting her feelings? Cynthia lived in a world of fantasy that changed on a whim.

In the large reception room at Westlake Hall, couples were assembling for pre-dinner drinks served by attentive waiters. Christmas had passed quietly at the flat, and they had hardly ventured outside preferring the warmth inside. Still, without a car, something they intended to remedy in the New Year, they caught a train to a nearby station and a taxi to Westlake Hall.

When they arrived, they found both Sir Peter and Lady Faulkner circulating amongst the guests welcoming each in turn. It soon became apparent that Dominic and Michelle were the youngest couple by far; most of the others were mature and established members of the business community. They became somewhat of a curiosity, for their presence at the Faulkner's old years night celebration, marked them as unusually young people of substance.

'It's good to find people here from home.' They found themselves in the company of a suave black man with a grey-flecked beard, twinkling eyes, and a white-toothed smile.

'You must be Jeffery's sister Michelle,' he continued, 'and you're Dominic, his business partner.'

'And you must be Mr Jacob Gomani,' Michelle said.

'Yes, I am. Pleased to meet you both,' he said as they shook hands.

'We're pleased to meet the person who played such a major part in our success,' Dominic said.

'It was a pleasure to help; we need homespun entrepreneurs if our country is to succeed. Sir Peter has very generously invited my wife and me to stay here on holiday at his expense for the next week. But I'm sure you both will be joining us for business meetings during that time. There is still much to be done.'

Jacob Gomani slipped a packet of cigarettes from the inside pocket of his jacket.

'Product of Northern Rhodesia,' he said, offering them one. Neither Dominic nor Michelle smoked, so they declined, while he patted his pocket searching for a light. Dominic pulled the Zippo out of his pocket, thumbed the lid open, and flicked the flint wheel. A tall flame rose up for Jacob Gomani to light his cigarette.

'Be careful you don't lose that it has the powers of a talisman. Without it we wouldn't be here,' Michelle claimed with an enigmatic smile.

At that moment, Lady Faulkner arrived at Michelle's side and said, 'Come on, Michelle, come with me. I'd like you to meet some of the ladies. By the way, congratulations.'

'What was that about a talisman,' Jacob Gomani asked as the two women walked away.

'It's a long story,' Dominic replied.